[Nothing happens here]

[Cat Connor]

ISBN Print: 978-0-473-55757-7
ISBN Kindle: 978-0-473-55759-1
ISBN ePub: 978-0-473-55758
ISBN D2D: 978-1-7385851-5-1

For permissions contact: 9mmpressnz@gmail.com

For My Knight of the Order of Chrome ...

"THE TRUTH IS YOU DON'T KNOW WHAT IS GO-
ING TO HAPPEN
    TOMORROW. LIFE IS A CRAZY RIDE, AND NOTH-
ING IS GUARANTEED." - EMINEM

Chapter 1
[EMAIL]

Rain hammered the windows. I listened to the stormy night. Something woke me and it wasn't the rain. Under a rumble of thunder I heard a knock. And then another. Two more followed in close succession and increasing loudness. The display on the bedside clock glowed orange in the dark.

Heavy rain pelted against the windowpanes with renewed force.

Three in the morning and someone was banging on my front door.

That wasn't good. I rolled out of bed and peered out the window. The security lighting flicked on. Pools of light cast eerie shadows over the steps to the porch. No police lights outside. Probably not bad news then?

A big part of me wanted to ignore the noise but each bang rattled the windows. Annoying. There was no sign of the noise dissipating. Under sufferance, I crawled out of my warm bed.

Shivering in the cool air, I shoved my arms into my dressing gown sleeves, and then tied the belt. Flashing whoever knocked at my door wasn't on the agenda.

I reached the bottom of the stairs just as a dark shape on the porch raised an arm to bash the glass again.

"For goodness sake. Hold your horses!"

"Hurry up, Ronnie," a snappish voice replied.

Mystery solved.

Cousin Donald.

I twisted the lock and the door handle.

Donald spilled over the doorstep and dripped onto the hall carpet.

"Why?" I asked, locking the door behind him and flipping the outside lights off.

"I was in the area. It's late. I'm tired," he said. "Spare room made up?"

"Where's your key?"

"I left it here the other day," he replied. With one finger, Donald hooked a set of keys from the bowl on the table near the front door and jangled them. The keys slid from his finger and fell with a clatter back into the bowl.

"You're welcome," I called after him as he disappeared upstairs. "And you smell like a brewery."

"Tomorrow, we'll talk," he replied, his voice floated on a haze of booze. The door to the spare room closed.

I muttered unflattering things about Donald on my way back to bed.

Morning came a lot faster than expected and brought with it large puddles and general sogginess. I sat in the dining room with my coffee and surveyed the boggy backyard. It did not bode well for the carpet. I looked at the sleeping greyhound on his warm bed in the living room. He didn't like rain.

A bedroom door opened. Romeo opened an eye and looked at me.

"It's just Donald. You want to go outside? It's raining."

He closed his eyes and pretended to be asleep.

Smart dog.

The front door opened and closed.

Donald swept into the room.

He dropped the morning newspaper on the table in front of me.

His hands flapped in all directions as he launched into details I didn't want to hear about his night. I made him coffee and waited for a lull in the excitable gesturing.

"And you woke me up why?"

He started to explain about leaving his key here but the phone rang.

I silenced him with a look and answered the phone.

"Hey Ronnie, it's Jenn, are you coming into the office today?"

"Not unless you need me. This is my week to work from home, problem?" I replied.

"No. Just wanted to know where everyone is this week," she said, there was a brief pause. "So, no Romeo at work then?"

Oh, I saw what was happening. Wasn't me that was missed, it was the dog.

"Not this week."

"I'll be in touch if anything crops up," Jenn said. "Unless of course you need someone to swing by and walk Romeo. I could bring him into the office, you know, to keep him occupied while you're working ..."

Nice try.

"Yeah. Nah. I was looking forward to spending the

week at home with him. I'm sure you won't miss him that much."

"I think I might ... he is our work mascot."

"Get your own greyhound," I said with a laugh.

"One day ... and I will call her Juliet."

"How very fitting."

Jenn should get a greyhound. Romeo would enjoy the company and mascot wise, two hounds are better than one.

"Bye."

I hung up and informed Donald he could resume his tale of the night before.

He immediately launched into a mega rave about his latest crush.

Fifteen minutes after he began, he ended and flew out the door declaring he was late for work.

Romeo and I watched him rush down the path from the living room window. I don't know what he thought he was doing but it wasn't running. Skipping maybe?

Could've sworn the dog smiled.

I put a warm fleecy jacket on Romeo and encouraged him to go out the back. There was a pause in the rain.

All was right with the world as I drank my coffee and began to read the newspaper. That was when I saw the headline that sent my civilised start to the day scurrying out of sight. The lead story seemed a little like something from a bad television series. Don't get me wrong, I'm quite fond of bad TV; in fact, sometimes it makes excellent entertainment. I just don't expect to see 'Law and

Order' episode plot lines in the newspaper here.

It's Upper Hutt, nothing happens here. Well, not in recent years anyway. We've had our share of headlines in the past with an armoured car heist, a few murders, and even an embezzler. The headline and article I read stunned me.

Taking into account how often newspaper stories contained the wrong information, the story in front of me was still a stunner.

An elderly woman, bashed to death in Silverstream.

Who bashes anyone to death in Silverstream? Unbelievable.

I read on. The assailant used a garden ornament, beating the eighty-five year old woman about the head and face.

She died from her injuries in Lower Hutt hospital late last night without regaining consciousness.

It did not sound like a Silverstream crime.

Stokes Valley or Naenae maybe, yeah, definitely more a lower valley type of crime. A cop told me once that we have a better class of criminal in Upper Hutt.

Bashing an elderly woman to death was strange behaviour for one of the nicer upper valley suburbs.

I folded the paper in half, making it more manageable, and read the rest of the story with morbid curiosity.

They even said what street it was; I could easily visualise the area. Kiln Street was predominately occupied by the elderly, to be fair, the whole suburb was getting on in years.

Images of the street and surroundings filled my mind. It was a short walk across the road to a small shopping centre containing a bar, chemist, travel agent, doctor surgery, dentist, beauty salon, physiotherapist, bakery, and a magazine shop. There was a supermarket nearby. The train station was on the other side of the houses and there were bus stops handy as well.

Perfect for older people.

Unlike a good percentage of the population of Silverstream, I'm nowhere near old enough to find the location appealing. Truthfully, I will probably never be old enough to find the location appealing.

There would be quite a panic in the inhabitants of Kiln Street now. To be fair, it would cause some unease with me too. Violence takes away a person's sense of security. The journalist surmised the woman had gone outside to investigate a noise and disturbed a potential burglar. I scoured the story for mention of anything taken.

Burglars don't often kill people. Yet I found no reference to anything missing. I didn't know what the situation really was but it wasn't a burglary.

The victim was discovered crumpled in the garden bleeding from serious head wounds.

Her eighty-seven year old husband found her when he came back from the dairy. The reporter went into detail about the bottle of cream he'd purchased and how he went for a short walk most nights to the local dairy. He was reportedly gone for only twenty-minutes.

Nothing in the story sat well with me. A niggle in my

gut said there was a lot more to it than was stated. What I'd read felt like a bit of scare mongering, not journalism. Not enough facts present to make a real story.

My thoughts turned to Nana. Thank goodness she had her own apartment in a retirement complex at the other end of the city. I didn't have to worry so much about her knowing there were people keeping an eye on her and she was out of harm's way.

I put the paper into the recycling bin, rinsed my cup, and went out the back door.

A red fleecy blur galloped around the garden shed, mud flying under his feet.

Three times he raced around the shed and washing line at seeming break neck speed. He was playing silly buggers and clearly needed to go for a proper run to stretch his long legs.

"Romeo!" I called. "Romeo."

He bounced toward me with his tongue lolling out the side of his mouth looking extra special. His whip like tail wagged.

"Good boy." I patted him for a minute before holding the door open. "Inside and wait."

Romeo frolicked up the steps and into the house. He waited on the towels in the hallway for me to wipe his muddy feet and take his coat off.

"Done, off you go." I ushered him into the warmth of the living room. With his usual grace, he folded himself onto his bed. His shiny dark brown eyes watched me moving around the room. I picked up his toys and tidied up.

A few minutes later, I sat at my desk and gazed out the window. At the very end of the street, I noticed a pale blue car parked on the far side of the intersection near the shops. Being an unusual colour made the car stand out.

I'd seen a car that colour twice in two days. The odds of the sightings being different cars were slim. I hurried upstairs to get a better view.

Yesterday I felt like a pale blue car followed me down the street. There was a chance it was innocent and the driver had been looking for an address and just appeared to be following me.

I recalled scrawling the license plate in my notebook just in case it was something.

Maybe that was a good thing.

From my bedroom window, I could clearly see the car. There was no doubt in my mind that it was the same car I'd seen the day before.

Seeing it again didn't seem so innocent. The creep factor increased. No one wants creepy near their home. I went back downstairs and resumed my position at my desk. The car hadn't moved.

Romeo stood and stretched. He moved with two long even strides to my side. He too gazed out the window. I didn't doubt his ability to see the car. My money was on him being able to identify the driver. Romeo is a sight hound and it was only two-hundred and fifty metres to the parked pale blue car from the front window of the house.

I slipped an arm around the big hound's neck. "Are we being watched?"

The dog maintained his position puffing air from his cheeks gently. When the car left he gave me a nudge with his long nose and lay back on his bed.

Chapter 2
[THE PHONE CALL]

Music erupted from my desk.

I grabbed my cell phone without looking at it and pressed the green button. Nothing happened. The music continued.

Confusing.

I looked at the screen, it was dark. What witchery caused my phone to ring but the screen to remain dark? I pressed the green button again.

Nothing happened.

The music continued.

Staring at the phone in my hand and willing it to stop didn't work.

The noise went on and on.

Stupid annoying tinkling song.

I pressed the button again with more force.

The tune continued.

"Damn you crackberry!"

A horrid thought occurred. A big dollop of stupid landed on my head. With a groan, I picked up the receiver for the landline.

The music stopped.

It occurred to me that I need to change the ring tone on my cell phone to something completely different to my landline or get an iPhone.

I glanced at the dog.

He looked amused.

"Never speak of this," I whispered holding the phone close to my chest. "Never."

Stifling a laugh, I took a deep breath and answered the phone. "Wherefore Art Thou satellite office, Ronnie speaking."

"Veronica, it's Reede."

A shiver ran up my spine.

"To what do I owe this horror?"

She ignored my comment.

"I've got a job I'd like you to work. Someone will be in touch shortly," Reede said. Her raspy two-pack a day voice grated on my nerves.

"Isn't that interesting," I replied glancing at my day planner. I had two jobs on for the week, neither of which was urgent or particularly interesting. I wouldn't mind passing them onto Jenn and Steph at the office if something better came along. "And the reason you called me with a job is?"

"He asked for you."

That was a pretty good reason but having Reede call me was almost as unsettling as answering the wrong phone.

"Here was me thinking I'd retired from the Service and was in business for myself." I paused. "Did you forget I don't work for you anymore?"

We've danced this dance before but not in a long time.

Reede's voice sharpened, "I didn't forget. This is an exceptional circumstance. Someone will be in touch. I expect you to keep me in the loop."

I don't think that expectation should be made.

"My opinion of you hasn't changed. I'm disturbed by your generosity in passing on this case."

"You never did master tact, did you?" she said.

Choosing to ignore her comment I carried on, "Whose pay roll would I be on?"

"Department of Homeland Security."

Hang on a cotton picking minute. Last time I looked this was New Zealand. If DHS were playing ball a long way from home then that put a serious spin on the job offer. I wasn't entirely sure I wanted to be caught up in something that sounded that grim.

"Why didn't Justin call me?" Something niggled away at me. Could've been because Reede called me herself and I didn't share the department's admiration for her work ethic. Or maybe it was that she wanted me to take a job for the Americans and keep her in the loop.

"Justin is overseas."

A standard line that meant he was working and contact wasn't possible.

"Someone from DHS will contact you. He needs help locating someone."

That's what I do, I find people.

I considered that sometimes Yanks can be fun but I had a few questions.

"Why DHS and not CIA? Aren't they over stepping their bounds way over here?"

"Homeland contacted us. No doubt CIA will be involved somewhere."

Interesting.

Serious jobs from other governments usually came with a hefty budget.

The people they misplace are often more interesting than runaway teens. A big pay packet and interesting job, now they were enticing thoughts.

Also, sometimes Yanks can be fun.

"I'll look forward to the call."

"Keep me in the loop Veronica," Reede said and hung up.

I replaced the phone in the cradle on my desk. There was much to think about.

Thoughts ran rampant. I hadn't heard from Reede directly since I left the Intelligence Service and now twice she asked me to keep her in the loop. Her request to keep her in the loop was odd; surely Homeland would see to that? Reede and I didn't see eye to eye on most things. Even so, I knew she'd authorised some of the missing person cases that Justin had given me. But I hadn't heard from Reede herself at all. I assumed she didn't like me any more than I liked her. I spun around in my chair a few times.

Nope, didn't work. Reede giving me a job still felt weird.

I wouldn't think twice about it if it had been Justin.

Justin and I were old friends who ended up working for the Security Intelligence Service.

He still worked for them, but I left eleven months ago

to start my own private investigation business. Often the cases he passed over to me were because the missing person was someone they couldn't be seen looking for or someone of special significance and everyone came up blank.

I have a knack for finding the unfindable.

I spun my chair again. There had to be something funky going on for Reede to make that call. My mind wandered back to when I left the Service and founded my own business.

It's not entirely my business. It's a partnership. Stephanie takes care of the accounts and keeps things running, when she's not watching the cricket, rugby, or answering the fire pager.

Then there is Jennifer, she is the other full time investigator and a volunteer fire fighter like Stephanie.

We do regular PI type things that include security work for companies, drug testing, loss prevention, and investigations into suspected sabotage/foul play. As well as that, there are always the unfaithful spouse cases that keep bread on the table and coffee in our pots. And I do some occasional locating work for various government agencies.

Until fairly recently, I used to be an intelligence officer. Steph worked for Inland Revenue and Jenn worked for a major telecommunications company.

I joined the Security Intelligence Service, a few more years ago than I cared to admit to. Young keen and seduced by the glamour of being a spy.

Turns out, it's like any other job.

Mostly not that exciting.

But it sure had its moments.

Most people never come across the service.

And why would you, unless you're a spy from another country or in need of a high security clearance; the service also gathers information, works to protect the country from threats etc.

I slotted in nicely with my own little area of expertise.

I'm pretty good at locating people who may not want to be found or whom someone is hiding. Often they're high risk targets. Got quite a bit of practice and perfected an unusual skill set that gave me an astonishing success rate.

It is what I am good at.

I was always good at it.

But I'm better at it now that I don't have so many rules governing what I can and can't do. Now Steph makes the rules but they're more about how much we can spend while on a case than anything.

She's all about keeping us in the black and she does a damn fine job at it.

It's also easier knowing I am free to use my skills without having to come up with more suitable explanations as to how I found someone.

I leaned back in my chair and considered the new job, which I knew nothing about. The consideration part didn't take long.

Nothing didn't take a lot of thinking.

The phone rang again.

This time I picked up the correct phone. It was hard not to smile.

"Wherefore Art Thou satellite office, Ronnie Tracey speaking."

"Ms. Tracey. I'd like to discuss a job."

Here we go with the mysterious American. I was all ears. Curiosity ignited. I mean, who doesn't love a good mystery with a sexy accent?

"And you are?"

"Benjamin," he replied.

There was something just a little familiar about his accent but I couldn't place it.

"Do you have a surname?"

"I'd prefer to discuss this in person, are you available this morning?"

No, I'm very expensive. I'll be charging you three-hundred dollars an hour and expenses. Or maybe a hefty flat rate plus expenses, I hadn't decided yet.

"I have a prior engagement at midday ..." I checked the time on my computer. "I can see you in an hour."

"Thank you. Where?"

I gave him my address. Working from home was one of my favourite things. I took a week out of the office every few months and worked from home. Mostly to allow me to spend more time with my Nana. She wasn't getting any younger.

I hung up.

Romeo was asleep. That was his favourite thing.

I called the office to check in.

"Hey Steph, I've got an overseas job coming in. Can you and Jenn hold the fort there?"

"Big fat pay cheque?"

"I think so."

"Then we can hold the fort. Jenn is working the Nugent case. She thinks she'll have enough surveillance by the end of the week."

"Good."

"She's had a few issues. That woman is high maintenance."

"In what way?"

"Jenn says the Nugent woman called her four times yesterday wanting to know where her husband was and started texting her during the evening."

That's one of the perils of giving clients our cell phone numbers.

The occasional nut job over stepped the mark.

"Give the Nugent woman a ring, Steph. Remind her of our policy regarding divulging information."

We don't divulge information to the client until the surveillance is over and report written.

Clients in marital cheating cases can get a bit wacky, and sometimes confront the spouse and put themselves and the private investigator in harm's way. We gather information. We collect evidence. We write reports. And we do it all while keeping everyone safe.

"Will do. Shall I point out that text messages after 6PM will be regarded as overtime and she will be billed for any communication?"

I smiled.

"That should shut her up. Do it. Also, remind Jenn that she can drop the case if the client gets too much."

"Of course, but you know Jenn, mate ... she'll see it through and give the Nugent woman a piece of her mind if she doesn't back off."

I laughed. That she would.

"Hopefully your phone call will set the client back on the right path. Right, I'll be in touch."

I hung up as my email program beeped at me.

Fifteen new emails seemed a bit crazy. Scrolling through them both amused and terrified me. Someone, let's blame my cousin Donald, had set Nana up an email account. Great. That's what I need spam from my ninety-four year old Nana.

Maybe if I didn't reply, she'd think she got the address wrong and give up? Another four emails arrived within seconds from Nana.

I groaned.

All the subjects were 'Is this working?'

Ignoring them was clearly not an option.

I picked up my cell phone and text messaged Donald: 'What have you done?'

He replied while I was reading all the mail from Nana: 'I don't know what you're talking about.'

And yet I had trouble believing him.

I text him back: 'I'm talking about Nana emailing me. How is this possible?'

The emails were almost identical in content. Nana wanted Romeo and I to visit today. Great, I was already planning on seeing her at midday.

My phone chirped again. Donald replied: 'I gave her my old laptop. Thought she'd enjoy the wireless internet they have at the retirement home.'

No, he didn't think. No thought happened there.

Another email arrived. I replied to Nana and told her Romeo and I would be there at midday. Then I replied to Donald via text: 'You'll keep!'

A nana with email capability was not ideal.

My Nana with wifi was definitely not ideal.

I spent the next hour writing a report for a client. It was a happy report to write. The woman hired me to find her long lost aunt. Found the aunt, arranged first contact, job done. Now it's time for the invoice, report, and the money to roll in.

After emailing the documents, I deleted another ten emails from Nana. I think she'd found her new hobby. Before I knew it, I was praying that she'd use her new found power for good and not for the continual harassment of me. More emails rolled in. I cast my eyes to the ceiling.

"Okay God, here's the thing, I know you don't micromanage but this is an extraordinary situation, my ninety-four year old Nana should not be using email to annoy the bejesus out of me. A little laptop smiting would go a long way about now."

God help us all if the woman ever gets a smartphone.

I sent a quick reply email to Nana's last epistle saying I wouldn't be near my computer for the rest of the morning. She had better never find out what phones are really capable of these days. God help anyone who introduces the woman to Twitter. I will not be responsible for my actions if she starts tweeting. Lightning didn't strike me down and on some level that surprised me.

The next half hour was spent tidying up my hard drive while waiting for the mysterious American to arrive.

Chapter 3
[A MYSTERIOUS AMERICAN]

Romeo and I watched from the living room window as a tallish man with light brown hair opened and closed the front gate. He walked up the path. I liked that he shut the gate. So many people stomp up the path leaving the gate wide open. Hello, it clearly says a greyhound lives here. Greyhounds run. Mine does not always have his ears on. Feet yes, ears no.

"That must be Benjamin," I said to the dog. "He looks like someone. Do you think he looks like someone we should know?"

Romeo wagged his tail in response. I touched his head with my palm. "Sit," I said.

Romeo sat.

I smiled. Yes, Greyhounds can sit.

A quiet knock at the door caused Romeo to lift his ears. "Stay," I said and headed for the front door.

He knocked again. I pulled the handle down and swung the door open.

"Benjamin?" The man on my front porch was a little over six feet tall. Blue-eyed, square jawed and clean shaven. Donald would say he was ruggedly handsome in a doable way.

Yes, he is as gay as that sounds.

In this case, Donald would be right.

"Ms. Tracey," he replied with a quick lopsided smile.

He definitely looked like someone.

"Yes," I replied. "Benjamin?"

He inclined his head in a subtle nod. "Yes ma'am."

"Come in." I stood aside and let him into the hallway, then pointed to the living room door. "Go through, you don't mind dogs do you?"

He hesitated at the closed door for just a second before turning the door knob. "I don't mind dogs, as long as the dog doesn't mind me."

"Guess we'll see won't we?" I followed Benjamin into the room.

Romeo was still sitting, waiting. "Good boy," I said, making eye contact. The dog stood and stretched, then meandered over for a pat. Meander is a bit of a mis-nomer; he took two strides and covered half the floor space in the living room.

"He's big," Benjamin commented as Romeo turned his attention to the newcomer, leaning against him to see if he'd pat him. Benjamin obliged. Satisfied, Romeo flopped back onto his warm bed and watched. "He's a Greyhound, right?"

"Yes," I replied.

"Did he race?"

"Yes, and he won a few. He's retired."

"Didn't realise Greyhounds were so big."

"Have a seat," I said pointing to the sofa. "He is a big boy. They tried to tell me he was medium sized for a male. But I don't think so. Can I get you a coffee?"

"No, thanks. "

"Okay, now what is it you wanted to see me about?"

I pulled my laptop off the edge of my desk and onto my knee, ready to take notes. I opened a new document and headed it Benjamin.

"You're a private investigator?"

"You asking me or telling me, because I know what I am."

"I'm looking for a private investigator. I have lost something."

Not someone?

"My speciality is people and I've been known to find the occasional lost dog."

"How about garden ornaments?"

"Pardon?" I could feel a frown puckering the skin on my forehead and worked hard to dislodge it.

"I've lost some garden ornaments."

"That's not something I've ever been asked to find before. What type of ornaments?"

"Gnomes," he said with a straight face.

"Gnomes? Are you serious?"

The lack of humour in his expression suggested he was serious. Could've sworn I'd seen that exact expression before. It irked me that I found him familiar but couldn't place him. Another more chilling thought popped up as I recalled the morning paper implicating a garden ornament in an elderly woman's death.

He nodded. "Very serious."

I got that impression.

"And this gnome can walk?" I hoped I'd kept the derision I felt brewing out of my voice.

"No, not without help," he replied. I detected a small amount of well-hidden impatience. "Are you interested or not?"

I really wasn't sure. Finding a gnome sounded pretty weird even for Upper Hutt. How hard could it be?

"Let's say I am interested, I'm going to need more information. Last known whereabouts, full description, any distinguishing marks, bank account details, cell phone number, and a list of known associates ..."

"You're not taking this very seriously, Ms. Tracey."

"I'm sorry," I replied, making a sincere attempt at contrition. It wasn't great but I tried. "You need to see this from my point of view for a second. Someone without a surname just asked me to find a gnome. And to get more cloak and dagger, the someone is an American and he looks suspiciously like a well-known actor."

I finally figured out where I'd seen him before. Tuesday nights on TV3 and before that Wednesday nights on TV One.

A smile played upon his lips for a fraction of a second. "I've heard about you."

"Great, I've heard about you too but not in the context that would have someone ..." I stopped myself. He flashed his boyish smile and it was disarming. "You're an actor. This is research for a role? Or have I just been punked?"

"It's not research. You haven't been punked."

"You're an actor though, right?'

25

"Absolutely."

"I don't want to appear rude, but an actor who has lost something has what connection with the Security Intelligence Service?" He must've had one or Reede wouldn't have rung me.

"A long standing one but not in this country."

The penny dropped. Being an actor was one hell of a cover.

"Interesting. That's one intricate backstop," I said. "Doesn't the acting thing attract undue attention?"

"Not really. I can go places that might otherwise be difficult and apart from fans mostly people leave me alone."

"Fascinating. But I think I prefer the PI gig."

Curiosity got the better of me.

"When did they recruit you?"

"Not long after my first acting job."

"You've been doing this a while then, twenty years or so ..." Yes, I knew how old he was.

"Yes."

"Doesn't the acting get in the way or vice versa?" He was an actual working actor, which meant auditions, rehearsals, being on set, travel and whatever else actors did. To be honest the profession was a mystery to me.

"Not very often." He grinned. "You have a lot of questions."

"I've never met anyone as famous as you before ..." That wasn't cool. Fan girl? Me? Looks like it.

"I'm just like everyone else."

You're really not.

"Lucky for you this is New Zealand and no one really cares who anyone is."

"I have noticed that. It's nice, you know?"

"I'm sure it is."

I glanced at his jacket. "But I will say it seems a bit strange to be carrying a sidearm in New Zealand, actor or not."

His eyes widened. "That's what I've heard. I heard your powers of observation are second to none."

Noticing a slight bulge in a jacket does not qualify as 'powers of observation' and finally figuring out who he was, was not exactly spectacular. Could do better.

"I'm going to need to see some identification before we go any further and it better have a last name on it." I really wanted to know if he used his real name while he was acting.

From his inside breast pocket he took a black wallet and passed it to me.

I opened it and looked at the gold shield and then the credentials sporting a blue eagle on a white background and a photo of the man in front of me.

"Awesome, I bought one similar to that from a souvenir store in New York," I replied. "Where is your passport?"

He smiled. "It's real." From his trouser pocket, he took his passport and handed it to me.

It looked like him. His name was the same as on the credentials, and the one the whole world knew. Benjamin Reynolds.

"Okay so, you're an actor and you work for the Department of Homeland Security and you've lost a gnome?"

Life is weird. Could be just my life though.

"Yes."

"I'd expect to be looking for a Daytime Emmy, not a gnome," I said. "You know how this sounds, yes? Put these words together and tell me what you see, actor, gnome, Homeland Security."

It's not my fault that it all sounded rather amusing and like a really bad movie. B grade would be pushing it.

"I'm aware how it sounds."

Good.

"Wouldn't you be better off enlisting police help to find this gnome?"

"We'd like this kept very quiet."

"And there are about twenty Private Investigator firms in the Wellington Region, what made you come to me?"

"Because I have heard of you."

Oh, that old line again.

"Who from?"

He appeared to be considering his reply. Almost a minute went by before he spoke. "A year ago, you found a missing woman. Her name was Bella Cross."

The chances of me forgetting Bella Cross were nil. That was my last case while working for the Service.

She wasn't easy to find because the person who took her really didn't want her to be found.

Bella was a teacher abducted from a school in Upper

Hutt and kept by her stalker in the basement of a house over in Mangaroa Valley.

Her disappearance was all over the newspapers for three months, during which time her abductor left clues indicating that Bella had moved away, possibly gone overseas. Her credit card and EFTPOS card were used at Auckland International Airport and then it all died down. People forgot about Bella Cross. When I found her, everyone but her father had given up hope. The newspapers carried the story again once I located her.

"Okay, my involvement in the Bella Cross case isn't a secret. It was all over the media." Plenty of other investigators have closed high-profile cases. "So, you want me to find gnomes, why?"

A small smile flickered on Benjamin's lips then faded.

"Bella's father was the one who told me about you. He told me that if I ever lost anything to call you and only you."

"What was his name?" I asked. That detail was kept out of the public arena.

"William MacKinnon."

Well, he could've got that from police.

"What else do you know about MacKinnon?"

"He used to be with another agency." He dropped his voice slightly before saying, "He's now my boss."

"Get him on the phone, and then we'll talk gnomes." I checked the time on my laptop. "Make it fast. I have somewhere I need to be in an hour."

Moments later, I was talking to William MacKinnon

for the first time in a year. I took the phone to the kitchen and conducted a semi-private conversation.

"Bill, you could have called me direct and warned me you were sending an actor."

"Thought this would be more fun. I would've paid good money to see your face when Benjamin told you what we've lost and when you figured out who he was."

"I must confess to already receiving a call from my ex-boss warning me someone wanted my help, but I had no idea it was you," I said. There was a chance Reede didn't know MacKinnon was involved.

"Does it make a difference?"

"I want to say no." I let a smile into my voice. "But it does make a difference. Also ... I might be playing with your man a little. He doesn't know who I used to work for, does he?"

"No," he replied. "You can tell him if you want to."

I don't think I will yet. Gnomes. Of all the things to find, gnomes!

"Thanks for sending the actor. It might even be fun."

I hung up, walked back into the living room and handed Benjamin his phone.

"Okay, let's talk. What sort of gnome am I looking for?"

"A regular garden gnome, except it's sealed. There is no hole underneath."

"Yeah I understand what sealed means."

"We're looking for three gnomes. I have taken the liberty of ordering three almost identical gnomes for you.

They will arrive by the end of the week. Once the gnomes are located, you are to uplift and replace."

"Three?"

"Yes."

"This is all very cloak and dagger for three missing garden gnomes."

"They're important gnomes."

"They sound it. Let me get my head around this for a moment." I scrutinised his face as I said, "You want me to sneak around peoples gardens looking for three gnomes, steal them, and leave dummy gnomes in their place?"

He nodded.

"And you know how stupid this sounds, right?" Especially coming from him. I mean really, how do I take an actor seriously?

"You will be paid well, and all expenses reimbursed. But I am going to insist that you tell no one of this job."

"Well, here's the thing. I own a company with my business partners." I proceeded to explain where I was coming from, "So two people are going to know we're working together. The money will go through our business. I'm not prepared to find myself in the shite with the tax department."

They may want secrecy but I want to cover my backside and the company's backside. Anyway, I was sure he was being a typical American and making it all more exciting than it needed to be. Gnomes!

"And your partners are trustworthy?" He had the good grace to appear uncomfortable at asking that question.

"Of course. You think I found Bella on my own?"

I actually did find Bella on my own but that's beside the point. "It was a company effort and MacKinnon knows that."

He nodded. "All right."

"One more thing. I will not be questioned about my methods nor will I tell you how I work."

He considered my statement for a moment. By the look on his face, I gathered he'd heard I used unorthodox methods and would not disclose details.

Again, he nodded. "I accept that."

Great.

"Now what's so important about the gnomes?"

"I can't tell you," he replied. "It's above your pay grade."

I smirked at his phrasing. No one but an American would say that.

"Nice. It's okay for me to find the damn things but I'm not allowed to know why ... maybe we don't need this kind of work," I said.

"Finding the gnomes is vital to the future of mankind."

Whoa, I would've done it because it sounded like a laugh and I knew the money would be respectable.

"You don't have to get super dramatic."

Although possibly it went with the territory.

"Do you want to do this or not?" he asked with a sigh.

I gave the impression of thinking about it for a second or two.

Money is good, it helps with things like food, shelter,

clothing, all things Romeo and I like to have. Jenn and Steph are rather partial to those things as well.

We are doing okay for a young company but money is not always as easy to come by in the private sector.

Not everyone settles accounts as quickly as we'd like.

"I'll do it. But I thought New Zealand and the Department of Homeland Security had an agreement, something to do with intelligence? So wouldn't you be better off getting the Secret Service involved. Pretty sure the future of mankind falls within their brief."

Sometimes I just can't help myself.

"We do have an agreement, we work together. This is a special case. The suggestion was made to utilise a private company and we'd like you to work with us."

"Secret Service rang me regarding this job."

"What details did they give?"

"None, apart from telling me an American would be in touch and that this was a Homeland job."

"We contacted them as a matter of courtesy."

Okay, business time.

"I need everything you have on the apocalyptic gnomes." I was pretty pleased with the way I kept all derision out of my voice as I said apocalyptic gnomes. "But right now I have to go visit my Nana."

"I'll email you everything you need. A parcel will be sent containing the replacements."

Benjamin stood and shook my hand. Romeo watched him leave but didn't stand up.

From the living room window, we watched him walk

down the path, open and close the gate, and drive away in his black sedan.

A black sedan. I love a good cliché.

"We've got a new job, might be a nice stuffed toy in it for you." Romeo looked at me. "Maybe that stuffed chicken you were coveting at the pet store last week."

I patted his head. "I know, I should've maybe mentioned Reede wanted to be kept in the loop."

I had about twenty minutes before we had to be at Nana's, time enough to take Romeo for a walk, so he would be all ready to relax with old people and stuff his face with treats.

It was warm enough to leave off his thick coat. I clipped his harness on then slipped a light jacket over the top and lined the D ring in the harness with a hole in between the shoulders of the jacket.

His lead clipped to the D ring. The jacket with the hole for the harness D ring was my clever invention.

That way if he got too hot I could easily remove the jacket without removing his whole harness.

That would be a definite safety issue on a busy street. Our usual walk was up Merton Street and down Ngata Grove to the alleyway at the end.

This meant Romeo had to suffer the mad dog on Ngata Grove that threw herself at the glass doors and went mental at the gate every time we passed.

As we approached the house, I whispered to Romeo, "Good boy, walk on."

The insane dog across the street threw herself headlong at the window with a thump. I could see her from the corner of my eye, foaming at the mouth, trying to break the window, barking.

Romeo ignored the commotion.

He was too good for that sort of carry on.

I praised him all the way to the alley way and our escape from the crazy street.

"We'll go home the long way," I said. "That dog has anger management issues."

Of course, it could just be jealousy. I'd never seen anyone take her for a walk.

We rounded the bars at the beginning of the alleyway.

I gathered the lead in my right hand, moving the dog to my right.

There was less glass sprinkled upon the right side of the path. Romeo paused at the edge of the large field next to the church hall. His nose twitched. His ears perked. He gazed into the distance and so did I. I could see nothing moving. But he was definitely interested in something.

"Come on then," I said, walking onto the grass. "Let's go see."

Romeo bounced next to me then broke into a high-spirited frolic. The more I tried to take him down the middle of the field the more he tried pushing me toward the hall.

Strange behaviour.

He was not a pushy dog. He loved to walk but did so with decorum. He pranced along next to me when on his lead delighting in praise from random strangers. He's what we call an old-man-magnet. He attracts them like flowers attract bees. Romeo was slightly snooty, very proper, and never pushy.

His pushing became pulling as I switched hands with the lead and moved him to my left.

It was most peculiar.

"Okay, let's go see," I said.

As soon as he realised I was going with him he stopped pulling and walked beside me.

Nose twitching, crazy ears alert.

We circled the building twice.

He checked every gap under the hall.

Romeo stood on the ramp to the front door. I joined him, peering into the dark beyond our reflections. I could see no one inside.

Just because I couldn't see anyone didn't mean he couldn't. His eyes were far better than mine.

There were no cars in the car park. Even the church was devoid of human life. Romeo stood. I let him stand there for a few minutes then called him away. I walked him through the graveyard and out to Fergusson Drive. The whole way, he was looking back over his shoulder.

Sometimes I wish dogs could talk.

Chapter 4
[THE CRONIES OF DOOM]

I stopped by the reception at the retirement home.

"Hi, Margot," I said, putting as much perk into my greeting as I could. Considering where I was, I thought I'd injected plenty of perk. Romeo poked his head over the divide and waited for Margot to pat him.

"Hello, Ronnie. Day off?"

"Working from home, think I'll be working from home all week." Working from home and working with a hunky actor from television. Weird life. I shuddered as I thought how crazed Donald would get if he caught sight of Benjamin Reynolds.

"Lucky for some. Your Nana is in the main lounge room." Margot turned the guest book around and put a pen on it. "Hello, Romeo." She rubbed his head and stroked his ears.

"Thanks," I replied, signing the guest book. I stole a furtive glance around the reception desk looking for any warnings of the Norovirus that plagued rest homes. I knew of two homes under lock down due to the virus.

Nana's home seemed free of the disease.

Upon further thought, I decided that no self-respecting virus would be caught dead near the inmates.

There was an information sheet and some antibacterial hand cleanser, and a note saying that any visitors that had been recently unwell should stay away.

I read the notice with care. After all, I didn't want to put anyone's health at unnecessary risk.

Margot interrupted my reading, "Everything all right?"

"Yep," I replied. "I see you're still accepting visitors."

Margot smiled. "Yes, it's your lucky day."

"It sure is," I said, and plastered a grin on my face which I hoped hid my twinge of disappointment. There was no way out.

"Donald has just left. He's coming back tomorrow to help out our hairdresser."

I smiled, that was almost as good as a blast of lightning from above, Donald setting old ducks' hair and doing blue rinses. "How'd you rope him into that?"

"It was your Nana's idea. She told all her friends that her grandson was the best hairdresser in Upper Hutt and always did her hair. Now they all want Donald to do theirs."

Laughter bubbled up.

Smiting the laptop came a poor second to Donald doing blue rinses and tight perms all day. Could it be a karmic thing? On the plus side, the blue rinse brigade will be looking very smart indeed, as they vie for visitor attention.

"That's great."

"Wee heads up, Ronnie, your Nana and her friends are up to something."

Hopefully nothing more than tormenting poor Donald.

"Thanks. I'll see you on the way out."

Margot waved as Romeo and I walked into the main

lounge area.

I stopped in the doorway and scanned the room. Wasn't hard to spot Nana.

The thin, grey-headed woman was deep in conversation with a couple of old biddies. One of them looked up and nudged Nana.

Not much wrong with her eyesight.

Nana waved with the customary impatience of the elderly. "Come on Romeo, she's waiting," I whispered.

It was obvious the old biddies weren't about to leave as we approached.

"Nana," I said and bent down to kiss her papery cheek. I noted the laptop was on the floor under her chair. It would be very hard to accidentally jump on it while it remained under her chair.

Nana kissed me with her tight old lips.

"Sit Veronica." Romeo sat. Nana snickered, "Good boy."

"Veronica this is Ester Mulholland," Nana said. She indicated to the well-rounded woman on her left wearing a pale blue flower printed frock, her hair was blue, and she wore a blue sapphire and diamond ring.

"Hello," I said with a smile and reached forward to shake her hand. "Call me Ronnie."

I was in no hurry to sit.

Some days it felt like all they did in the retirement home was sit, and I just wasn't ready to sit, just in case old age snuck up on me while I wasn't looking.

The team and I had discussed how old age was tricky

and might catch us unawares.

I was the oldest. I sensed they were prepared to throw me under the old age bus, if it meant keeping the crypt keeper from their doors.

"Nice to meet you, dear." She had a slight accent, Scottish maybe.

"Veronica, please don't ask my friends to call you Ronnie," Nana said, her lips pinched and face sour.

"I like Ronnie, Nana." The argument was long standing. I think I was ten when I first introduced myself as Ronnie. Some decades later and Nana still hated it.

"It's too mannish. You are far too pretty to be a Ronnie, Veronica."

I let it go as Nana introduced me to the other woman.

Frankie Mount. I bet she wasn't really a Frankie, my money was on Francine. Ironic. Nana had no problem with her friend using a mannish name.

I nodded and smiled at Frankie. She was younger than Nana and Ester, maybe about eighty-five.

There was a hint of brown still in her hair and a nice tweed skirt with matching brown cashmere twin set. She wore a single string of off-white almost cream-coloured pearls around her neck.

It struck me as odd, how colour coordinated the old women were. I looked at Nana as the women chattered together.

Even she was coordinated. A charcoal grey skirt and deep red twin set. She wore a ruby and diamond ring and an onyx and ruby brooch. Her hair was platinum grey, not silver, or blue.

At least they still made an effort. It was likely that Donald chose their outfits.

I glanced around the spacious room. Romeo whined. "Okay boy," I said unclipping his lead. "Go visit." He ambled off to locate his favourite friends and the snacks they liked to ply him with. I watched him approach the first of his targets then move on when a snack didn't follow the petting. Clever dog. Not wasting his time with the no hopers. He moved in on an old biddy in the corner, sitting by herself.

On the far side of the room, comfortable chairs were arranged in large semi-circles. There were three such semi-circles. The majority of the inmates occupying the chairs seemed to be women. A few old men were scattered among them, they garnered as much attention as an edible centrepiece on a Christmas table. At the furthermost edge of the room, I glimpsed a pool table. Craning my neck, I saw two old men playing pool. They were nowhere near as decrepit as the ones sitting in the lounge. Several spry old women were watching the game with a lot of interest.

I wondered which one was offering herself as the prize. The thought triggered my gag reflex. Romeo appeared next to the men and waiting patiently for the fussing over him to commence.

Nana's voice interrupted my musings. "Veronica, dear."

"Yes, Nana."

"We have a puzzle for you. A conundrum of sorts."

I looked at the trio. They did look as though they were capable of scheming and puzzling. I suspect they'd read one too many Agatha Christie novels.

"Okay, tell me the details of this conundrum."

"Sit down dear, you're drawing attention to us," Frankie said, her voice not much more than a whisper.

I pulled a chair out of the semi-circle and placed it right in front of the women. Throwing caution to the wind, I sat. They nodded with approval.

The act of sitting seemed to slap old age in the face, or rather the nasty creeping virus that caused it. I'd formulated a theory that old age was in fact viral when I was quite young. I'm quite lucky it didn't turn me into a germaphobic freak.

My latest school of thought on the potential viral ageing conundrum was that the Norovirus acted as a delivery system.

I hid a cringe.

"I'm not sure how to put this," Nana started, and then paused. Her tongue flicked around her thin lips. "I'm dreadfully worried about Donald."

Here we go. I steeled myself for the rest because I knew Nana and nothing ever ended well when she was worried about Donald.

"Why Nana, what on earth has Donald done to make you worry." I trotted out my most intent concerned expression knowing full well that before she discovered the immediacy of email, worrying was Nana's hobby.

She'd long since given up knitting and needlepoint replacing them with worrying, gossip, and now emailing me. Nana was always worrying about something or other. Despite the worrying, she never seemed to come up with any solutions. This I also knew from experience.

My standard way of dealing with Nana when she'd tell me she was up all night worrying about something or other was to turn it back on her with a question. Did you find a solution?

Nana, had to my knowledge, never ever found a solution by worrying.

I did suspect that when Grandad was alive he used to provide solutions. It was that or not sleep, ever.

Nana fidgeted. Her answer came with reluctance, "He's never brought any girlfriends to visit."

"I see," I said, keeping my thoughts on the subject quiet.

"Frankie has a lovely granddaughter, she's about your age Veronica, and we were rather hoping ..."Nana petered off.

Frankie picked up the baton. "... We were hoping you could help us get the two of them together."

Oh my. That was not going to work.

I resisted the urge to laugh. Nana attempted something similar regarding Donald a few years earlier. Lucky, for Donald, Grandad was alive then and put an end to the parade of eligible women provided by Nana's long list of acquaintances. The list was shorter now. I imagined that was the drawback of living so long, she'd out lived a lot of her friends but not her family.

"Did you suggest this plan to Donald?"

"Not in so many words, no." Nana looked shifty as only a cunning old woman could.

"What words did you use?" I asked sensing the cunning old woman was holding back.

"I asked him to do my friends' hair."

"That's nothing like asking him to go on a blind date," I exclaimed.

"What should I say?" Nana asked with much indignation. "He gets so antsy when I ask about girlfriends."

I suppressed a smirk.

Nana carried on, "He has such high standards. I'm afraid he'll never meet the right girl."

Yes, high standards. That's why he's never had a girlfriend.

"Leave it with me, Nana. I will sound him out for you."

"Thank you dear, I knew you'd know how to help."

I made a move to stand up, only to find Nana's bony hand clamped upon my leg just above the knee.

"There was something else."

The three old cronies all leaned toward me, filling my personal space with old lady smell. A mixture of lavender and mothballs with a swirl of death. I tried leaning back but that encouraged them to lean closer.

"You remember my friend Martha," Nana said, as if she had no doubt that I knew whom she was talking about.

She was right. I knew Martha.

Nana liked to tell the story of how she met Martha; it became a not-so-cleverly disguised cautionary tale over the years. Poor Martha was an unfortunate soul from England who got knocked up by some Yank soldier during World War Two.

She somehow ended up on the Port Nicholson wharf in Wellington, New Zealand, hoping to find her Yankee lover.

Nana said that it was a funny place for a respectable woman during the war, or anytime really. Grandad was less charitable; he declared she was a tart and the open toed shoes she wore were proof of her low morals.

The more I'd heard the story as I grew up the more there seemed to be large holes in the plot. Grandad was a police officer back then, who reportedly found Martha on the docks. Despite his apparent disapproval of Martha's loose morals, she ended up boarding with my grandparents. They then married the poor woman off to a police officer friend of Grandads'. It seemed all very convenient, but at least the child wasn't born a bastard.

Martha, the redeemed scarlet woman and supposed friend of Nana's, was never someone Nana spoke well of. I lost count of the times I'd heard Nana say, "Poor Martha, she's no better than she should be." One day I'll figure out what that means.

Nana's voice interrupted my thoughts. "Martha lives in Silverstream now, in one of those little town houses by the railway line."

I hoped she wasn't about to tell me that Martha was

the dead woman from the newspaper, especially with what I'd been asked to help locate. I glanced at her; there was no sign of tragic news in her faded blue eyes.

"Does she, Nana? They look very nice those places."

If you like trains and having your china rattled every half an hour, along with gardens full of white-walled swans, concrete cats, and other ornamental atrocities.

Nana continued, "They're not nice places dear. All those trains and that licensed premise across the road. Bet that brings in an element."

I wanted to tell her I was being facetious but it seemed like a wasted effort.

Instead, I just agreed.

"So, tell me about Martha."

"Well, dear, Martha told me, she got up this morning to find one of her gnomes missing."

I blew out a silent sigh of relief. At least she got up. The gnome mention was worrisome and warranted more information.

"She didn't misplace it? You know, move it, and forget where?" It's been my experience that people never just have one gnome and Nana did say one of her gnomes. People who have gnomes tend to have all manner of oddities in their gardens. But still it struck me as ironic that there was a missing gnome now.

Nana shook her head. "That's what I asked her when she rang. She's adamant the gnome is missing."

"How odd."

"And then this …"

Frankie picked up a newspaper from her knee and showed me the front page. "Martha says it was two doors away from her house."

I read the headlines aloud, "Woman bashed to death in garden." I nodded. "I read this in the other paper this morning. Shocking." This paper seemed to have a little more information. Reading on, I noted they said the murder weapon was a garden gnome and that Police were canvasing the neighbourhood, hoping that someone might have seen the assailant.

A missing gnome and a gnome used as a weapon and I'm supposed to be looking for missing gnomes? There was a whole lot of crazy going on in the world of garden ornaments. Whatever next?

"That was so close to Martha's place. She's terrified," Nana said then rolled her eyes. "She always was one for the drama."

Pretty sure she had good reason to be concerned this time.

I opted for a soothing tone. "The murder and the theft probably are not related. Look they say here they have the murder weapon." Doing my best to downplay the whole thing. "Was Martha's gnome special in some way?"

It was possible that Martha's missing gnome could mean someone else is looking for gnomes. There a chance that whoever that person was had already found one. Or was Martha's gnome the murder weapon? I hoped she was an old lady who misplaced a gnome and nothing nasty was going on in her garden.

Nana's voice jolted me back to the conversation.

"I'm sure I wouldn't know," Nana said.

"Wouldn't know what, Nana?"

Nana tutted. "Pay attention, Veronica. You asked if the gnome was special in some way," she said allowing derision to sneak into her voice. "I have no idea what variety of horrendous ornament it is, other than a gnome."

"Just a question, Nana, that's all," I murmured.

"She's no better than she should be, that Martha," Nana grumbled.

I let Nana's words roll around my head for a few seconds. I still wasn't sure I knew what Nana meant but it was strangely comforting to hear her say it.

Changing the subject just a little I said, "Fancy a missing gnome and a murder by gnome, in sleepy little Silverstream."

And instantly regretted making the association out loud.

The whole gnome, Martha, murder situation writhed in my stomach like an angry eel.

"We were thinking of tracking down the thief," Nana announced with glee. "And maybe the murderer too. Could be the same person."

And there it was. The Nana bomb shell. I sucked back the urge to suggest she take up emailing the Prime Minister with invitations to afternoon tea. Perhaps she could use her new found email power to invite Prince William to the impending marriage of her favourite grandson Donald to Frankie's niece. That amused me more than it should.

Just then, I noticed there was something very Miss Marple about Nana.

I looked at Frankie, perched on the edge of her seat, the likeness to Angela Lansbury from the nineteen-eighty television series Murder She Wrote was uncanny.

I glanced at Ester Mulholland; she'd been very quiet throughout the conversations. I wondered what her story was but didn't have to wait long to find out.

Nana's face lit up as she announced, "Ester was a Police woman. She knew your grandfather."

"Did you work with Grandad?" I asked, welcoming the distraction.

"I knew your Grandfather. He was a sergeant when I met him. Police women didn't really work with the male officers." Ester sighed. "Back in those days we were mostly confined to our desks, nothing more than glorified office clerks."

It sounded like a dull job.

"Did police women ever get out from behind the desk?"

"Not often dear, we chaperoned female prisoners, filed reports, and made tea," Easter said. "It was a different world back in our day."

And Donald thought he had problems.

Nana and Frankie exchanged looks, and I waited to see if they had anything interesting to impart or anything that required sharing with the group.

Nothing more was said. It was as if the women were

waiting for some revelation from me.

I checked my watch. There was plenty of time for them to spill details of their plan and give me a chance to thwart it, with a touch of subtle underhandedness, of course.

The last thing I needed was the three ancient crones zapping around on their mobility scooters causing all manner of trouble.

I considered for a second how much of a charge those things held. Could they get from Northern Upper Hutt to Silverstream?

I doubted it.

I didn't imagine they had enough juice to travel from one end of the city limits to the other.

How else could the trio get to Silverstream to carrying out their investigation?

I jumped back to the conversation around me just in time to hear them discuss asking Donald to drive them. Oh no, that would never do.

I jumped in boots and all. "Haven't you three tormented Donny enough?"

"Don't call him that Veronica, it's so cheap sounding," Nana said, pursing her thin lips.

I suppressed my amusement, cheap sounding it maybe, Donny sounds more like a pillow biter than Donald but only just.

"All right. But haven't you?"

"We're not tormenting him, dear. We're assisting him to have a more fulfilled life."

I smiled, my eyes danced with amusement as I considered encouraging Nana in her pursuit of a girlfriend for Donald, so much better than her harassing me via email every two seconds and it would serve him right.

Bugger. I wasn't as mean as that. God preserve us all from Nana's ideas of fulfilment.

There was a chance for me to save Donald and keep a closer eye on The Cronies of Doom.

"I'll take you to Martha's in the morning. If the gnome hasn't turned up by then." And no one else shows up dead.

It was a two birds, one stone situation. I could use the outing as cover for my own investigation.

"That would be lovely, Veronica," Nana said, stretching her thin lips into a smile.

A little plan formed.

"We really need to know what the gnome looked like?" I suggested injecting as much nonchalance as I could into my voice.

"Yes, we do," Ester said with enthusiasm. "June, you should give Martha a ring and find out."

"Does it really matter?"

"It'll be hard to find it if you don't know what you're looking for," I replied.

"I suppose that is true." Nana thought for a moment. I could see the cogs turning. "Pass the phone dear."

I stood and looked around. On a coffee table not far away was a phone. I retrieved it and gave it to Nana.

She dialled Martha's number from memory.

After the longest minute in history, Nana finally spoke to Martha. I heard Nana's part of the conversation and murmuring from the phone. Ten minutes later Nana hung up.

"And?" I asked.

Ester had a pen poised over a pad of paper ready to jot down notes.

"Just one of those ugly foot high garden gnomes with a blue hat and red trousers, I believe," Nana replied.

"Anything else? Distinguishing mark of any kind?"

Nana chortled. "I doubt it had a scar or a tattoo, dear."

"Was there anything to narrow it down in a line up?"

Nana smiled at the question. "Sometimes, Veronica you remind me very much of your grandfather."

With a smile I said, "Answer the question please, Nana."

"She might have said the wretched thing had a pick axe or a shovel."

"Might have or did?"

"Oh, I don't know. How many different sorts of gnomes are there?"

"More than you could imagine," I said. More than I ever wanted to know.

And my plan involved a quick trip to The Warehouse to find a replacement gnome that I could plant in another part of Martha's garden and let Nana find it.

That would be difficult if I didn't know what the silly thing looked like.

"A shovel. The wretched thing had a shovel."

I saw Ester writing in her notebook.

"Tomorrow morning then?"

"Oh thank you, Veronica," Nana said, her voice took on a delighted tone. "It will be such fun."

I arched my eyebrows, fun?

Fun wasn't something I envisaged when I thought of supervising The Cronies of Doom. I was certain the three of them were no threat to the security of gnomes in general, but they were nosy.

Nosy had a way of inadvertently leading to trouble. I'd have to watch them and head off any rumblings of disquiet before trouble started.

"I'm off. I will see you three in the morning. Ten o'clock sharp at the reception desk."

I stood up.

"Romeo!"

He bounded across the long room wagging his tail and licking cream off his doggy lips.

He'd been conning creamed scones off some old duck in the dining room. I clipped his lead to his harness.

The trio smiled, their thin lips stretched to the maximum over teeth that now appeared too big for their mouths. Gruesome.

Uncharitable notions surfaced about Halloween and scaring children. It was no surprise that the big bowl of sweets at reception was still sitting there from last Halloween. What kid would try trick or treating at a retirement home? The inmates didn't need costumes to terrify people. It was like being stuck in The Evil Dead movie, without Ash Williams.

"We will see you tomorrow morning," they chorused as Romeo and I walked away.

I could hear the excited chatter filling their corner of the room as we exited through the wide doorway. Side stepping a Zimmer frame pushed by a fragile oldie, our escape lay directly ahead. A sigh escaped my lips as a gaggle of old folk shuffled into the reception area and blocked the exit to freedom.

Weaving through the crowd, it occurred to me that it wasn't going to be easy keeping The Cronies of Doom in check. They couldn't do much harm whilst supervised. Surely? As long as I kept Nana away from the murder scene, it'd be all good. There should be a cordon around the scene complete with scene guards and that would help keep the inquisitive oldies out. I hoped.

Opening the front door and stepping out into a cool fresh breeze, I took a deep breath, ridding my lungs of the dense air from inside the retirement home.

Heavy air laced with death.

"Breathe deeply Romeo, cleanse yourself."

I thought about the odd smells associated with old age as I attached the seat belt tether to Romeo's harness, safely buckling him into the car.

Really, old people shouldn't smell any different to regular people. However, they do. Old seemed to have its own special smells associated with it.

Old cars smell a certain way, all sunbaked leather and stale tobacco. Old houses smell of musty darkness mixed with rose potpourri and lavender oil. Very old people and old animals smelt a lot like death, as if they were rotting from the inside out.

I pushed thoughts of death aside.

For the second time that day, the pale blue car came into view. This time it was parked a hundred metres up the road from the retirement home.

Twice in one day seemed like less of a coincidence. I pulled out my notebook and jotted down the sightings of him. A shudder tore up my spine. Panic prickled deep in my brain. The car was trouble.

Bugger it.

Time I called the office.

"Hey, Steph, I could be imagining it, but I think someone is following me."

"Pale blue car by any chance?"

"Uh huh, why?"

"Jenn called in earlier. She's seen a pale blue car twice today, and she's on the job. She wanted me to check it wasn't the wife or another PI hired by the husband."

Reasonable query.

"And?"

"Not related. The car belongs to Daniel Shankle."

"Daniel Shankle."

That was a familiar name. He was a moron of the highest order and it wasn't the first time he'd drawn attention to himself.

I'd even run a quick criminal check on him once but that was a few months back and primarily to satisfy my own curiosity.

His name felt all sharp and pointy as I said it again, "Daniel Shankle." He was never going to amount to much with a name like that. "His parents must've hated him."

Steph laughed. "I'd say so."

"What do we know about him now?"

"Not much, he's still unemployed as far as I can tell."

"Let's do some digging. Maybe that'll unearth a few clues as to why he's so interested in what we're doing."

"I'll get back to you."

I hung up.

Pushing all thoughts of the horrible man out of my mind, I scanned for traffic and pulled out heading south. A few minutes later I parked at Pak n' Save.

Because I am such a good cousin I texted Donald warning him of Nana's hare brained scheme to fix him up with a nice girl. Donald texted back wanting to know how to put an end to it.

I laughed and replied, 'ever thought of telling her the truth?'

I didn't expect a reply to that text, and the reply didn't come. The truth concerning Nana was a touchy subject for Donald. He didn't give Nana enough credit for knowing how the real world worked and I had weighed in several times with that particular observation.

I cracked the back windows an inch and left Romeo snoozing on the back seat while I shopped. I exited the stupid market with two bags of groceries just as the same pale blue convertible cruised through the car park. Three times in one day, I was going to have to do something about him and his stalking ways.

I dumped the bags in the boot. Romeo watched as the blue car crept from the car park.

"Let's go home. It's creepy out here with that blue car around."

I could've sworn Romeo nodded.

Chapter 5
[DEVIL IS IN THE DETAILS]

With Romeo out in the back garden making the most of the sun, I settled into work mode. With an equal amount of dread and excitement, I opened my email program. Another six emails from Nana; she was excited about the investigation.

Yay.

Under Nana's emails I spotted the email I was waiting for from Benjamin with a bunch of attachments.

I read it, and then opened the first attachment. It was a Jpeg of the gnome I was looking for. Unremarkable, garden variety gnome. No shovel or pick axe in sight. Nice and easy then. Didn't look like the one missing from Martha's, if Nana was right about that one having a shovel. Martha was at least ninety years old so there was a good chance she'd misplaced it or miscounted or simply forgotten what had happened to her gnome.

The second attachment contained a contract and security briefing. I checked the phone numbers on the briefing and added Benjamin's to my phone.

Yeah, I have an actor's phone number in my phone.

What of it?

Twice I read the amount on the contract. Expenses plus two hundred and sixty-five thousand American dollars to find three gnomes.

Just over quarter of a million US. That was a crazy

amount of money. It would go a long way to keeping our business afloat for quite some time.

I also sensed a holiday on the horizon.

I had a hankering to buy a round-the-world ticket and travel for fun. Before the thoughts of exotic places carried me away, I hauled my mind back to the task at hand.

Locating gnomes was even weirder than delivering fairy dust to pixies. And that was the weirdest case I'd had to date.

I pondered on the fairy dust thing. Obviously, I hadn't really delivered fairy dust to pixies. It was Anthrax that I'd delivered to a pixie. Because that's so much better than delivering fairy dust. The memory of the case caused a ripple of laughter as it surfaced.

The transfer took place in a fairy grotto created in a local park the year before last at a medieval fair. The recipient was a pixie with green pointy ears. Parts of my life are too weird to tell regular people about. It bordered on fantasy and one day I knew I would write about it. I can call it fiction. No one would believe it otherwise. And now I'm working for an actor who isn't just an actor. Yes, fiction it would have to be.

Back to the task at hand.

There was a form to fill in. Jenn would love it. She had forms for everything. Pretty sure, she has forms for forms. I filled it in.

They also required a bank account number for payment.

I typed in the company bank account number and

emailed the form back to Benjamin. I also gave him a run down on the news and the missing gnome in Silverstream.

I surfed the internet for about ten minutes before a reply arrived from Benjamin.

Yes, he'd seen the news about the woman bashed to death and supplied the actual police report for me to read. His advice regarding the missing gnome was to keep a close eye on the situation.

Again, I asked why he didn't just send police to hunt for them. Couldn't they put out some kind of gnome alert? Imagining it to be like an Amber Alert for missing kids caused another ripple of amusement. I love my life.

My phone rang. I didn't even get a chance to say 'wherefore art thou' before I heard my name.

"Ronnie?"

"Benjamin?"

His name felt quite formal. Perhaps that was his intention. I hadn't come across a Benjamin in years. Not really a name that's common.

"We want you to locate the gnomes, police have other things on their plate, and you are the one recommended for finding things."

I find people. I might suck at finding gnomes.

"I'll be in Silverstream tomorrow. It will give me opportunity to look around gnome

filled gardens. Also, regarding the missing gnome, who else is looking for the gnomes?"

Silence.

"Benjamin?"

"There might be other factions interested in this situation."

I was skimming the police reports. "Other factions who don't mind bashing an old woman to death when they're disturbed while fossicking in someone's garden?"

"We don't know if that is what happened."

"Guess what my money is on?"

Silence again.

"Do your best," he said.

"And the shipment of replacements?"

"It will arrive by courier tonight. I've moved it up. You might need one tomorrow," Benjamin said.

"Is there a time frame on this?"

"Just find them before anyone else does."

"How do we know someone already hasn't?" It seemed feasible to me that someone may have found one already. It could've been at Martha's.

"Chatter. We'd know."

I hung up. It didn't seem quite so funny now someone was dead. Something nasty was going on. Something involving chatter. Terrorism jumped to mind, sending a cold chill down my spine. Well it was never going to be a good situation, not with Reede asking me to take the case and with DHS involved.

I read the police reports thoroughly. It was great having both the murder report and the theft report. The stolen gnome was different to the gnome that someone used as a weapon.

So it probably wasn't that gnome?

The husband identified the gnome as one from their garden.

I checked the story about the stolen gnome again just to make sure that Martha gave a description that didn't match. She hadn't seen the gnome that did the damage to her neighbour but hers definitely had a shovel. I presumed the murder weapon was messy and not something Police would want an elderly lady to see.

From the description of the gnome weapon, it seemed indistinguishable from the ones I was looking for. I had a horrible feeling. What if they had the description wrong for the ones I was supposedly trying to locate? What if someone beat me to it? My poor choice of words continued to smack into the sides of my skull.

To clear my head and allow some fresh air in my lungs I decided I'd take the dog for a walk.

I called Romeo, put his harness and lead on and we went for a walk to the park. He was happy and I was getting much needed time away from Nana's emails, the constant chiming as another one arrived grated on my nerves as I tried to consider all possibilities regarding the gnomes.

The joy of Greyhounds is they don't tend to like walking too far. Twenty minutes and a fast run three times around the cricket pitch was more than enough for Romeo, and then he was ready for another snooze.

He stopped on the porch when we got home and stared off down the street. I followed his line of sight. Daniel bloody Shankle and his pale blue car.

This was stupid. He'd become a problem and I didn't like it. Having someone watching me right now wasn't the best idea. But why was he watching Jenn as well?

I called Donald.

He'd know if this were an overreaction on my part or not.

I launched into conversation without bothering with pleasantries, "Hey. You remember that guy who tried to pick me up in the Seven Bar a few months ago?"

"Which one?" Donald asked.

"The one I called the hobbit."

"Ewww, him, the Humpty Dumpty look alike with the enormous hairy feet. Oh, that man needs shoes," Donald said, his voice thick with disgust. "He's not trying it on again is he?"

"Not exactly."

"Then why bring his fat troll arse up?"

"Yes, that's what he is, a troll. Thank you! And as to why, I've seen him three times today. It's creepy."

"Is he stalking you?"

"I don't know. Just seems like a huge coincidence that he's everywhere I am all of a sudden. It's not just me, though. Jenn has seen his car as well."

"He's watching both of you? This has to be connected to the business."

"That's what I was thinking."

"Be careful – he was a crazy fat troll and it doesn't sound like he's improved."

"Call you later, cuzzie."

If it accomplished nothing else, at least Donald now knew about the hobbit slash troll stalker. Security wise it made sense to have someone else aware that Shankle the troll was lurking at the edges of my life.

He could even be an Orc, an escapee from The Lord of the Rings movie set, perhaps?

Gross.

That made me think of the secret hobbit set that once inhabited the old General Motors site out by the army camp and Benjamin the actor. He was too good looking and tall to be a hobbit. I pushed the movie thought away.

My next task was to find a map of Upper Hutt. Took a bit of searching but I eventually found one among my extensive map collection. I smoothed the map across the dining room table, making sure there were no creases or folds in awkward places. Then I took the quartz crystal on a silver chain from around my neck. Most people never noticed it. I'd worn it under my clothes for years.

My right hand closed around the crystal. The cool stone warmed as I closed my eyes. Concentrating on my breathing, I asked my guardian angel for protection and to guide my hand.

Opening my fingers the crystal dropped until all I was holding was the silver chain between my thumb and forefinger. My eyes opened and I asked for confirmation of an affirmative swing. The quartz spun in big clockwise circles.

"Stop."

It stopped and hung absolutely still.

"Show me no."

The quartz swung forward and back, tugging the chain in my fingers.

"Stop."

It stopped dead.

I started in the north of the town, with the farthest suburb and asked, "Show me the gnome."

The crystal hung still.

I moved along the map in small increments, pausing to allow time for the crystal to react.

Nothing.

The process was slow because the universe worked at its own pace. I steadied my hand and my breathing and concentrated on moving without causing the crystal to wobble.

As my hand approached Silverstream, the crystal began to move in circles.

I stopped over the suburb. Street by street was the best way to go.

The crystal swung with ever increasing speed in clockwise circles. The circles started big, and then became smaller, until the stone was swinging in tiny fast circles over an area near the railway station.

Interesting.

I thanked my guides and asked for another gnome. This time I started in the south. The stone did nothing until it was over Pinehaven.

So now, I knew there was one gnome near Silverstream railway station and one not far from the Pinehaven tennis courts.

My hand was drawn to another suburb as I worked my way north on the map. Totara Park.

All three places held a connection which made the gnome situation all the more intriguing. Not only were there many gnomed gardens in the chosen suburbs but the suburbs themselves held meaning to me. Justin popped into my thoughts and I wondered where he was. Once upon a time, when we were young we flatted together in each of those suburbs.

Chapter 6
[GARDEN OF GNOMES]

I checked my smile in the rear vision mirror after parking in the driveway of the retirement home. The smile came off like a scary grimace. I smiled again. It still looked like a grimace. I took a breath and put everything I had into it. The result wasn't much better.

Romeo sighed, huffing air out the sides of his mouth. I twisted around and eyed him.

"If I have to go, so do you."

He sighed again.

Finally, a smile that would satisfy the fussiest of grandmothers slipped into place. If it didn't slide off the smile might even fool The Cronies of Doom.

The day was warmish and sitting in the car amplified the heat. Not bad for autumn; at least the rain had stopped.

Troll's stupidity crowded my mind. I needed to work harder than ever to maintain the smile and get rid of the image of Daniel Shankle and his car. But I did it.

From where I'd parked, I could see three old women gathered about the reception desk and a real smile crept over my face.

I saw Margot surrounded by The Cronies of Doom and imagined they were pestering the hell out of her.

Even knowing that they would soon be in my car didn't stop the amusement.

"No need to hurry," I whispered to the dog. "They'll happily pester Margot while I get the car sorted."

I reached around and took Romeo's bed from where I'd left it folded over on half the back seat, and climbed out of the car. I opened the rear door and spread his bed in the very back then moved Romeo from the back seat to his bed, and reattached his seat belt. He lay down.

It was a pleasant day and I intended to enjoy every quiet, warm, step of it. I breathed in the scent of the roses growing near the driveway, and the jasmine climbing the arch by the front entrance. My nose tickled as the warm Jasmine smell reached the very back of it. I fought back a sneeze. Birds twittered, a cat skulked by, sirens screamed.

Toward the road, the siren grew louder and louder. A police car tore by followed by an ambulance. Lights and sirens mingled, all in a blur of activity. Someone's day just ended badly.

The old women poked their heads out the door at the commotion and spotted me.

Behind them, I caught a glimpse of Margot's relieved face. I waved over their heads and yelled out, "I'll drop them back in an hour or two."

"No rush," Margot called back. "There's not much planned for today."

I laughed. An hour or two is more than enough for me.

"That colour is pretty on you, Veronica," Nana crooned. "You should wear red more often."

I eyed her with suspicion, as anyone would with a

Nana like mine.

Often her compliments were thinly veiled snipes, or a tool she used to soften someone up before the axe fell.

I knew Nana and I had a feeling there would be an axe before the end of the day.

"Glad you think so, Nana."

"You could be out on a date wearing that pretty top, Veronica," Nana replied with a thin smile.

"One day my prince will come, Nana. Isn't that how it goes?"

She nodded. "One day. I might be gone by then."

"Where are you going, Nana?" I replied. We'd been having this same conversation since I was eighteen. Nana often said she might be gone soon.

"You know, dear," she said with a heavy sigh. "I won't live forever."

Same old conversation heading to the same answer from me.

"You'll be around a long time yet, Nana and I don't need your help when it comes to dating," I said with firmness. "When the right man comes along, I'm pretty sure I'll know what to do with him."

Nana huffed. "You're not getting any younger." She narrowed her little beady eyes. "I want to see my great-grandchildren before I go."

"You better hang on for a few more years, then, Nana, because I've not found any suitable contenders for fatherhood."

"Perhaps you are too picky ..."

Time to pretend I couldn't hear her. We were fast approaching an argument. According to Nana, I was either too picky or not picky enough. Win win for her.

If she didn't let it go, I was prepared to sacrifice Donald.

I turned my attention to the cronies. "Nice to see you ladies," I said, smiling at them. "Shall we go?"

Frankie smiled. I realised she still had her own teeth. Amazing.

The other woman, the one who seemed quite forgettable said, "Good morning, young Veronica."

I had to think before replying, "Good morning, Ester."

It bugged me that I had trouble remembering the woman's name, even though she used to work with Grandad. It flustered me. I don't like forgetting names. Maybe it was Alzheimer's setting in early? I imagined that I'd caught the old age virus from the retirement home and shuddered. I should've used more hand sanitiser.

More likely, recent events coupled with the horror of spending the next few hours in the company of my loving Nana and The Cronies of Doom and I simply forgot the woman's name.

A shiver zapped up my spine. I didn't want to be around when the crypt keeper came looking for the crones.

Despite that, I began the process of easing the women into my car. I drove an SUV. It was a capacious car, with wide opening doors both front and back; in other words, it was perfect for getting older folk in and out of. Except, it was more truck than car and old girls don't climb so well.

Nana needed help into the front passenger seat.

Frankie and Ester chose a side each and managed to get themselves in with little fuss.

I did help pass the seat belts to them.

Fair enough though, it's not always easy to reach around and wrestle seat belts even for the more able bodied.

I swung into the driver's seat. "Everyone buckled in?"

"Yes," chorused my charges.

Old people in Surround sound, I didn't know my own luck.

"Where to?" I asked.

Not wanting to be presumptuous by suggesting going to Martha's straight off, I rather hoped the thought of freedom would dissuade them from a gnome hunt. Perhaps a nice morning tea out somewhere or a trip to the mall. Nana loved the mall.

The women in the backseat muttered together. It struck me as odd that none of the three needed hearing aids.

It was especially odd when Nana joined in the discussion.

I could've sworn that just last week Mum was telling me that Nana couldn't hear anything said, and never turned her hearing aid on.

More Nana games?

The week before Mum insisted Nana had lost the rest of her marbles and was now deep in senile dementia territory.

That was due to Nana's inability to recognise her and because Mum heard Nana referring to Donald as Donovan.

Nana confessed her naughty behaviour to me the next evening.

She also said it was jolly hard to keep a straight face throughout the episode.

Nana is a wicked woman. I want to be just like her when I grow up. Perhaps that should be if I grow up.

I waited for the in depth discussion of protocol regarding the investigation to end. It wasn't easy to remain calm and unhurried. But I had experience with older folk and it left me very aware that the slightest thing could turn them nasty.

That wasn't something I wanted. Trapped in a car with three nasty old women sounded a lot like hell. I'd need a weapon. A Taser would be ideal. Zapping old people into submission or a heart attack felt like a good option. Either way it would be quiet.

Then it happened, my phone rang. The soft old voices came to an abrupt stop.

My phone rang louder. I regretted my choice in ring tones immediately. Right Said Fred's 'I'm Too Sexy' blared from my handbag. I cowered in terror as I fumbled for the phone. There was no need to check the caller ID that was the ring tone I set for Benjamin. It seemed fun and whimsical at the time. I undid my seat belt and opened the car door as I answered the phone. All eyes were on me.

I waved at the cronies and shut the door.

Benjamin spoke, "Everything all right at your end?"

"Sure, why wouldn't it be?"

I leaned on the car, soaking up the sun's rays.

"There's been some chatter this morning."

"Chatter?" I repeated.

I love a good gossip as much as the next girl but sensed that wasn't what he meant.

His type of chatter was never good.

The Cronies of Doom would be chattering by now, too, and that wouldn't be good either.

"Some chatter has been intercepted, regarding the packages."

I stifled a smile because it wouldn't do to have a smile resound in my voice. Even though the thought of chatter mentioning gnomes was amusing.

"Who intercepted?" Not that it mattered. I rather hoped it was the CIA because that would be funny as hell to me. Every CIA officer I'd ever come across had zero sense of humour. Just the thought of those deadpan faces having to send out alerts regarding gnomes was almost too much for me.

"NSA and GCSB."

Bugger.

That was not anywhere near as funny.

NSA and GCSB worked with the Intelligence Service

and helped set up the whole fairy dust thing. They all proved they had a sense of humour when it counted.

"And the chatter said what?"

"They confirmed there is a terror cell involved and they are searching for the same packages as we are."

"I'm on my way to Silverstream. Do we know if the murder is related?"

"Yes."

"I'll keep you posted."

Ester knocked on the window.

I looked into the car. The three oldies and Romeo were sitting in full sun, in a closed car. I felt awful.

"One second," I said into the phone.

I opened my door, turned the ignition key, and hit the window releases, opening the windows and filling the car with fresh air.

I indicated to the phone in my hand, "Sorry, work. It's rather important."

The women all nodded, as if they understood. I heard Nana explaining to her cronies about my job as a private investigator.

Unable to now talk by the car, I casually waked a few feet away and continued the conversation with Benjamin. I looked toward the road just as the troll's pale blue car cruised past doing well under the speed limit. I sighed. He was going to make the job tough.

"What was the sigh about?" Benjamin asked.

"Nothing much."

"Who were you talking to a moment ago?"

"My Nana. I'm taking her out this morning," I replied.

"That's nice," he said, taking a sharp inward breath. "Did you get the replacements?"

"Yes, I have one with me." I doubted our missing gnome would still be around waiting for me to find.

"How long will you be?" he asked.

"A few hours. How far ahead of the cell are we?"

"Judging by the murder, they think there is a gnome in Silverstream but don't know where."

That was what I thought, too, but I wasn't going to tell him how I came to that conclusion yet.

"And you're sure they didn't find it when they killed that woman?"

"From what we can gather they're still looking."

"We don't know where it is either."

I considered how much he needed to know. Technically, he was my boss.

"So far all I'd been able to turn up is the possibility of a gnome being stashed in Silverstream and one in Pinehaven, and I'm leaning toward Totara Park for number three."

If I'm right then I think I know who hid them and that makes for one hell of a perplexing situation.

"We need to meet."

I heard the questions in his voice lurking under the words and wondered how long it would be until he asked how I knew their potential locations so fast.

"Coffee, movie, bar?"

"Movie. I'll book and get back to you," Benjamin said.

"Okay." I watched the same pale blue car cruise back on the other side of the road and decided to tell Benjamin about the car. "I may have a small problem. I think I'm being followed."

"That's not good."

"No. It's not ideal by any means."

Neither of us said goodbye.

I scanned the road. The pale blue car was out of sight. While talking to Benjamin, I'd walked farther away from my car than I realised. Nana waved as I walked back.

Benjamin's movie idea made me smile.

Nice. I wondered if he'd be in it. Would that be awkward? Do actors watch their own movies and shows?

Even though I knew it was business, it was still good.

The thought of a movie with Benjamin made the hours that stretched in front of me with the cronies seem a tad less daunting.

My thoughts returned to more pressing things: where exactly was the Silverstream gnome and could I find it before someone else was killed?

And was Martha's missing gnome the gnome. It didn't match the description but who's to say the description was correct? Or who's to say that Martha remembered her gnome correctly?

Taking three elderly ladies to the place where the gnome may or may not be was:

A/ Dangerous?

B/ Stupid?

C/ Completely insane?

I chose D/ all of the above.

The women were champing at the bit when I clambered back into the car.

"To Martha's," Nana commanded.

"Yes ma'am," I replied, zapping the windows up and switching the air conditioning on to a comfortable eighteen degrees. It didn't do to have old people get too chilled, or too warm, or to sit in drafts. "Off we go."

The backseat remained a lively chattering place on the drive down to Silverstream. Nana joined in a few times from her perch up front, but I got the impression she just wanted to chat to me about Donald. And I wanted to clear my mind and prepare for possible trouble.

It was one of those times that I wished for more than a Swiss Army Knife.

My current wish list included pepper spray, a stun gun or Taser, a Glock, or maybe a Sig Sauer.

Any kind of firepower or defensive weapon thing would be good with confirmation we are up against a terror cell.

I stopped myself from speculating on the contents of the gnomes. It was enough that it was something terrorists wanted as bad as we did.

If anyone was still watching for activity in Silverstream, my arrival with a carload of old women wouldn't look suspicious. Nothing odd about an elderly day out. Couldn't see how it would spark alarms and trigger a response. As far as we were aware, no one knew about my involvement in the situation, with the exception of

Homeland that is. I hadn't told Reede so that meant the Secret Intelligence Service didn't know. My plan was that I appeared as nothing more than a chauffeur and possibly a relative to one of the old folk. Part of me wondered if anyone would be watching.

I kept careful watch on the traffic looking for the troll; I deemed him the biggest immediate threat to the operation. And the sort of attention he would bring was not helpful.

I parked as close to Martha's as possible so the oldies didn't have far to totter.

Police cars parked on both sides of the road and officers milling about, pointed to an ongoing investigation.

Crime scene taped stretched across a gate, of the crime scene.

Outside the gate was a van. I could see police working in the garden beyond the low fence, still collecting evidence and conducting a scene examination.

"Veronica," Nana said, pulling my attention away from the scene outside.

"Yes, Nana." I turned my head to find Nana standing on the footpath.

That was quick.

"Do come along," Nana said.

I hustled from the car and assisted Ester, then Frankie. With all three safely standing on the footpath, I took Romeo from the back and locked the car using the remote on the key ring.

"We never had such things in our day, dear," Ester said

watching with interest as the car's indicators flashed and the alarm chirped letting me know it was armed. Compared to the horse drawn carriages they had in Frankie and Nana's day, I supposed, just having a steering wheel was high tech. I remembered Nana telling stories of how they went to school by horse drawn buggy. Of course, there were cars, but few people had or used them out in the small country town where Nana grew up.

"They're fairly new." Compared to horse drawn buggies and stone tablets.

"Do they do other things or just make a noise?" Ester asked.

"This one immobilises the engine so the car won't start unless you disable the alarm first."

"Isn't that clever?" Ester said, and nudged Frankie.

Frankie agreed it was clever.

I surveyed the area as the women made their way up the path to Martha's front door. It was almost painful to watch, the slow, deliberate small steps. Frankie put on a burst of speed and arrived on the doorstep first, she knocked. A firm knock for an old duck.

They all waited for Martha to answer the door.

I watched the street. While I watched, the troll drove past.

He turned at the roundabout outside the shops to cruise back again. Romeo whined as the car disappeared down the street.

I pulled a notebook from my bag and jotted down the registration and time. I also made a few notes on the morning's troll activity. None of the old women noticed my notebook or interest in the street.

Nana clicked her tongue and trotted out a tut of disapproval about the garden ornaments in the small overloaded garden. From inside the house I heard a shuffling of feet and scuffing of slippers across a polished surface. They waited.

A few minutes passed before there was a rattling near the lock of the door and then finally a click and a squeak as the door was unlocked and handle turned.

"Yes?" said the woman inside through the security chain.

"Martha it's June, and the girls."

The door rattled, closed, reopened and this time opened freely. Martha peered out.

"June? Is that you?"

"Yes, dear," Nana replied. "Put your glasses on."

"Oh, I don't know where I left them, silly things," she replied, stepping aside from the doorway. "Come in, come in."

"You need one of those string things to hang your glasses around your neck," Nana told her. "There is quite a to-do at your neighbours."

"It's awful, June. Poor poor Patricia." Martha ushered the group in doors. "Go through to the living room, I'll put the tea on," Martha said.

"You like dogs, don't you, Martha," Nana said through tight lips. I got the impression it wasn't really a question.

"Yes, yes, of course. I had my old Billy for eighteen

years."

Nana scoffed none too quietly, "Bony old bag of fleas that he was."

"Who's this?" Martha questioned, grabbing my arm with a gnarled claw like hand. Romeo looked at the woman, and then walked on following Nana into the house.

"My Alan's daughter, surely you remember Veronica," Nana said.

Martha peered at me, her wrinkled eyes squinted. Faded blue and old. "I don't think so, June. Your Veronica was only a wee lass when I saw her last."

Nana saw fit not to argue. She turned to me and waited for Martha to scuffle off to the kitchen. "She's quite mad, poor thing."

"Pots and kettles Nana, watch out."

"Whatever do you mean, Veronica?" Nana said, again I heard the forged innocence in her tone.

"Nothing at all, Nana," I replied, smiling.

The three of them sat in the living room.

Romeo found a comfortable spot on the carpet in the sun and lay down.

I considered that once upon a time, we would've sat in the front room. A room reserved solely for guests.

However, with downsizing to a retirement flat, there was no front room anymore. They all had to make do with the less formal lounge room.

Martha crashed about in the kitchen; clattering and banging as old people tend to do.

After five minutes of the interminable noise, that the Cronies of Doom duly ignored, I excused myself and disappeared to help Martha.

"Martha, can I help?" I asked, careful not to scare the woman into a heart attack or stroke.

"Yes, yes. How lovely. Who are you again?"

"I'm Veronica, June's granddaughter."

"Oh yes, June. That's right."

I glanced out the kitchen window and noted it overlooked the area of garden that once housed the missing gnome. How the woman knew anything was missing was beyond me.

I saw several gnomes that fitted the description of the one I was looking for.

"Shall I make the tea?" I asked, and then noted the teapot stood steaming on a wooden board on the bench. "Ah, I see you've already made the tea."

Martha was fishing around in a cupboard under the bench, bringing up cups, and finding matching saucers.

"Or would you like me to help you get the cups?"

Martha didn't answer as she carefully counted the cups and matched them with their saucers.

"I'm afraid I haven't baked for some time. I only have bought biscuits to offer." A flustered panic gripped the woman and resounded in her voice. "Your Nana always had something in the tins, no matter when a body called in."

I smiled.

Martha and her Nana had been friends for sixty or

more years and yet she didn't know that Nana's baking came from the local bakery or at least had for the last thirty years.

"Your Nana was famous for her creamed sponges," Martha said with reverence as she wrestled open a packet of Vanilla wines and laid a few on a pretty plate.

"Yes, I remember," I replied.

My childhood memory regarding sponges was one of Nana buying them at the local New World supermarket. And Grandad whipping the cream, then slicing the strawberries and decorating the sponge cake.

The only memory I had of Nana actually baking was making the shortbread for Christmas, and the Christmas cake. The delicious booze soaked moist dark fruit cake Nana had made every year, except last year.

She didn't have the strength to mix the cake batter anymore, nor the inclination to bake it now that Grandad had shuffled off this mortal coil. I don't know that she used the oven or stove in her apartment at all now. She seemed to have all her meals in the communal dining room with her friends. I would, too, if I had a choice.

Martha touched my arm. "And that Christmas cake, people came for miles for a sample of that cake."

Yes, that's right, that's what Nana used to say. I could not confirm any truth in that statement. Her cake might have been as famous as she said but somehow I doubted it.

I looked out the window again. The high fence prevented anyone from on the street or footpath from looking in, unless they stood directly in line with the gateway. The gate itself was only three feet high, about half the height of the fence.

Martha filled a small flowery cream jug with milk, and poured sugar into a matching sugar bowl.

Half the sugar cascaded onto the bench. I wiped it up before she noticed.

She was going to a lot of trouble and it all seemed to be to garner the approval of Nana.

It was somewhat confusing. It's not as if Nana was the Queen or anything. Why did Martha treat her with such reverence and worry so much about impressing her?

I loaded a tray with the milk, sugar, biscuits, and teaspoons and then carried it through to the living room, then unloaded the tray onto a central coffee table.

I picked the empty tray up, and then leaned forward to the group and in a conspiratorial way asked, "Where do you suppose the gnome was?"

They looked from one to the other. No one had any idea.

I whispered again, "Do we know if she even had another gnome?"

Again, they looked at each other.

"Just asking, she seems a little vacant and lonely," I said, and then added, "And how could anyone tell what was missing from that garden? I noticed no gaps." I scooted back to the kitchen with the empty tray.

Seeds of doubt lay strewn about ready for pecking at by the Cronies of Doom.

It was possible that Martha imagined she had a gnome go missing and called the newspaper, to get someone to come out and stop for a cup of tea. Old people did weird things out of loneliness.

With a tray loaded with tea and cups, I returned to the gaggle of women, and set the tray on the table.

I did the polite thing, and passed everyone a cup of tea, then offered the milk and sugar.

Martha passed the biscuit plate around, apologising for her lack of baking. I watched Nana carefully to see if she showed any disdain.

There was a subtle tutting.

The women began to interrogate poor Martha before she'd even sat down.

It was bad enough she'd lived her life trying in vain to measure up to Nana, who wasn't half the saint and perfect wife, or perfect mother, she'd led everyone to believe. Now the poor woman was undergoing a grilling by the Cronies of Doom and I had helped by the sneaky way I cast aspersions on. I'm a bad person.

There was no enjoyment in planting the seeds of doubt; I simply wanted Nana and company out of there as soon as possible. Preferably, I wanted them to leave believing there was no missing gnome. No missing gnome and no mystery and this whole thing was nothing more than a lonely old woman in need of company.

A little bit of subversive coercion to keep some oldies safe versus a terror cell, it worked, when I justified it like that. My mind began to drift, looking for somewhere to hide so it didn't have to witness the interrogation. It was time to snoop about the small town house.

"Excuse me, Martha, could I use your bathroom?"

"Goodness, yes. Down the hall on your right."

"Thank you," I said. I exited, shutting the door quietly behind me.

The questions continued. I could hear them and still hear Frankie's pen scratching on her stenographer's notebook. It didn't take long to tour the house, checking the view from every window.

Living room, bathroom, toilet, and laundry, and bedroom all looked out toward the railway lines.

There was a clothesline out there too, and a park bench.

The bench was set on a small square of short grass. Beyond that, a wire fence covered in climbing roses.

Over the fence lay the railway line. I looked toward Upper Hutt and saw the station. The only access to the small backyard was through the house or across the railway lines. It'd be fairly easy to be spotted while crossing the tracks.

I smiled and returned to the main living room. It was quite easy to surreptitiously check out Martha. A sneaky look to see if she had some sort of emergency unit on her person. She did, a Never Alone pendant hung from a cord around her neck.

Brilliant, I relaxed a little and listened to the endless banter and haranguing of Martha by the women.

Cringing with every jibe, I took the opportunity to take

Romeo outside and check out the gnomes.

"Excuse us, Romeo needs to stretch his legs," I said and called him to me. I hoisted my bag onto my shoulder.

Nana commented, "Are you leaving us?"

"No, Nana, his poop bags are in my bag. I might need them."

Nana screwed up her nose. "Rather you than me dear."

We left through the front door. Romeo wandered the gnome filled garden and peed on a few of the uglier specimens. I followed Romeo around the garden.

No one appeared to be watching us from the house or the street.

The fence was high enough to block all but the very top of my head.

Anyone seeing my head ducking and popping back up would hopefully just think I was picking up after the dog.

I checked the gnomes that looked similar to the photo I'd seen. Twelve gnomes later, I was getting very tired of lifting gnomes out of the garden and then carefully replacing them. I did not want the garden to look as though someone had systematically checked gnomes. Then I saw him, a gnome identical to the photograph sent by Benjamin.

There were several others that were identical in appearance. The big difference was weight. I used both hands so I didn't risk dropping it as I turned it upside down and I saw it had a sealed bottom. Something moved inside it. I tipped it right way up. Something moved again. Interesting.

My plan of leaving a gnome to replace the previously lost gnome so Nana could find it, crumbled before my eyes.

I needed to use my spare gnome to cover the disappearance of the heavier sealed gnome that I stashed in my bag. Who knew I'd need two gnomes?

Looking up I saw Romeo hunched over next to a large fat gnome. Nice. I pulled a poop bag from the front pocket of my handbag and waited until he was finished.

With warm dog poop safely contained within a small blue plastic bag and the heavy gnome stashed in my bag, I called Romeo and headed for the gate.

After putting him in the back of the truck, I climbed into the driver's seat and reached over to open a drawer under the passenger seat. I placed the heavy gnome inside the drawer, almost toppling off the seat. Using two hands to position the gnome made balancing while leaning forward difficult. Once the gnome was safe I rang Ben.

"I have the first package."

"You're sure?"

"Nope, but it's ugly, heavy, sealed and there is something in it that moved when I tipped it ... what do you think?"

"Sounds like it."

"That's what I thought."

And with that, the call ended. I smiled, shoved my phone in my pocket, cracked the windows an inch for the dog, relocked the car and ran across the road to drop the poop bag into a public rubbish bin.

Back inside Martha's I washed my hands in the kitchen sink and then joined the gaggle of old ladies in Martha's living room.

Nana resembled a dog with a bone. She hammered away at Martha trying to determine if in fact there was a gnome.

Nana even asked for photographs as evidence. Poor Martha could not produce photographic evidence.

Photos? She didn't have a camera. I waited with bated breath for a garden plan to materialise with every hideous ornament and its placement documented. With a minor sense of disappointment, I realised there was no plan.

Frankie remained silent except for the scratching and scrapping of her pen and the turning pages.

I half expected to see caricatures of Nana emerge as she flipped the pages over the spiral spine. I stared at the white pages. Blue ink showed through in neat straight lines of perfectly formed handwriting. That was a lot of writing, more writing than Martha had done talking. I decided that Frankie was writing a novel with the story gleaned from the scraps of information Martha parted with.

Nana broke into my thoughts with a triumphant, "Veronica!"

"Yes, Nana," I replied trying to sound perky and not bored.

"Did you hear what Martha said?"

"No, Nana."

"She said, she inherited the gnome, and it was here when she moved in."

"I see."

"Well, I think that solves the missing gnome mystery," Nana announced, folding her hands into her lap and setting a self satisfied smile on her lips.

"Indeed," Ester agreed and followed suit.

Frankie finished the sentence she was writing and closed the pad.

I wanted to get my hands on it and have a read. It may be more interesting than what actually transpired in Martha's living room.

"It's obvious," Nana said with an air of absolute knowing. "The original owners came back for it.

For the life of me, I can't imagine why anyone would want a ghastly garden gnome enough to return for it." Nana paused long enough to get her second wind.

"One can only imagine what horrors they have in their new garden to come back for a hideous old gnome."

Martha's face fell. I watched her wrestle with something, then eventually cave and let it go.

"Thank you, June," Martha said quietly. "I am grateful for your help. It was such a worry thinking a thief had been in my front yard."

"You're welcome, Martha," Nana replied.

There was a sense of smug achievement in Nana that I hadn't witnessed for a long time.

"I'm sure a few things rubbed off from Timothy's time

on the force. You can't be a policeman's wife without learning a thing or two about investigations," Nana said with wee smile.

"Yes," Martha said. "I'm sure I should have taken more notice of Bernie's police talk."

Nana moved to the edge of her seat. "We should be leaving," she said, making a show of checking her watch.

I took her cue and helped Nana to her feet, then set my sights on Ester, who seemed well stuck in her chair.

"Thank you dear," Ester said, shuffling toward the door. After a few shuffles her stiff body loosened up and walking became easier.

Frankie stood with more ease than the older two, and pushed the stenographer notebook into her large black handbag.

Martha was slow to stand. I helped her up. It was then that she clamped her bony hand onto my arm and squeezed. They watched the three women leave before Martha spoke.

She whispered, "They can't have, you know?"

"Who can't have what?"

"Come back, they can't have," she said with a quiet desperation.

"Why not?"

"Well, he died, you see. And she went into a secure care facility, she has Alzheimer's," she said, watching the door as she spoke, her eyes fearful.

"I see."

"I couldn't say anything to June," panic rimmed her

already shaky voice.

"Why not?" I asked. If Nana was wrong then she should know she was wrong. Even though I was secretly pleased, Martha hadn't said anything. Nana never took kindly to being wrong.

Her voice dropped to a lower, more panicked whisper, "June is never wrong."

"Sure she is. She's fallible like anyone else," I said.

"No, Veronica, no she isn't."

"What do you mean?"

Nana's voice called out from the front garden, "Veronica where on earth are you!"

"Hurry along child. Don't keep her waiting," Martha said.

I turned to Martha and asked, "What is it you are afraid of?"

"The thief that stole my gnome," she replied. "It's a dreadful business the murder and the missing gnome." "Martha, do you think the missing gnome is related to the murder?" I asked.

"Yes dear, don't you?"

I certainly did.

"I'll keep an eye out for you," I replied. "Just don't tell my Nana." Knowing what I found in her garden meant I had to keep an eye out. I felt an obligation to the old duck and considered it would suck if my actions got her injured or worse.

"Oh no, I can't ask you to do that."

"You didn't ask me, I volunteered." I reassured the old

panicked woman. "I will drive by a few times during the night, just to make sure everything's quiet."

"That's too much trouble," Martha protested.

"I want to do it," I replied in a tone that let Martha know she wasn't going to hear any more argument. "I won't mention this to Nana and you shouldn't either."

Martha looked relieved. "All right dear."

Nana's voice called out again, "Veronica, come along!"

Then again, "Chop chop, Veronica."

I rolled my eyes, and smiled at Martha.

"Stay inside, I'll get that lot out of your hair," I told her, hurrying off and shutting the front door behind me, before Nana could come back in to see what the hold up was. It really was no trouble for me to pop back and check on Martha later. I did want to keep an eye on the poor old thing.

Silverstream was no longer a sleepy village. Serious crime had arrived and Martha was inadvertently in danger.

There was time for some silent contemplation as I drove the old folk back to their very attractive prison. I didn't feel like talking, nor did I feel like listening to Nana crowing about how clever she was. The temptation to put her straight was too much.

All in all, the result was a good one. Nana solved the case to her satisfaction and they were all home safely. So long as the Cronies of Doom never found out about the other gnome all would be well.

And I was free to go home.

Chapter 7
[THE PLOT THICKENS]

I took the gnome inside and set it on the kitchen bench. From the mobile under my desk in the living room, I took a finger print kit. I wanted to know who hid the gnomes and no one was telling me.

My suspicions were mounting because of the location of the first gnome and because dowsing told me there was one in Pinehaven and another in Totara Park. I dusted all the surfaces of the gnome, plenty of prints. The ones underneath were of the most interest. I knew I didn't touch it there. I lifted a clear index finger and a partial middle finger print from the bottom of the gnome. Next, I photographed the prints and uploaded them to my computer. Running them through databases would take a little while. That was fine and gave me time to have a coffee.

I glanced at the bench beneath the windowsill.

The troublemaker in a red hat, blue trousers, and cheery rosy cheeks stared back.

"You are causing quite a stir," I said. "Looks like someone did take one of Martha's gnomes and they thought it was you. I'm thinking the same person also bashed that other woman to death. Have you anything to say for yourself?"

The gnome didn't reply. It just stared. Painted eyes unblinking, yet somehow those cold painted eyes indicated superiority.

"Don't get all uppity," I muttered. The jug boiled, spitting hot droplets into the air. I made my coffee and went through to the living room to check on the finger print identification progress. Romeo lifted his head from his bed and wagged his tail. I bent down and gave him a quick pat.

Sitting in my chair sipping my coffee and watching the computer work was akin to watching paint dry. I finished my coffee at the same time as the program alerted me to a match.

Justin. As I feared. Knowing it was Justin who potentially hid the gnomes didn't tell me what was in them, but I knew it was nothing good. Something terrorists wanted and Justin for whatever reason hid them from both sides. That made no sense to me at all. Why hide it? Why not just hand it over to the authorities? He was an officer with the secret intelligence service, he knew people. I wondered how Justin came into possession of whatever world altering shit was in the gnomes to start with.

I pulled his file. No doubt, a few alarm bells rang somewhere, but too bad. If I had to find what he'd hidden, I figured I deserved to know what he'd been working on.

Turned out his current work was a highly classified project with a combined Defence Force team.

No project lists of any kind were available, so I had no way of guessing what it could be about. It probably wasn't good if it involved the Defence Force.

Digging a little deeper I discovered it was a combined

Defence Force team and it was international.

That made sense as I was contacted by Americans. The shakiest part of the puzzle was Justin's whereabouts. If he was in trouble and had gone to ground, even I probably wouldn't be able to find him.

As much as it irked me, Justin wasn't my problem. Yet.

There was still plenty of day left, and I needed to use it to find another gnome.

I put my cup in the sink, filled it with hot water, and then tapped the gnome gently on the top of his pointy hat.

"Have a nice afternoon, shorty," I said before calling Romeo and leaving.

Romeo and I headed to Pinehaven.

Finding the first gnome so fast was a little bit more luck than investigating or planning. Although not entirely, the crystal pointed to it being near the railway station and that was where I found it. This one would be legwork. Growing up in the suburbs meant that if anyone knew which houses were likely to contain gnomes in the gardens it was me. As a child, gardens full of ornaments were a source of joy and delight. As a teenager, they were fun for other reasons. Gnomes used to take world tours when I was a teen. I recalled one in particular, pinched from a garden. Postcards of the gnome at various world famous landmarks were sent to the owners. Fun times. Thinking about the world traveling gnome caused memories to bob to the surface.

Justin and I were eighteen when we took off on our big

OE with a gnome in tow.

That thought led me back to wondering why no one mentioned Justin could be involved in this situation.

Okay, so, it wasn't exactly hard finding gnome number one, but it was a bit of a fluke and a bit of good old Wiccan dowsing. No need to ever mention that to anyone.

Justin hiding the gnomes was even more concerning than not knowing he was involved. If he hid them, then maybe he didn't know who to trust? That was worrisome.

I had a few ideas of where gnome number two could be and I promised myself that once I found it I'd go looking for Justin. There had to be something very wrong for him to do this. Very very wrong.

I remembered a few properties that were accessible from the bush path behind the tennis court as containing gnomes; they were well out of the way. A good place to hide things. Also, some of the more colourful homes on the way in on Pinehaven Road had the sort of gardens that harboured gnomes and the occasional white-walled tyre swan. Some of them had giant plastic butterflies clinging to their chimneys too. From where did we liberate the gnome that we took to England with us? Pinehaven Road, that's where. Seemed a good place to start.

I glanced at a few properties on the drive down Pinehaven Road. Not as many gnomes around as there used to be.

Romeo whined in the back.

"We'll go for a walk soon," I said and chose a suitable parking space.

Romeo eagerly jumped out of the truck as soon as I swung the back door open.

He bounced onto the footpath and waited for me to lock up. My plan included starting with the houses that were accessible from the streets.

Even though the crystal indicated the gnome was near the tennis courts. I intended to be thorough, and give Romeo a decent walk.

We walked up and down two streets that I knew contained gardens of horror.

Concrete borders, tyres sunken into closely cropped lawns with trees planted in them and gnomes. One or two even had giant wooden butterflies attached to the house, much classier than the plastic variety.

My favourite was the house with the concrete cat stalking the concrete bird on its roof. Think it also had concrete bunnies in the garden and a large concrete lizard by the low decorative gate. A real treat of a garden that one.

A rumbling engine caught my attention. Looking up I saw the same pale blue car idling at the end of the street. The fat troll stared at me.

I flipped him off.

Daniel Shankle you're a dick.

He had to go. This stalking, interfering, and being in my business, was detrimental to the job. Romeo glared at him until he drove away. We carried on with our innocent walk. I came across a few older folk who were in their gardens. They asked about Romeo and wanted to pat him. He made the most of it, loving every stroke and happily encouraging more of the same.

I entered into more conversations about gnomes than I ever thought possible.

Despite finding an abundance of gnomes, none of them looked like one sitting on my kitchen bench.

Not that I expected any of them to, yet.

The crystal indicated that the gnome I was after was over near the tennis courts.

Satisfied I hadn't missed any hidden gnomes, Romeo and I turned our attention to the park.

I let him run for about ten minutes, enjoying the spectacle of my Greyhound in full flight. In all seriousness, ten minutes was his lot. I didn't want him so tired he couldn't drag himself through the bush and then back to the car.

"Romeo, Stop!"

He skidded to a halt and turned around. He must've been in the mood to listen. Often, he was not. Running or listening, it was rare for both to happen at once.

"Good boy, come!"

Romeo bounded across the grass, ears perky, tail high. He bounced around me as I praised him for returning, gave him a chicken treat and sat down on the grass with him while he ate it. Five minutes later, I clipped his lead back to his harness. I had his camouflage coat in my bag. I slipped it over his head and threaded his lead through an opening between his shoulders, then fastened the large Velcro belly strap. His coat performed double duty. It stopped his muscles cramping by keeping them warm after his run and was just the thing to conceal his white and black self as we walked sedately into the bush.

As kids, Justin and I played in here. We also played tennis at the courts below the path. Romeo and I walked past several bush clad back yards. Some containing swing sets, some with dogs who lunged to the very edge of their chains barking insanely as we passed.

Romeo, as always, ignored the fuss. Barking dogs did not interest him. He was above that kind of palaver.

I took careful note of which houses had crazy dogs.

They don't bother Romeo but I didn't want any nasty surprises should I need to come back.

We stood at the edge of the seventh yard, something caught my eye.

It was half way up the section and poking out from a bush.

A gnome.

A gnome like the one I was looking for.

People moved about in the downstairs of the house. We shrank back into the bush. I knew Romeo's camouflage jacket would come in handy one day. So much for Donald declaring it was an unnecessary extravagance and that Romeo was spoilt. He may have a point.

Kids raced out a sliding door and into the yard.

Bugger.

I took a spray can of glow in the dark spray paint from my bag. Never leave home without glow in the dark paint. It would be barely noticeable during daylight. I walked Romeo back toward the tennis court. We walked slowly.

At the edge of the property with the gnome, I tagged two trees low down by the leaf littered ground. At the next property I marked one tree, again low down, and carried on doing the same thing all the way back to the entrance by the courts. I rammed the paint back in my bag. I'd need the markings to be able to stay on the path after dark.

There were no streetlights in the bush.

Knowing I was coming back after dark to retrieve the gnome didn't thrill me.

Also, the finding of them seemed too easy to me. Why could I find these silly gnomes so easily?

Because I know where gnomes like to gather in Upper Hutt? Because I had insider information from the universe and knew how to use a pendulum to find more than water. And because I now knew who hid them. I wasn't zeroing in on the gnomes, I was zeroing in on residual energy left by Justin.

Romeo looked at me with his knowing dark brown eyes. He knew too. So where was Justin and why hadn't he told anyone where the precious gnomes were?

Back at home, I phoned Benjamin.

"Benjamin?"

"Yes, Ronnie."

"I have located the second package. I will retrieve it tonight."

"Excellent. What time are you intending to pick up the package?"

"After dark."

"Do you have any plans for the evening?" he asked, his voice never wavering.

We'd already discussed going to the pictures, so I expected he had found us one to see.

"No."

"Would you still like to go to a movie with me?"

In a way it'd be fun. He wasn't hideous and there was a hint of a decent personality in him.

The grin on my face was hard to remove. Going to the movies with an actor made it difficult not to smile.

My life is weird. It made more sense to go with it and enjoy the ride than fight it.

"Sure," I replied.

"Good, I'll meet you at the theatre in Upper Hutt tonight, at six-thirty?"

"Any idea what's showing?" I asked with casual disinterest.

"No, does it matter?"

"Not at all," I replied. There went my theory that he'd found us something to see. There were four theatres in the cinema complex so there was bound to be something worth watching.

"See you there."

I hung up. Face to face was the perfect opportunity to discuss Justin. Justin's involvement was just the sort of information I needed to help me do my job. Unless, no one knew he was involved. Perhaps Benjamin didn't know about Justin? I gave that some thought then decided to hold off mentioning him, until I knew more about the situation.

The gnome was still on the kitchen bench. That was a good thing. The two replacements were in a box in the laundry. I took one and put it in my backpack, so I wouldn't forget later.

My next task was to make contact with Justin. I checked his Facebook page. There had been no activity for four days. Same with his Twitter account and his Foursquare account. No logged whereabouts for four days. Prior to that, the last place he logged was a café near Defence House in Wellington.

I picked my cell phone up and ran through the directory until I found his number.

I hit the call button and waited. It went to voice mail. I didn't leave a message.

Using the landline, I punched in a number I knew by heart and waited. A woman answered.

"Hello Mrs. Vandyke, Ronnie here. Is Justin around?"

"Hello, Ronnie. We haven't seen you for a while," she said, her voice lilting as it usually did. "Justin is away on business." Nothing in her tone indicated concern for his whereabouts.

"That'll be why I can't get him on his phone," I replied. "Any idea when he'll be home?" I was going for an old friend wanting to catch up tone and hoped it was working.

"You know what he's like, he doesn't say much." She paused. I could almost hear her mind ticking over. "Or not to me he doesn't. You two have always been thick as thieves." Surprise edged into her voice. "Of all people I thought you'd know more about Justin's current job than anyone."

I needed to throw some water on the small flames of concern I felt brewing in Mrs. Vandyke.

"I've been out of town," I lied. "Work, you know. Incommunicado and all that."

"Of course, Ronnie. I've been around you two and your secret lives long enough to know how work goes."

I laughed.

"Did he say where he was going?" Long shot.

"Australia."

"If you hear from him, could you tell him I called, please?"

"Of course dear. Last time I spoke with him, he mentioned catching up with you. He had some things he wanted to talk over, I believe."

"Oh really?"

"Yes, I should let him talk to you but he won't mind me saying that he wants to speak with you about leaving the Service."

"Must be time he thought about leaving," I said, hoping I sounded casual about the life change.

"I'm trying not to get my hopes up. But I would like to see him in a job more conducive to having social interactions and potentially a family one day."

She should get together with my Nana.

"Thanks Mrs. Vandyke. Let him know I called!"

"It's high time you came to visit. How about dinner

when Justin gets home?"

"Sounds great. Bye for now."

"Bye, Ronnie."

It was time to email. We had a special email account. It pays to when you do what we do. I sent an email asking that he contact me A-SAP, I also mentioned I'd visited a few gardens lately near places where we used to flat.

A car cruised past the house. Romeo looked out the window. He grumbled. I stopped surfing Justin's known online hangouts and followed Romeo's line of sight.

The same blue car. Romeo grumbled again as it drove away. He wasn't a dog that grumbled or growled, or barked. Noise was not his thing. The blue car was clearly upsetting him. Hell, it wasn't doing much for me either.

Daniel Shankle needed to pull his head in and leave us alone.

In fact, the more times I saw that car the crankier I got. Thing was he hadn't actually done anything. Seeing the same car all over the area wasn't proof of any wrong-doing. I had nothing that said he was stalking me. His word against mine. Coincidence. Not a police matter.

Well, I'm not police. I unlocked the top drawer in the mobile unit by my desk. The drawer rolled out freely at the merest touch. Lying on top of a ream of printer paper was a Glock 17 in a holster. My fingers played upon the web of the holster. Calm descended. I pushed the drawer closed and locked it.

A little voice in my head, which sounded suspiciously like Nana, told me I couldn't just go around shooting people I didn't like. Although really, I couldn't see why not.

My Grandfather growled in agreement.

I groaned.

Chapter 8
[SPY TRUCKS]

At five-thirty, I fed Romeo and drew the curtains. It was still sunny outside, seemed nuts to shut the house up so early but I wouldn't be home until late and I had a stolen gnome on the kitchen bench. I showered, changed into tidy jeans but not too tidy, and a pair of black sneakers. I'm not stumbling through bush at night in anything with a heel.

I flopped back on my bed and rested my eyes for a few minutes. My hands sought the crystal around my neck. Where was Justin? It wasn't long before I drifted off to sleep, a dream filled sleep.

* * *

A large tree illuminated by a bright green light, glowed in the darkness. There was nothing else to see but the tree and the eerie glow.

I scouted around the dark graveyard. No signs of life. As one would expect. This is where the dead people live and they're not ones for partying or making a fuss. I stumbled over fresh dug ground. A new grave? My torch played on broken headstones.

This graveyard was not in use. The beam from my torch wandered across the ground until it disappeared into a long deep hole.

A new grave.

I ducked into a shrubbery close to the huge spooky tree. If there was a fresh grave, there might be someone else around, the digger for example.

The moon stumbled across the sky, ducking from cloud bank to cloud bank, sliding drunkenly behind a building storm front.

From my position, I could crouch out of sight and scurry through the back of the shrubbery. Undetected. I emerged from the edge of the bushes as the moon broke free. I stood bathed in brilliant white light, waiting for the inevitable booming voice to render my judgment.

For maybe half a minute I stood stock still staring up at the moon, waiting.

Lightning flashed across my field of vision.

A warning?

Had I angered the Gods? It was a possibility.

I waited.

The pool of light shrunk. Spits of rain flew.

In the shrinking pool, I shrugged my backpack off and removed the filth smeared blue jacket.

With a smile, I turned it inside out. It was now a clean black fleece jacket.

The new trend that seemed to make almost every article of clothing reversible these days was great. Just the ticket for midnight adventures.

The nylon side of the jacket was cold against my tee shirt. I zipped it up to my neck, and pulled the hood over my hair.

Reversing it to start with would've been smarter, I'd be a lot more comfortable snuggled in the fleece side now – dirty or not.

I felt better with the dirt smears safely hidden from unintentionally prying eyes.

You never can tell who is watching.

Rain splattered my jeans and shoes. The last rays of moonlight illuminated running red streaks on my white Reeboks.

I pulled a folded umbrella from my backpack then slung the bag over my shoulders. It wasn't overly heavy but thumped into the small of my back regardless. With minimal pressure on the release mechanism, the umbrella rose with Mary Poppins precision.

The last moon rays pointed toward the path. I had no idea where the torch I had earlier went. I felt my pockets and pulled out my Two Dollar Shop mechanical torch.

With a few squeezes in the palm of my hand, a strong beam of light sprang forward.

As the last moon rays disappeared and rain poured from the dark sky, I tightened my grip on the umbrella, and pointed the torch beam to the path in front of me.

The rays of light bounced off rain drops and shimmered across puddles.

Without further ado, I began winding along the well worn track through the graves.

Somewhere ahead of me was a parking area, the church hall, a field and an alleyway.

I knew the area. Romeo and I walked here all the time.

Rain splashed up from the wet grass and puddle ridden asphalt.

Muddy water splashed over my sneakers rinsing away the last of the red streaks.

At the road edge of the car park, I felt a small amount of relief. Now I just needed to get down the alleyway, down the street, around the corner, and then I would be, good as, home safe.

There was no traffic. There was no one else around. Not even dogs were wandering the rain soaked streets tonight.

It seemed pertinent to question my sanity as I moved quickly down the street.

Walking five kilometres in the middle of the night to steal a garden gnome from a particularly over gnomed garden two suburbs away seemed crazy. Water seeped into my shoes and my socks squelched. Not only did my socks squelch but I felt sure they'd be stained red from the red laces in my shoes. If the dye ran down my sneakers it was sure to have seeped inside as well.

Five kilometres to steal a gnome.

The whole job made no sense. What the hell would anyone want with a gnome? And why stop at a gnome? If garden ornaments are a hot item these days, why not take the hideous swan made from an old white-walled tire? Or one of those large ornamental butterflies?

Such temptation.

Alas, I couldn't have spirited them away anyway. They simply would not fit in my backpack. It was the gnome that he said was important.

An unremarkable ugly garden gnome.

I growled to myself as I quietly opened her front gate and dripped up the porch steps.

The security lighting flicked on, nearly blinding her as I shoved my key in the lock and turned the key and handle simultaneously.

* * *

I woke expecting to be dripping wet.

The crystal was still in my hand. I was dry and laying on my bed. The last question I'd consciously thought was about Justin.

The new grave.

I shuddered. Justin was in trouble. I suspected he was blocking me.

My eyes closed again, this time my dream walk took me back in time, back to my childhood.

* * *

A loud rumble shook the street.

"What was that?" I asked.

"The street sweeper truck," Mum replied.

I looked around, "I can't see it."

Fog obscured everything except within a ten-metre circle around us. Misty rain settled on my gloves.

The truck rumbled again. I held Mum's hand tighter as

we walked closer and closer to the grumbling hidden in the fog. I tugged Mum's hand pulling her closer to her, and away from the roadside of the footpath.

"Don't pull me, Ronnie," Mum reprimanded gently, she knew I was afraid of the noises in the dense fog.

I whispered, "It might get you."

Mum held back a chuckle. "It won't get me, I don't think the street sweeper trucks can suck up people."

I held tighter to her hand.

My eyes opened.

* * *

I was back in my room. Fading sunlight slipped between the closed curtains. I took a breath and cleared the memory. The rumble of the street cleaning truck filled the room. I jumped up and flung the curtains open. There was no fog. It wasn't morning. It wasn't raining or even overcast. It was a clear evening and it would be a clear moonlit night.

I frowned.

It was well after five-thirty. Since when did street sweeper trucks work after five-thirty?

I dredged my memory banks. However, I couldn't come up with any memory of seeing a street cleaning truck operating after about four in the afternoon. Early morning, midday, in the afternoon, but never during rush hour, it was anomalous.

There was a theory to consider, one I'd pondered upon

before. That street sweeper trucks were actually spy vehicles in disguise. Who would suspect them?

I hated the horrible smelly trucks even though I was well grownup and even less likely to be sucked into the rotating brushes.

Nana told me it was noise that scared me as a child.

Possibly.

Either that or they were the tool of Satan and out to get me. I had potentially done things in my life to draw Satan's attention to me.

Although not usually out of any kind of maliciousness.

Stealing a gnome from an old woman, even though it wasn't hers to start with, would possibly bring me to the attention of Satan, if he existed.

I shut the bedroom curtains as the street sweeper truck turned in a large circle at the intersection and came back. No more thinking about spies, Martha, or Nana. I felt an urge to check on the gnome. He stood on the bench staring at me with his black eyes. At least he hadn't hopped down and run away. I checked the box of replacement gnomes, hidden in the laundry. One left. It lay face down in the box. I picked it up and turned it over. It had a small crack down the front of his face.

Damn.

How'd I not notice before?

Something pressed into the back of my left leg. I jumped; the gnome flew across the room smashing into the tub.

"Shit!"

I looked down, Romeo sloped away.

With a sigh, I cleaned up the broken pieces and tossed them in the rubbish.

Chapter 9
[A NIGHT AT THE MOVIES]

I drove the six minutes to the picture theatre and noted every car and every person I saw. Paranoia was now my constant companion. I also tried to recall what Daniel Shankle did as a job, I was sure he'd told once upon a time in a pub. He'd tried and failed to pick me up. Funny how people get shitty when you point out things like their criminal past. It only took a text with his name and date of birth to the office to get a call back within minutes stating he had several arrests for male/female assault, two for theft, and one for illegal possession of a firearm.

The street sweeper truck rumbled again when I entered the picture theatre car park. There in the cab of the truck was Daniel bloody Shankle. He worked for the city council. It was a spy truck and he was driving it. I wished all the trolls had left Middle Earth. I knew there was no hope of ever being troll free. The hideousness was here to stay and now woven into the fabric of New Zealand life thanks to Sir Peter Jackson.

The truck crawled up the street. A feeling of cold dread crawled up my spine. I parked my car and then scanned the area looking for Benjamin.

A dark coloured car in the furthest unlit corner looked like his. Of course, where else would he be?

I locked my car and waved to Benjamin as I walked over. Friendly. Old friends happy to see each other.

Be obvious.

Hide in plain sight.

They were things that didn't draw suspicious looks from passersby.

Sulking toward a car in a dark corner and furtively glancing about, however, sent normal people's alarm bells ringing. I didn't want to be memorable. I didn't make eye contact with anyone walking toward me. Instead, I smiled brightly in the direction I was going and carried on toward the car.

Friends off to see a movie.

Certainly not about to steal another unsuspecting gnome from some unwitting person's yard.

The door opened as I neared the car. He climbed out of the vehicle. Grinned in my direction then pressed the fob in his hand. The cars lights flashed, alarm chirped, and doors locked. I whispered, "Greet me like an old friend."

Benjamin smiled and hugged me. I returned the hug just as another couple appeared from nearby Logan Street.

"Shall we?" he replied, placing his hand in the small of my back to guide me.

"Yes, let's," I said. "Any idea what movies are playing?"

"We have a few to choose from. I'm sure we'll find a movie that suits us both," he replied.

I choose to break the news about the smashed gnome right away.

"Can you get me a replacement gnome?"

He looked at me, and said, "Something I should

know?"

"Accident."

"I'll find one for you. Can you try not to have any more accidents, please?"

"I'll do my best."

We chatted as we crossed the car park and up the stairs to the cinema. I warned him to speak softly. "Your accent is memorable. Don't want someone remembering there was a Yank at the pictures tonight."

"Sure," he replied, with a smile.

He opened the door for me. As we entered the brightly lit lobby, the smell of hot buttered popcorn hit me. My stomach growled.

He laughed.

I shrugged.

He might not be so bad. Benjamin was certainly easy to look at, and be around. He was a few years older than me and a few inches taller too.

"Better get you some popcorn," he said as we scanned the movie posters.

"How about that one?" I offered, pointing to a colourful poster.

"Isn't that a New Zealand movie?" he asked, turning to the poster.

"Yes."

Then I saw it, a poster with him on it.

Just great.

Benjamin leaned close and whispered, "Don't even think about it."

"Is it good?"

"Yes, and we're not going to see it tonight."

I stifled a laugh and scanned the board above the ticket and confectionary counter looking for session times. Our timing was great.

"I'll get the tickets," he said.

"I'll get the popcorn," I replied.

We went to separate tellers. True to form, mine was the slowest. I stood in the small queue at the counter searching the shelf and racks behind it, for a telltale yellow bag of Clinkers. Not a Clinker in sight. With much disappointment, I ordered popcorn and a bag of Pineapple Lumps.

Benjamin was waiting for me by the entrance to the cinemas.

He pointed out cinema two as ours.

I looked around as we entered the dimly lit theatre. Dotted about the theatre in little pockets, I counted eighteen people. The session was due to start in ten minutes. Not a big crowd. It suited me better that way. I followed Benjamin to our seats. We were seated toward the back with no one in front of us to block our view, and no one close enough to overhear any snippets of whispered conversation.

Perfect.

I settled into the comfortable chair. My intention was to enjoy the free movie and the company.

My escort settled into his seat. He tossed a few pieces of popcorn into his mouth and chewed softly.

This pleased me. Noisy eaters and slurping drinkers were not welcome.

Benjamin's hair brushed mine when he leaned close.

"This might even be good," he said, his breath tickled my ear.

"Yes, it might," I replied matching his hushed tone. With the movie about ready to start, I thought it best to open the bag of lollies, pre-empting any complaining from patrons that was bound to ensue if I waited. Pascal's lolly bags fight back. True to form the pineapple lumps put up a bit of a fight. Experience kicked in; up ending the packet, I opened it from the bottom.

"Pineapple Lump?" I offered, holding the bag out to Benjamin.

"Pineapple what?"

"Pineapple deliciousness covered in chocolate. We have to make do. There were no Clinkers."

He took one and dropped it into his mouth. He gave a few chews before handing out his verdict.

"They're good. Are Clinkers better?"

"Do gnomes have pointy hats?"

Benjamin laughed.

Scrunched down in our seats, chewing lollies and whispering as we watched the movie. I rather hoped that we would blend in with the rest of the crowd.

To anyone in the theatre our posture probably appeared nothing more than the conspiracy of lovers. We're not going there. So I refused to think anything else along those lines.

Mix business with pleasure?

No.

Anyway, I hadn't even assigned him a nickname yet. Although, Ben was probably going to be it, because Benjamin just didn't roll well off my tongue and Benjie sounded like a dog.

The theatre plunged into darkness. Noise bellowed from all angles.

I relaxed, happy to have found his nickname and ready to enjoy the movie.

Ten minutes later, he nudged me. "Okay?"

"Yes, thank you," I whispered back.

Nothing more was said until the movie was almost over when Benjamin leaned close and said, "Hang back a bit when the movie finishes, make it look as if we've had a good time and aren't in any hurry."

I nodded.

It wasn't much of an act. The movie was good and I enjoyed his company. Being around Benjamin was easy.

We made our way from the theatre at the back of the leaving line of patrons. I reflected on why being in his company felt comfortable. Several thoughts floated about in my head. The most obvious being, there was no expectation. It wasn't a date.

The movie simply gave us a reason to be seen together and was a fun interlude. Nothing overly exciting about that. As long as Nana didn't get wind of me attending a movie with an unknown escort, all would be well.

I surreptitiously watched the other patrons as they all

filed out the main door.

No one appeared familiar.

No one appeared to be over fifty years in age.

A quiet sigh of relief escaped my lips.

Nana's spies were probably not among the movie attendees. It was a rare night that the spies weren't out and flying monkeys securely caged.

"Can I call you Ben? Benjamin is so ..."

"So?"

"Long and formal. You're more like a Ben."

"Sure, you can call me Ben," he said, amusement resounded in his words. "Guess it's like you being more of a Ronnie than a Veronica."

Guess it is.

"Thanks."

Ben spoke as he politely escorted me to his car, "Where's the next package?"

"Not too far away," I replied as I let him open the car door for me. "I'd suggest we have a drink somewhere as it's still a little early to make the pick up, but I don't know if that's such a great idea." I reached for my seat belt and clicked it into place. "If you can drop me back here later I'll pick up my car."

"No problem," he replied shutting the door.

A familiar pale blue car crawled through the car park. I ducked down before the driver could see me. Ben watched the car and never so much as glanced in my direction until the car was out of sight.

"Explain," he said tapping my shoulder. "Something

you'd like to tell me about that blue car?"

I sat up, straightened my clothing, and settled back into the seat.

"The driver of that car may be stalking me."

"That sounds like a problem."

"It will be if he follows me while I'm working," I said, glancing in the wing mirror. No sign of the car.

"Can you deal with it?"

"Yep."

As soon as I figure out what the weirdo wants.

The conversation ended.

A few minutes later, he pulled out of the car park and asked for directions to somewhere that sold decent coffee.

I laughed, "I think the only place open now is McDonald's."

"Really? It's not even late."

"It's Upper Hutt midweek and a bar wouldn't be the best idea. McDonalds."

"Drive thru?"

"Yes," I replied pointing right. Much safer than eating in the restaurant. "Take a right, and then another right at the end of the street, right at the roundabout, then left at McDonalds."

"What is with New Zealand and roundabouts?"

"They're cheaper than traffic lights ..."

"Really?"

"I have no idea, but now that you mention it, we have a lot of roundabouts."

"You do."

I gave it more thought. I only saw one roundabout while I was in the States and that wasn't even in a city.

"We do." We are roundabout mad.

The thought of the drive thru made me hungry.

"I might need something to eat with that coffee," I said.

Ben nodded as he turned into the drive thru. "Me too."

I fished my wallet from my bag. "My treat," I said and pulled out some cash.

At the drive thru window, we decided upon meal choices.

"One Big Mac combo extra pickles and One chicken Royale combo both with coffee not soda," Ben said clearly into the brown box outside his window, the box and the night swallowed his accent.

The box crackled and hissed as the employee read back the order. Upon confirmation, we moved through to the next window. I handed the cash to Benjamin.

He duly paid and handed me back the change, then dropped two bags of food into my lap and passed the tray containing the coffees.

"Where to?" he asked.

"Maidstone Park," I replied without hesitation. We could eat in the car, undisturbed and it was far enough away from the target area that no one would make a connection. Probably no one would see the car anyway.

Directing him to the park was easy. It seemed smart not to stop in front of the well lit skate park, with all the skater boys, their cars, and the operational security cameras. Police monitored the cameras from the local police station.

Instead, he parked in the shadows more or less in front of the cricket pavilion, a much less populated area of the park.

Unfurling the top of one of the bags, I spied the Big Mac box. My mouth watered. I handed Ben his bag.

Biting into my burger sent special sauce and lettuce falling into the box on my knee. Not the tidiest of things to order. I plowed through the burger in record time and started on my fries. Mopping up the dripped sauce with a few fries, I popped them in my mouth. So good.

Ben sipped his coffee and asked, "How long have you been doing this?"

"Eating fries with special sauce or the other thing?"

"The other thing," he replied, grinning.

"I've been a private investigator about eleven months," I said.

"And before that?"

Oh, you know, Intelligence Service. Nothing much.

I wasn't entirely sure I wanted to go there yet, so I went with an umbrella term. "Law enforcement."

It was my turn to ask questions. "How long have you been in New Zealand?"

"Three weeks," he replied.

I gave him, a sidelong glance. "You were brought over for this assignment, weren't you?"

He smiled but didn't answer.

"So what's your cover?"

He grinned. "I'm an actor."

"Yes, yes you are, but you're here why?"

"A few meetings with directors and so forth, talking about a possible mini series and television movie set here."

That sounded reasonable. I'm sure customs enjoyed that when they asked why he was visiting our beautiful country. Or maybe they don't ask when it's someone like him.

"You known MacKinnon long?" I asked.

"A little while, I suppose," he said, his voice remained noncommittal. "Who'd you used to work with?"

"Had a government job."

"Yeah? Me too."

I laughed. "Unless Homeland Security is now private you still do."

He nodded. "Good point. I still do. Sometimes it feels like a side job."

"And you've known MacKinnon how long?"

"Long enough to have his confidence."

I wiped my mouth on a napkin, then balled it up, and tossed it in the paper bag. Time to flash some inner knowledge. "Have you taken over Jared Forbes' unit?"

He covered his momentary surprise well.

"No, not officially anyway. I came out for this. I'll go back when we're done." Ben smiled and drained his cup. "That was truly disgusting coffee." He leaned back in the driver's seat. "Tell me how you know Jared Forbes."

Time to come clean?

"Until eleven months ago I was with the Security Intelligence Service. I not only know Jared but I know what he ate for breakfast, how long he spent in the shower, and which tie he wore for important meetings."

"Now it starts to make sense."

"I could have told you earlier. But MacKinnon said I could play with you."

He chuckled. "Why'd you leave the service?" His eyes roved over me then snapped back to mine. "Not old enough for retirement. Problem with authority?"

"Decided I could do more on my own." I preferred to use my unique skills for my benefit. Then I need never explain how I came by the information.

"Encouraged out or was it voluntary?"

My eyebrows rose.

"It was voluntary." But probably wouldn't have been if I'd stayed much longer. Reede was pretty keen to see the back of me.

Our conversation continued for almost an hour, during which I wrestled with the part of me that wanted to tell him about Nana and her cronies. It was the section of my mind that governed how I conducted myself during operations. It was happiest with full disclosure. But full disclosure wasn't always the best thing for everyone.

Until I knew a bit more about how Benjamin Reynolds operated the less said about the cronies' attempt to investigate a missing gnome the better. Happy that the sensible part of my mind won. I didn't mention Nana. Three old women were not about to crash our job, especially when Nana believed she'd solved the mystery of Martha's missing gnome.

Anyway, I'd already told him about the troll stalker and that was enough news for one night.

My mind wandered to the gnome who was happily sitting on the kitchen bench.

"Are you taking the packages tonight?" I used a tone that suggested it would be a good idea.

"You want me to?" He turned to face me.

His eyes seemed to wash out to a very pale blue but in daylight they were quite bright. Marvelling at the change in his eye colour I completely missed his mouth moving.

"Ronnie?"

"What?" I tore my eyes from his. "What?

"Do. You. Want. Me. To. Take. The. Packages. Tonight?" he said with care.

"Yes please, it's less for me to worry about. I don't want two packages sitting on my bench. That's twice the responsibility."

"Note taken."

I sank back into the seat and drank my cool coffee without looking at him.

There wasn't so much as a glance in his direction until I'd finished the last drop and shoved the empty cup into the bag that contained other rubbish. I held my hand out to Ben, indicating I wanted his rubbish too. He passed it over.

Screwing the bags up tightly, I got out of the car,

ducked inside the park and tossed the rubbish in the closest bin.

I paused long enough to scan the area for potential trouble.

Maidstone wasn't my favourite park, especially at night. It wasn't as inviting as Trentham Memorial Park. It didn't bother me to traipse through Trentham Park at night, moonlight or not. Funny really, I didn't even like stepping through the gates at Maidstone park after dark. It wasn't that anything bad had ever happened there, not to me anyway.

The park felt off. Off, in an evil way.

Possibly that wasn't helped by my behaviour of late. Hoodwinking an old woman out of a gnome and asking God for a quick laptop smiting. Not my finest moments.

Chapter 10
[IN THE DEAD OF NIGHT]

I jumped back in the car and shut the door a little too quickly.

"Alright?"

"Yes," I replied. "The door got away from me. Let's do it."

He turned his face toward me. His unusual eyes paled more in the fading interior light and he seemed to take stock of me for a moment.

"Which direction?" Ben asked.

"Head south, we're going to Pinehaven."

"This time I know where I'm going," he said.

"Good," I replied, watching street signs as he drove. Seemed a good idea to make sure we were heading south. I held my breath as he turned under the underpass that took us into Silverstream and right by Martha's place. I snuck a quick look as we drove by. All quiet. We carried on through Silverstream village. I kept an eye out for any signs of the blue car; it would not be a good time for him to show up.

"Head for Blue Mountains Road, but go up Fendalton and down Chichester turning right onto Blue Mountains. Pull over just down from the intersection."

I watched the road and said nothing else.

I'll admit to being impressed that Benjamin certainly did seem to know where he was going. I supposed he had to be fairly smart to be an actor and an agent with Homeland Security. I was also sure he had GPS on his phone and had probably already checked out all the Upper Hutt suburbs.

He took a left when the road forked, heading up Blue Mountain Road, and then another left into Fendalton Crescent.

He slowed.

Moonlight filtered through the trees on the hills on the left.

He carried on up the road, turning right at the top of Fendalton onto Chichester which climbed over the hill.

Pine trees loomed in front of us as the road met with Blue Mountain Road again. Ben slowed. He turned right, and parked a safe distance from the intersection. I waited to see what he was going to do next.

"You want me to come?" he asked.

"No, thanks, I'll draw less attention and can move quieter alone."

"How long do you need?"

"Ten minutes, meet me on the other side of the school, by the shop." I could get there in six but walking was preferable to running. It drew less attention and made less noise.

"Down this road, turn left, follow Pinehaven road to the school?"

"Yes. Before the shop, there is a long driveway on the left. It intersects the park and leads from Pinehaven Road to the Scout Den and tennis court, that's the way I will be coming." Straight up the road and into the car. That was my plan. Quick, quiet, trouble free.

I opened the car door and picked my bag up from the foot well.

As I alighted from the vehicle, I slung my bag over my shoulder.

In a bright voice I said, "Thanks for the ride." And shut the door.

I waved, just in case someone saw him drive away. Making as if I was heading into a house down one of the long driveways near the trees, I ducked sideways into the bush and hurried down the dodgy steps cut into the hill. After a few metres, trees and the dark night hid me from prying eyes

The steps led to a path through the bush to the tennis court, scout den, and rugby clubrooms. It was also a much used short cut to the primary school.

The path forked. I took the left path. The less used path gave access to the backyards of a number of properties. I paused long enough to pull my trusty torch from my bag. It would help me get to the first of the yards where I'd be able to see the marks I'd spray painted on the boundary trees earlier.

I hoped the houses with dogs had the dogs inside at night, and not running free. Just in case, I had a secret stash of little pieces of fresh meat laced with tranquilliser in a ziplock bag squirrelled in one of the pockets of my bag. My preference was not to leave sedated animals littering the bush. It would draw attention, and that I did not want. I drew a deep breath and hoped nothing barked at me.

Approaching the first yard, I flicked my torch off. I stopped to drop the torch into my bag and listen to the sounds of night around me. For a moment, it was pitch dark.

The canopy of trees above blocked all the moonlight. My eyes adjusted and I moved on, stepping with care, knowing twigs and branches lay on the leaf covered path.

The sound of a snapping branch carries a long way in the dead of night. Tripping or falling may well attract an unwanted response. I passed the outer markers of the first back yard. So far so good.

If anyone came across the marks after tonight, it wouldn't matter. Several markers later, I saw the boundary double mark I'd made. This was the yard. From the bush, I could see the clearing that was the back lawn. The clearing afforded moonlight and starlight to provide me with enough luminosity to spot the gnome. It sat close to the bush, partially hidden under a large lavender bush. I waited a few seconds, visually checking all was clear whilst listening for any sounds of movement.

I held my breath as I stepped from the edge of the bush. I counted my steps to stop myself from running.

Fourteen paces to the lavender bush.

Counting equals calm.

I picked up the gnome.

It was heavy and sealed underneath like the first gnome. I replaced it with the lighter gnome in my bag.

Then turned and disappeared into the dark bush.

Moving back the way I'd come, I passed the outer markers while still clutching the gnome in my arms. Ten metres later, I was sure it was safe and stopped for a moment. I took the torch out of my bag and shoved the heavy gnome in it. The gnome was considerably heavier than the one I'd left in its place. I adjusted the shoulder straps to accommodate the extra weight I now carried.

A deep cleansing breath flowed through me and I realised I hadn't breathed properly since approaching the houses.

Snatches of the story I'd read Nana last week surfaced. Half expecting to stumble onto a decomposing body in the woods, I found myself walking faster down the bush edged path. The bush winked and blinked as moonlight filtered through leaves in the canopy above. Every flash of light felt like eyes watching.

I joined the main path and took a deep breath to calm myself as I walked down the last of the hill toward the tennis court.

Moving fast was easier on ground that was more open. It didn't take long for me to reach the end of the path, and another set of stairs carved from the hill. I scanned the area in front of me from the top of the steps. There was no one around and no movement. I knew that down the steps and to the right, stretched an open playing field. At the bottom on my left were the tennis courts. Somewhere beyond the edge of my vision was the scout den, set back a little into the trees. I walked on, following the open path to the driveway that led to Pinehaven road. As I skirted the tennis court, I heard voices near the public toilet.

Chapter 11
[THIS COULD BE BAD]

I paused on the grass to listen, hoping no one heard my approach. There were no cars in view. The voices continued. A male voice, loud and insistent but hard to understand. A female voice, pleading, panic edged, and frightened.

Buggery bollocks.

Not good. The longer I listened the more I heard terror in the woman's wavering voice. My thoughts spun back to the contents of my drawer and how I wished I'd slipped the holster and Glock onto my belt earlier. But I hadn't. I did a quick mental inventory. I had keys, a phone, and a Swiss Army knife. That'd do.

I snuck around the outside of the toilet block to determine where the voices came from.

The women's toilet.

After a few more seconds of careful listening, I was a hundred percent certain the woman was in trouble.

I slipped my bag from my shoulders, catching it before it hit the ground. I fished in my bag pockets and took out my knife, and cell phone. I shoved the phone into my jacket pocket and held the knife, closed in my hand.

I stowed the bag under a bush a few feet from the toilet block, hoping it would remain safe. If there was a scuffle, I couldn't risk anything bad befalling the precious cargo.

I opened the blade on my knife and locked it in place.

A girl can never tell when a pocket knife will come in handy. I pushed the knife handle first up my sleeve, perfectly positioned so when my arm dropped, the knife would slide down into my hand. Blade first. I didn't want to enter the toilet looking armed and that was the best I could do in a hurry.

I listened for sounds of life by the door.

A muffled scream.

Time to move.

Taking a breath, I kicked the outer door, hitting it squarely by the flimsy lock with my heel. Wood splintered. The door flew open, taking both occupants by surprise.

"Whoops," I exclaimed, then dropped my voice an octave, letting as much menace fill my voice as possible. "Didn't know this was occupied."

The woman's eyes widened in terror. The man hauled himself off the woman and scrambled to his feet. She moved back and tried to cover herself. I flicked my eyes over him but could see no obvious weapon.

The light wasn't good but I could clearly see red marks on the woman's face. An obvious handprint across her mouth. He must've used a bit of pressure to prevent her screams filling the night air. Bruising around her throat. Bruises on her upper arms where she'd been pinned, possibly by his knees.

I positioned myself where I could see the man in my peripheral vision but also could seemingly ignore him.

"Are you all right?" I asked the woman, as I reached

out and helped her to her feet.

She shook her head. Her body trembled. Her clothing ripped and barely holding together, as she pulled at the torn fabric to cover her exposed flesh.

I noticed blood on the floor where her head had been.

I detected movement in the corner of my eye. The man lunged for me. He over extended.

"Bitch," he yelled as his fist came up short of my head. "You're next. Going to enjoy taking my time with you."

That's not going to happen.

He stepped forward onto his right foot and smacked me with an open hand across my face.

My head snapped back.

I palmed the knife. Play time was over.

With a push of my foot, I encouraged the woman to move out of the way. She shuffled against the wall. I levelled a stare at the male and maintained eye contact.

A mean mouth cut across his face like a deep gash. How fitting. The blade flashed in the yellow light from the bare bulb on the ceiling. His eyes moved to the knife in my hand.

"I don't like you," I said, stepping forward and shoving the knife into his jugular. Hard and fast. I felt the warmth of his neck on my hand, for a moment. I gave one sharp twist of the blade.

He squealed like a stuck pig. I pulled the knife and repeated. A hot gush flooded my senses with a metallic stench. Blood poured forth.

Steaming deep red cascaded as I pulled the knife from

his throat. Stepping back quickly I dropped the knife into the nearby sink. He clutched his throat. His mouth moved by no words followed.

He fell with a thud onto the concrete floor.

Spurting blood created a puddle that trickled toward the door. His gagging last breaths filled the small space. I leaned over him and said, "Whoops a daisy. Bit of bad luck there, bro."

The frightened woman backed to the doorway. Her slim ragged shape was silhouetted by the moon. I couldn't see her face, as it was in full shadow, but I was aware the young woman was looking at the crumpled pile of death on the concrete floor. I also found it hard to drag my attention away from the death. It was a curious situation.

His bloodied body filled me with disgust. Aware that taking life should elicit more than a feeling of disgust didn't bother me as much as it should have.

Panic and terror lit the room like a beacon, flowing freely from the young woman. Even though I knew she was beaten, almost raped, and then witnessed her attacker die, I needed her to calm down.

Calm is good. Panicked, erratic flailing and screaming, not so much.

Outside, tyres crunched as a car rolled over stones on the driveway. It took me a split second to determine it was coming towards us.

I turned the tap on in the sink and hurriedly washed the knife and then wiped everything off with a wet paper towel. The car sounds edged closer.

"Come on," I said, grabbing the woman by the arm. I half dragged her around the dark side of the building. "There," I whispered, pointing to deep shadows near bushes. "Stay there." The woman slipped into the bushy area and hunched down as small as possible.

I peered around the corner fully expecting to see a police car doing a routine patrol, or maybe even investigating sounds of a woman screaming. The noises would have carried a fair distance in the still night. Someone probably heard something before I came along.

The hills around Pinehaven made sound bounce and directional information tricky. It'd be hard to pinpoint the location of the distressed noises.

I inhaled sharply and checked my watch. The numbers glowed a soft green in the moonlight. Three minutes late for the rendezvous. Felt like longer.

A dark coloured sedan crawled over the gravel and down the driveway toward us. What were the chances of another dark sedan being in the area? I couldn't tell if it was black or very dark blue.

The car passed the toilet block and moved to the tennis court area. I blew out a sigh of relief. It was black. Ben was driving. He should have gone, three minutes ago.

I stepped out from my concealed position, knowing he'd see me in his rear vision mirror. He did.

Ben swung the car around and pulled up next to me. He leaned over and swung the passenger door open.

"I need to get the bag," I said. Turning I got my bearings and found the bush with the bag under it. I opened the back door and placed the bag on the floor.

"Problem?" Ben enquired, watching me.

"Yes," I said. There's problem. "A less than ideal situation. I need your help, and so does a woman – I found."

Ben raised his eyebrows. "Found?"

"Found? Rescued? Do we have time for semantics?"

"This is what I was warned about," he muttered, clambering from the car to follow me.

I ignored the comment.

"Female toilet," I said, pointing to the entrance. "Sorry."

Ben entered the room. I encouraged the woman from her hiding place. Straightening up was difficult for her. I held her arm, allowing her to lean on me.

"What's your name?"

"Kirsty," she said. Her voice was little more than a raspy croak.

It didn't surprise me; there was a lot of bruising around her throat.

"We're going to get you medical attention," I said, guiding her gently toward the car.

Kirsty began to protest but shushed when Ben appeared. She froze.

He pulled a cell phone from his pocket and pressed three numbers. As he did so, he scrutinised the woman.

There were plenty of people that would've walked away. Plenty that wouldn't have given the woman's plight a second thought. Even if some people could help without jeopardising their cover or job, they wouldn't. This time, I knew I should've walked and not become involved. But that's not in my nature. The look on Ben's told me that he wouldn't have walked away either.

The phone in his hand stopped ringing; I could hear a low voice but not the words. Ben spoke for a few seconds and then hung up.

He stepped toward the woman. She stiffened beside me.

"It's okay. No one will hurt you," I said, touching her arm. She looked from me to Ben.

"What's your name?" Ben asked.

"Kirsty."

"Here's what's going to happen, Kirsty." Ben kept his voice soft and low, a no nonsense tone but gentle with it. "We're going to take you to a doctor. We'll pay for your medical care, and make sure all this goes away." He waved an arm toward the nearby restroom.

Kirsty's eyes widened.

"Him?" she rasped.

"He'll go away too," Ben said his voice still soft. "Do you know who he is?"

"No."

"Do you have a vehicle anywhere near by?"

"No."

"Does he?"

"No."

"Let's get you in the car."

Ben opened the backdoor for her and carefully helped

her in. I scooted around to the other side and retrieved my bag, best to keep that close. The door closed softly. Kirsty leaned back in the seat, firmly held by the seatbelt Ben fastened for her.

I placed the bag on the floor in the foot well of the front passenger seat. I took my phone and Swiss army knife from my pockets and pushed them into the small pockets on the outside of the bag. Looking around I saw Ben open the boot.

Something about Ben's whole manner seemed familiar. I gave his soft tone, caring behaviour, and not getting too close to the victims personal space, some thought. A smile rallied. He reminded me of David Caruso's character in CSI Miami. The character I detested because of his manner. Here it was at work in front of me and getting results. I wondered if he watched CSI Miami, or came upon his nonthreatening soft voice and a way of calming terrified victims by himself. That was something I'd ask him, another day.

Ben opened the back door and passed a water bottle to Kirsty.

"Sip this. It will help your throat."

She hesitated before taking the bottle.

"It's just water with some electrolytes added." Ben's quiet reassurance made all the difference.

"Thanks," she croaked, accepting the drink and taking several long sips. "It's a little salty."

"That'll be the electrolytes. It'll help."

He closed the door, leaving Kirsty drinking the water

in the car. I walked over to him. He took latex gloves from a box in the boot.

"Do you want help?" I asked when I heard him snap the latex against his wrists.

"Sure," he replied. "Glove up."

I did and shadowed him. He scooped up large handfuls of stones and carried them into the toilet. I followed suit.

"What are we doing?" I asked entering into the bathroom behind him.

"Blocking the toilets," he replied. Dropping stones into one of the toilets. He left to gather more stones.

We dumped as many stones as we could scrape up in both toilets. Ben flushed the first toilet, opened the cistern and broke off the ball cock. I did the same in the second. Water flowed freely into the toilet pans and rose rapidly. Ben turned his attention to the body. I could hear the water spilling over the toilets onto the concrete floor. He patted down the body. He found a wallet and shoved it into his own pocket. There wasn't much else in his pockets except a few receipts for recent purchases. Ben took those. It made sense to take everything. We didn't want to make it too easy for the police to name him. Even a tentative link between the victim and the dead guy could make things tricky for us. I hoped there wasn't one.

Ben took paper towels, wet them, and wiped down all the surfaces he could've possibly touched the first time he entered the room. I used wet paper towels and wiped the door handles, doorframe, and anywhere I may have touched. We both stood in the room, and turned in a slow circle making sure we got everything.

Where would Kirsty have touched? The floor, doors, basin? I wiped the whole room except the floor, which would flood soon enough.

Water was spilling out from the cubicles and across the bathroom area. To help it along we jammed paper towels in the sinkhole and turned the tap on hard.

There was a drain hole in the floor. I stuffed it full of soggy paper. Satisfied the room would soon be awash, I had one last look from the doorway.

"Let's get out of here," Ben said.

I followed him back to the car.

He opened the driver's door, and pulled the boot release.

From the boot, he took a roll of tape.

Yellow tape that had a single black word repeated along it, Danger.

I hurried over to the toilet block and took one last look inside; the water reached the body.

Ben taped off the whole toilet block with the yellow danger tape. It was the kind the councils used, and often seen around work sites and problem areas.

I smiled at his handiwork, this toilet block definitely qualified as a problem area.

Satisfied we'd done all we could to cover our trail, we peeled our gloves off and dropped them into the boot of the car. Ben shut the boot and slid behind the wheel.

"Let's get out of here," I said. I turned my head and checked Kirsty in the backseat. She looked almost asleep.

Ben drove up the long access way to the street.

He glanced at me before pulling out onto the road.

"Where's your bag?" he enquired lightly, the softness in his voice replaced by a conversational tone.

"By my feet," I replied.

"Everything else go okay?"

"Without a hitch."

He gave a small smile.

I knew it was cold relief after the whole ladies' room incident. I was well aware that I'd jeopardised my mission by saving the woman. Times like that made me glad I was no longer an intelligence officer. I liked to be able to make my own decisions. Reede would have ripped me up and down and then kicked me all the way home, figuratively speaking of course. I could take her. She wasn't a field operative.

Reede got to where she was with ruthlessness and by clambering over the backs of everyone above her. I think she wore rugby boots, stuck those sprigs right in. There was a rumour that she'd slept her way to the top but I don't believe she could've faked that many orgasms.

Reede had no heart. She was a backstabbing, goal orientated mega bitch.

Justin jumped into my head again. Reede was his boss but he didn't go to her with whatever was going on that led him to be in possession of gnomes. Why didn't he go to her?

Ben tapped my knee.

"Yes?"

"You okay tagging along? I'd sooner keep you with me. I'll drop you back to your car later."

"In for a penny in for a pound ..."

I wanted to know that Kirsty was okay and that I helped.

"That's what I thought."

There was a niggling feeling of horror in the back of my mind and I really didn't want it to become something I had to deal with yet. Killing someone was a lot easier than it should be, but living with it, that's something else. My attention turned to the woman and how she came to be in that situation. I really wanted to know.

But Kirsty's voice and throat were not up to talking and from a professional point of view the less interaction the better.

Chapter 12
[CLEANING UP]

It was a quiet trip into Wellington city. Mid week, there wasn't a lot of traffic heading for the city at or around midnight. For that, I was grateful. Nice that there wasn't a compulsory breath testing stop either. No sign of the booze bus or even a single police car as Ben negotiated the city streets to a private hospital.

We could be very grateful for that.

Ben called ahead and notified Wakefield hospital that a guest of the embassy required urgent medical care. As soon as we entered the gates, we saw a gurney and staff waiting by the main entrance.

"If you like, we'll stay with you," Ben said to Kirsty while opening the back door of the car. She didn't respond.

"She asleep?" I asked, turning in my seat.

"Don't think so," he replied and scooped her into his arms. He lifted her effortlessly from the car.

I swung my door open and exited the vehicle in time to see her head sag against his shoulder. That wasn't right.

"She's drifting in and out of consciousness," Ben said to the group of people by the door. "She could've been drugged."

What? Really? She seemed okay earlier.

A man wearing white and pushing a gurney came forward, along with two women in pale blue scrubs.

Ben laid Kirsty on the gurney. It was the first time I had seen the women in proper light. Her long wavy brown hair, matted with dried blood. Blood. Wouldn't a head injury be more likely to cause her sleepiness? It seemed odd to me that Ben suggested drugs. Now wasn't the time to explore that. I wanted to commit her face to memory. Fine featured, high cheek bones, oval face. Young. Twenty to twenty-five. Her clothes were nice, not super expensive, but good nonetheless. It looked like she shopped at Farmers or Glassons rather than The Warehouse. A woman in blue scrubs covered Kirsty's battered body with a blanket.

I stayed silent until the team hurried away, with Kirsty to the emergency room.

"I think we'll wait," Ben said, quietly. He indicated to the doorway, and led the way to a waiting room. Guess he'd been there before. "In here."

I entered the small well lit warm room. A vending machine full of chocolate bars and lollies stood against the far wall and next to it a coffee machine on a bench.

"Coffee!" I said, unable to hide my joy. "And chocolate."

Ben looked long and hard at me.

"Do I have something on my face?" I rubbed my hands over my face.

A smile crept over his lips.

"Stand under the light for me," he said.

"I do, don't I?" Thoughts collided. None of the hospital staff looked at me strangely. "Ben?"

"I just want to check your clothes."

I obliged without further comment. He indicated for me to turn around with my arms out.

"The cuff of your right sleeve," Ben said.

"That's all?" I asked inspecting my cuff. Red edged in places. And that was all. How I managed to escape with minimal mess was a mystery. I can't eat a cream donut without squirting cream all over myself. You never want to see me negotiate a custard square.

I reciprocated. His shoulder bore a smudged bloodstain.

"You've got a smudge from Kirsty's head. That should come out with a little cold water," I said.

I looked around the room. There was a small sink, with a liquid soap dispenser, and paper towels in the corner of the room. I took a closer look at the bloodied cuff. I could scrub it without even taking my shirt off. That was a blessing.

Ben handed me his jacket.

Are you kidding me?

"Shall I clean that for you?" A little bit of snark infected my voice.

I could imagine Nana tutting and telling me to clean the jacket. Her words circled me. 'He's a man, what does he know about cleaning anything?' My eyes rolled as I took the jacket from Ben.

I wet a towel, added some soap, and rubbed at the smudge, trying to recall if Nana ever said anything about removing bloodstains. Nothing popped up. I dabbed at the smudge, adding more water. It was a given that I was doing it wrong, but Nana wasn't with me, so it'd have to do.

"I can do that, you know. I can," Ben said, watching with interest.

"I'm sure you can, but I am doing it," I replied. Have to clean my cuff anyway. "Coffee would be good."

He got us coffees, which he set on a small table between two chairs. A few minutes later, I shook his jacket a little and handed it back to him.

"Hang it on the back of the chair to dry," I said as I washed my cuff with lots of soap and plenty of cold water. All I could see, when I was done, was a slight pinkish tinge. I washed my hands in hot soapy water and sat down next to Ben.

"Thank you for cleaning my jacket."

"You're welcome."

It really was the least I could do. He took care of everything else and hadn't so much as raised his voice at all the trouble I'd caused.

"She can identify me," I said, nodding my head toward the door.

That was the thing that'd been playing on my mind the whole time. Well, that and the killing. Upper Hutt wasn't that big a city. It covered a large area but population wise it wasn't that big. The minute you do anything stupid, you find out just how many people recognise you in a city of only forty-thousand people.

Running into Kirsty again was on the cards.

"It'll be all right," Ben replied. His soft tone edged back in.

I watched him without watching him, a trick I'd learned years ago while still training. How to observe someone using peripheral vision was an excellent skill to have.

He was interesting.

He was shaping up to be someone I could like. That pretty much meant he wasn't an arsehole. He seemed relaxed, even when I knew he probably wasn't. He had the ability to soothe and make everything seem all right when it probably wasn't. Good skills to have.

He was few years older than me. He'd hit the magic forty a few years ago. There was no grey in his light brown hair, his eyes were clear and bright, his skin slightly tanned. Manicured nails but calloused palms. He didn't confine himself solely to indoor pursuits. I noted the callous pattern on his inner left palm and finger tips as he set his cup down.

"Do you play guitar?"

Ben lifted his head and turned to face me. A smile stretched across his face. "I do."

He didn't question my question.

I added something else. "Do you play a lot?"

"Not as much as I used to. But I play most days," he replied, picking his cup up again. He glanced at his fingertips then grinned at me.

"Giving myself away."

I shrugged.

"Unlike you I don't have a dossier to refer to."

But I really did, if I chose to use it. Wikipedia had everything there was to know about Benjamin Reynolds, and a good deal of it was made up by crazy people. The only thing not mentioned was his sideline career as an agent with Homeland.

He dialled back the grin. He looked almost shy. There was something quite charming about him. Behind the charm, I saw he'd worn braces as a child. His smile showed something else too. The light reflected oddly from around his pupils. He was wearing contact lenses. I could just make out the edge of the lenses in his eye.

Somehow, it was comforting to know he wasn't perfect, and sure wasn't born perfect. He had shaped up to be quite a human. The way he took charge and dealt with my mess was comforting.

"Are you all right?" he asked.

"Yes."

"Do you want to talk about what happened tonight?"

"No." Let's not delve into that assortment of problems.

Ben leant down and reached into his jacket pocket. He pulled out the wallet he had removed from the body earlier.

He opened it. I moved the coffee cups to the floor. Piece by piece, he laid the entire contents on the small table between us. I cast my eyes over the contents. A driver's license. A scrap of paper bearing a cell phone number. National bank EFTPOS card. Massey University student identity card and a VIP card for a Spotlight Store.

He moved the scrap of paper so it was no longer in the midst of the cards and hummed softly. A smile bounded across my face. It had been a long time since I'd heard that particular Sesame Street song. He was right. One of those things was not like the others. I reached forward and touched the Spotlight card.

"Not the kind of thing I'd expect in the wallet of a jerk like he appeared to be."

"What is it for?"

I racked my brain for an American equivalent to Spotlight.

"Jo-Ann, it's like Jo-Ann fabric and craft stores but big like Michaels."

He smiled. "How do you know that?"

"I go to Spotlight all the time ..."

"That's not what I mean. How do you know about Michaels and Jo-Ann?"

I smiled back and winked. I didn't know him well enough to tell him all my secrets.

Ben moved on. "Maybe he made rainbow tutus in his spare time?" he said. "Perhaps that was his thing. He made tutus and attacked women."

They probably looked better in them than he did. I could see it was a jealousy thing.

"Got a laptop handy?" I said.

"Why?"

"Wanted to check and see if Massey University does a design course that might explain the VIP card." He might even be a graduate and be working as a designer in

Wellington somewhere. No doubt, there was a profile somewhere. Facebook was the likely place.

"I'll go get it, won't be a minute."

He was right he wasn't a minute. He was several minutes. I amused myself by counting the ceiling tiles while I waited. Counting keeps the mind from panicking. Counting stopped me thinking.

Ben strode through the door with a laptop under his arm. He slid it on to my knee.

"They have Wi-Fi in here," he said as he sat back in the chair with his jacket hanging on it.

"Cool, I thought they would, being a hospital and a private one at that. Doctors use laptops, and I guess they also Google?" I replied. The Google School of Medicine popped into my head as I fired the laptop up and clicked on the Firefox icon. The jury remained out as to whether I liked that doctors could look things up or not. It just seemed a bit like cheating. All those years of schooling reduced to a Google search.

I typed Massy University design school in the internet search box.

"Here look," I said turning the laptop toward Ben. "The Massey University School of Design has a campus here in Wellington. But it's not much help otherwise. I'll try Facebook."

Sure enough, I found his profile.

He was indeed a designer working for a company in Wellington. His profile was interesting. He'd been with the same company since graduating from Massey University. His ultimate goal was to appear on Project Runway.

"Guess that explains the Spotlight card," Ben said, reaching for his coffee.

"Maybe it does. Never thought of designers being violent like that."

"I don't know," he said taking a sip of his drink. A frown creased his forehead and he put the cup back on the floor. "Ever watched Project Runway, you know that reality show fronted by Heidi Klum?"

"Ah no, can't say that I have."

"You wouldn't be saying designers weren't violent if you had," he said while barely holding in a throaty chuckle. "Although I have to say, they're more inclined to tantrums and shedding tears than physically attacking each other – maybe a bit of hair pulling."

I laughed. "Let me guess, you watch it to see Heidi Klum?"

"Naturally. It sure isn't to see designers have melt downs and bitch slap each other."

"Good to know," I muttered under my breath then asked almost nonchalantly, "How old was Bruce Wilson?" My teeth sank into my lip to stop me adding 'when I killed him'.

"Thirty-five, his birthday was three days ago."

"Hope he enjoyed it," I said.

I shut the lid of the laptop. My knee was getting warm so I moved the computer to the coffee table. A yawn escaped. I stood up, arching my back, and stretching my hands to the ceiling. I was overly warm and uncomfortable, not to mention genuinely tired.

I shucked off my jacket and hung it carefully over the side of the chair I'd been sitting in. My cuff would dry better without it on anyway.

Private hospitals were overheated and stuffy feeling just like public ones. No wonder people feel so bad when they're in hospitals. Even visitors end up feeling like crap.

One more big stretch and I sat back down.

"Now what?" I asked. My question caught Ben yawning and that made me smile.

"I'll take you back to your car then follow you home and pick up the other package. Once I'm sure everything is all right here, we'll get going," he replied.

A question burned. I almost didn't want to know but asked to see if he'd tell me.

"You said she was drugged when we arrived here. What was that about?"

"I gave her a drink in the car." He smiled a little. "She won't remember ever seeing us or anything of what happened."

"Should I even ask what you used?"

"Rohypnol in the water bottle."

It all fell into place. I remembered him saying the water contained electrolytes, that would've been so she wouldn't balk at the taste.

"Remind me never to accept a drink from your water bottle," I said. The revelation that Ben had a date rape drug with him was a smidge disturbing. "Do I want to ask why you had Roofies handy to start with? On second thoughts, don't tell me. It's exactly what I'd expect an agency to use, that or ketamine."

Scary but clever really. Knock her out, take her memory, and leave her at a private hospital in the city. It'd take quite some figuring to connect Kirsty to a dead guy in a Pinehaven public toilet. Or at the very least, it wouldn't be as simple as it could've been.

I studied him carefully yet inconspicuously.

A question rolled around my head, picking up speed as it revolved.

Why did he have drugs on him?

I shoved it aside. It seemed smarter to be thankful he could deal with the situation and safeguard our involvement than worry about the origins and intended use.

"We should probably get moving," Ben suggested as he stood up. "I'll go see if I can find someone and get an update on how she is, then we're out of here."

I nodded.

It had been a long day, and a longer night, and I was tired. Sleep would be more than welcome. But not the sort of sleep Kirsty was having.

My attention turned to finding another more super hero nickname for Ben. His super power was memory loss. Where'd I heard of someone who could alter memories or erase them before? Partial clips of a television show entered my head. Once Upon a Time.

Mr. Gold, otherwise known as Rumpelstiltskin, could erase memories with magic. As tempting as it was to call him Gold I decided I should stick with Ben. After all, Mr.

Gold wasn't the nicest of characters. I tried other versions like Benjie and Benny, but even in my head they sort of got stuck somewhere behind my teeth and came off sounding special. Kind of like the word oblong sounded special.

Yeah, I liked Ben, as a person and as a name.

I just needed to block the whole carrying memory zapping drugs thing out.

He was perfectly fine as a man and a damn good actor. An actor. Ha. Life is weird. I knew I'd never look at actors in the same light again, I'd always be wondering who they really worked for.

Chapter 13
[DEATH IN THE CHURCH YARD]

I flung my arm out and smacked the alarm clock until it stopped making its infernal noise.

"Ouch," I muttered, shaking my hand. "Stupid clock, I hope you're broken. You hurt my hand."

I opened my bleary eyes and inspected the damaged hand. There was nothing to see. I struggled to a semi sitting position and grasped hold of the offending clock. Holding it close so my tired eyes could read the face. I peered at it. My eyes finally focused and the clock hands came into view.

Seven. God. It was only seven o'clock. I dropped the clock back on to the bedside table. It hit with a crash and fell onto the floor.

I rolled over, tugged the duvet higher up and snuggled into it.

Half an hour later I threw the duvet back and jumped out of bed, panicked that I'd slept in too long. Romeo would need to go out. I opened the back door, and then the living room door and called Romeo. He took his time stretching before loping out to greet me before galloping out the backdoor to relieve himself.

I slouched off to the kitchen and made coffee. The kitchen felt empty.

The absence of the gnome on the bench reminded me of the previous night's escapades.

Liking gnomes might be my guilty secret. I missed his pointy blue hat and scrunched up face. But having two of them on the bench would've been bordering on creepy. I whipped the curtains open and let the warm sun bathe the room. Wouldn't be long before winter moved in and sun became a sad drippy grey affair blown in on a southerly gale.

I sat at the table with my cup of coffee and flicked through some junk mail. Half way through the latest Warehouse mailer I stopped.

Strange. How did the junk mail get to my kitchen table? My mind scrolled back over yesterday. The evening shone as a less than spectacular life moment. Setting that aside for a moment, at no point last night or yesterday, did I stop at the letterbox to gather the junk mail?

Did Ben? My mind conjured images of our arrival home.

He parked on the street. I pulled up the driveway. Ben shut the gates for me and walked beside me up the path. I was on the letterbox side. He didn't go near it, let alone empty it. What a liberty that would've been. People don't randomly empty another person's letterbox. People don't carry Rohypnol on the off chance either. I shooed that thought away, fast.

My attention wandered to the troll slash stalker. Would he show himself today? That wasn't a helpful line of thought either.

I stood up and prowled around the house going in and out of all the rooms. The guest bedroom door was shut. I always left it open. I turned the handle and pushed the door. At the end of the bed lay a black leather trench coat. Very Matrix.

Next to the bed were black leather boots, sporting rather pointy toes, an inch high heel, and silver Marshall Stars on the ankle. In the bed lay a dark haired shape. Face down and snoring.

Donald.

He must've remembered his key.

I shut the door and went back to the kitchen.

When did Donald arrive?

Was it before or after the gnome left?

Did he see Ben?

Either of those instances could spell trouble for me. A mental berating began. I should've hidden the gnome in my room rather than leaving the little bugger on the kitchen bench. There was a way to find out when Donald arrived. Leaving sleeping beauty to his dreams, and went down to the kitchen. Didn't take long to find and open the alarm company's app on my phone.

From the menu, I chose to view the daily use lists, bringing up a list of times the external doors were opened and closed on the house. Donald may have had a key but I had a way of checking when and who accessed the house.

When I adopted Romeo, I changed the alarm system from audible to a tracking system with a silent alarm component. Opening any windows or doors from the exterior without a key triggered the alarm at the monitoring company's end. All keyed access was recorded as well as any attempted access. I just had to read the access times over the last two days and I'd know which was me and which was cuzzie Donald.

According to the site, someone opened the front door with a key at four minutes past midnight then there was no other activity until zero three hundred.

This meant Donald arrived home just after midnight.

We didn't get home until nearly zero three hundred.

Donald would've been well asleep in the spare room by then. He probably didn't see us arrive home.

I knew he'd been in the kitchen. He wouldn't have missed the gnome on the bench.

I began to form a plan in case Donald asked about the gnome. Pocketing my phone, I decided it was time to rummage in the wardrobe and find something to wear.

Nothing fancy, but I needed to be tidy and suitably attired. It may be Upper Hutt but I don't leave the house in my pyjama pants and slippers. I do maintain some standards. Plus, there was a chance I'd be seeing Ben again. It wouldn't do to be slovenly.

The morning plan was to take Romeo for his walk, try and locate the third gnome, figure out why Justin was missing, and there was the obligatory Nana visit. I also needed to get hold of the office and see if we had anything else on Daniel bloody Shankle. Finding clothes wasn't hard; tidy dark blue jeans, a teal blue shirt, and black shoes. I dropped a black jacket on my bed. I couldn't decide if it would be too warm for a jacket or too cold without one. There was no telling what the weather would do.

I showered, dressed, and added minimal makeup. Just enough makeup to disguise the tiredness in my face and to add some length to my eyelashes. It wouldn't do to have Nana telling me how tired and sickly I looked. Although Nana preferred to use the term peaky.

I heard Nana's voice as I applied another coat of mascara, the words echoed in my head. "You're looking peaky dear. What you need is a tonic. Perhaps some cod liver oil or malt extract with Halibut oil."

I cringed.

I brushed my long hair vigorously with a pig bristle brush then leaned forward and stood up quickly, tossing my dark hair back as I did so.

My reflection in the full length bedroom mirror smiled at me.

"Fabulous," I crooned, delighted to find no trace of anything remotely peaked.

"Yes you are," said a voice from the doorway.

I jumped, Donald's reflection appeared over my shoulder.

"Don't sneak up on a person like that!" I flapped my hair brush at him.

Donald smiled. He stepped behind me and smoothed out a few wayward waves in my hair.

"Did you have a good night?" he asked, throwing himself theatrically onto my bed, to end up propped on one elbow with his legs stretched out.

"Not bad," I replied, sitting on the edge of the bed and putting my shoes on.

"What's on the agenda today?"

"Have some work to do, but Romeo needs walking, then I'll work for a bit and then it's Nana and The Cronies of Doom," I replied with a sigh.

"That explains the teal shirt and scowl on your face."

I shot him a filthy glare. "I was not scowling."

"You are now."

"Smart arse."

"Shall I tag along?"

"Not unless you want Nana to fix you up with someone nasty."

"She'll be over that now, hasn't she got some mystery to solve?" Donald said with as much innocence as he could muster.

I looked at him. He knew.

"Not now, she's already solved that," I replied, waiting for him to say something about the gnome.

How could I be so stupid as to have the thing sitting on the bench? Bad enough I killed a man and caused a slight clean up problem. I stopped thinking.

Best not to go down that path.

Dead is dead.

No regrets allowed.

Donald sat up. "Shall we have coffee? You have time, especially if you're taking the car."

"Walking the big guy first though, remember?"

"You still have time ... Nana isn't going anywhere."

I nodded and followed him to the kitchen, coffee did sound good. Nana might not be going anywhere but I couldn't guarantee the gnome I was after wouldn't vanish. My eyes avoided the empty bench.

Donald watched me with a newfound interest. I could feel his questions and his eyes. Bugger. I was going to have to conjure something up so I was ready for his questions.

He made coffee and placed a mug in front of me at the table.

"I'll get the paper," Donald said.

He disappeared out the door and down the hall leaving me to my coffee and the empty gnome free bench.

Donald came back a few moments later and dropped the paper on the table.

"It's warm out," he said. "I'll take the entertainment section, you have the front."

Donald removed the back of the paper and handed me the front.

"Thanks," I said, scanning the front page for anything that mentioned Pinehaven. There was nothing. I laid the paper on the table and opened it up.

Most of the news involved the Government debating tax cuts. Like I cared. The Prime Minister was apparently blaming treasury for not giving him the correct information on the financial state of the country and that was why the country was in so much debt. It all seemed very pass the buckish and typical of politics. I skimmed the rest of the articles on tax. I'm pretty sure the

Christchurch earthquakes played a big part in the debt, but what do I know? Could there be a more boring subject? Then I found a more boring story, asset sales. I glanced up at Donald.

"Water rights?" I said. "Again?"

His left eye brow rose. "You don't want to go there before you've had your coffee made with my water," Donald said with a flourish of his hand toward the kitchen sink.

"Unless you peed in the jug it isn't your water, end of story," I replied with a smile. "Although, it is a very clever way to disrupt the government's asset sales agenda."

Donald grinned. "Score one for us."

"I have no comment," I said and settled into enjoying the colourful human interest articles. At least they weren't murder stories or water rights stories or anything to do with any treaty or tax increases.

Half way down the third page, I spotted a small news story. It was about the missing gnome of Martha's.

I groaned.

"What?" Donald asked looking up from his gossip column page.

"Nothing," I replied and turned the page. "Boring tax talk."

"Swap?"

"I'm not done yet," I said. "Thought you were reading gossip columns and getting caught up with the rich and famous?"

"Same old same old. Someone is always getting divorced, changing gender, or having a baby, Kardashians

I'm looking at you." He flicked the page with his index finger. "I really don't think I can take any more Kardashian anything."

"Over it?"

"Very much so. Oh what on earth?"

"Now what?"

"I never did like that Paris chick. Don't you think she's rather horsy looking?"

"I find her a wee bit too strange," I said, scanning the page I was reading for more news of gnomes.

"This is not a good photograph," Donald said holding the newspaper up for me to see. "She looks like Romeo's dinner."

I grinned. Yes, she did.

"Yes." I also thought she'd had her fifteen minutes. Years ago, I tried to understand why she caused such a stir and decided it was because she was easy.

"I can't believe they're dragging her back up now."

"Apparently you don't need to be attractive or smart, when you have money and put out," I said.

Donald high-fived me. "You bitch, I love it."

"Time?"

Donald made a huge show of checking his watch. The sun bounced off the diamonds that surrounded the face and nearly blinded me.

"I see you're wearing the man magnet watch," I commented with a wink.

"I really am."

"It's gorgeous," I replied.

Donald flapped his wrist and sent little rays of light all over the kitchen.

"Michael Hill, diamond collection. And it's nine-fifteen."

"I am meeting the cronies at eleven," I said, folding the paper in half and turning my attention back to Donald as another ray of light blasted my eyes. "So did you attract something fabulous with your watch?"

"Like a gorgeous moth to a flame baby," Donald replied. "He was tall, tanned, and scrumptious."

"And what brought you here?"

"He lives around the corner, how marvellous is that?"

"You went back to his place?" I looked at him.

He was smiling wistfully and admiring his own watch. He appeared happy, relaxed, and to be reliving some kind of memory.

"Don't give me details, just yes or no," I warned.

"Yes, oh, yes."

I laughed. "I'm glad you had fun."

Donald dragged himself out of his memory and poked a finger at an article in the folded newspapers in front of me. "Did you see that?"

I looked where he poked. How did I miss that?

"Another gnome, this time in Pinehaven."

Donald glanced at the bench, as if he expected to see something.

"Didn't you have a gnome sitting there last night?"

"Pfft, seriously? Me, a gnome? You must've been seeing things. Since when have I ever had gnomes, inside or out?"

Donald winked, smirked, and said, "I don't know your sexual preferences, darling, what you do with gnomes is your business."

My hand flicked out and smacked his arm. "Sicko."

"But really, Ronnie, I could've sworn there was a gnome on your bench."

I watched Donald's confused face and almost felt bad then found a way to spin it to make him feel better.

"You are so silly. Goodness, by the sound of it you had such wonderful time last night, you hallucinated."

Donald smiled, a satisfied, cat got the cream smile. Bile rose in my throat.

"Oh, I did. You're probably right. I could barely get the key in the lock."

Donald went back to reliving his memory of the night and forgot all about the gnome.

I read the article about the missing Pinehaven gnome. Funny, that anyone noticed. It was not the best kept garden in the area, and I doubted the gnome was visible from the house, and I replaced it. I replaced it. Did that mean someone stole the replacement? If so, then that someone's going to be pissed off.

The whole gnome thing was beginning to take on a life of its own. I could almost guarantee that Nana would see that article and be all fired up. I scanned the article several times. There was no mention of where in Pinehaven the gnome disappeared from, just that it was assumed stolen. The journalist mentioned it was the second gnome to go missing in Upper Hutt. They thought children were responsible.

My fingers crossed and I hoped Nana and The Cronies of Doom missed the whole article. It was a short piece, only eight lines, and didn't draw any comparison between the Silverstream gnome disappearance and the Pinehaven one or the death of the woman.

Maybe it was a different gnome to the one I'd taken.

How would anyone have found the gnome I replaced? Unless they knew exactly where to look. I surmised that someone took a gnome from another garden thinking it was the gnome.

The other interested party.

Someone has the wrong gnome. I suspected that would cause quite a stir in the chatter department. The sooner I could locate that third gnome and keep it out of the damn newspapers the better. I had a feeling it wasn't going to be easy. The only person I'd noticed in both Silverstream and Pinehaven was Daniel Shankle. He didn't strike me as smart enough to be working for anyone in an intelligence gathering capacity but what if he was? Perish the thought.

"I need to make a call," I said and hurried into the living room with my cell phone in hand. I called the office. Sure enough, Jenn and Steph were in.

"Do you have anything further on Daniel Shankle?"

"Yes, we do," Steph replied. "You're not going to be impressed."

"Let me have it." I prepared myself for bad news.

"He has applied for his Private Investigators license. Police are running the required checks and get this, his application is before the Private Security Personnel Licensing Authority."

Bollocks, that's not ideal.

"Hang on, he has criminal convictions. He can't get a PI license, can he?" I asked. Surely, we don't allow convicted criminals to hold PI licenses.

"He could. His convictions were all more than seven years ago and he has the right to explain himself and convince the powers that be that he's reformed."

Damn.

"Who is he working for?"

"A PI firm in Wellington has him on their books as a file clerk. They have had him on the books for a year."

"And I think he's working off the books for someone unsavoury," I replied. "Damn, thought he was just a creepy stalker but it's starting to look like he's tailing me for a reason."

"How can we help?" Steph asked.

"Put Jenn on him, tail him, and make it obvious."

"Might take both of us."

"Then do it."

"I'll rope Beck in to cover the office," she said. "We'll keep you posted."

"Cheers."

I hung up. Counter surveillance time. The Shankle guy had become a liability.

"Earth to Ronnie? What was all that about?"

"Work, just work," I replied as I spun around to face Donald. "Thinking about Nana. I'd better get moving. Will you be here when I get back?"

"Yes, you should, and no I won't. I have a lunch date."

"With him? The mysterious, tanned, scrumptious one?"

"Yes!" Donald almost squealed with delight.

"You have fun!"

"Kiss Nana for me."

"If I have too," I replied. "Ring me later."

I called Romeo, fitted his harness on him, snapped on his lead, and grabbed my keys, cell phone, and jacket before calling, "Bye."

"Watch out for nasty hairy trolls," Donald called after me.

I saw the troll's car the minute I stepped over the threshold. Bloody Donald jinxed me. There it was, idling across the road. Shankle pulled out and drove off fast when I glared at him.

Something poking out of my letterbox gave me reason to pause.

Reaching in I pulled out an envelope. Seeing my name scrawled across the front in spidery handwriting didn't please me any more than the lack of stamp.

The envelope contained a folded piece of white paper. I extracted and opened it. It was a piece of A4 printer paper. In the middle of the paper were the words 'You think you're so fucking clever. You and that dog of yours. I'll be watching.'

Definitely not good.

I pulled my cell phone from my pocket and called Steph. Romeo whined and leaned on me. He wasn't happy about the interruption to his walk.

"Shankle just left my street heading south," I said. I tightened my grip on Romeo's lead. We crossed the road. "I'm walking Ro. We're going to head down Ngata Grove via Merton Street. I'll let him have a run by the church hall or at least a good explore, then bring him home via Fergusson Drive."

"Jenn is closest to you," Steph said. "I'm nearly in Upper Hutt."

"Let Jenn know?"

"Yes, have her stick close to my route. I have a feeling he'll be popping back up."

I hung up. There was no one out on the street. Romeo and I walked to the shop before I decided I needed to make another call. This time to Ben.

"Small problem – this note was in my letterbox. It reads, 'You think you're so fucking clever. You and that dog of yours. I'll be watching.'"

"And?" Ben asked.

"This guy could be feeding information to the other interested party."

"If so, then he's making this job more exciting than it needs to be. Be careful."

"I always am," I replied and hung up.

Romeo and I headed to the churchyard. I had my pendulum around my neck. We passed the lunatic dog throwing herself at the glass doors and got safely into the alleyway. At the edge of St John's field Romeo began pulling. He slacked off with one warning tug from me but it didn't last long. He pulled again, this time harder.

Lunging toward the far end of the field.

"You want to run, big boy?" I asked. He pulled, twisting in his harness. "Guess that's a yes." I looked around. There was no one about and the field was big enough for Romeo to run. I bent down to his ear. "You sure you want to run?"

He whined.

I unclipped his lead, but held his harness. With my other hand, I rubbed his haunches. He bounced. I let go. "Go!"

He careened toward the high corrugated steel fence. I watched. A greyhound in full flight is impressive. I knew I'd never tire of seeing him run. Romeo turned at the last second and came back to me. Panting.

I patted him.

"Go!" I said, sending him off again. This time he ran to the fence and braked hard, sending muddy dirt flying up from his feet. He shoved his nose in the mounded grass clippings and mulch by the fence. No amount of calling made a difference. His nose was on and his ears were off.

"Is there a rabbit hole over there, Ro?" I asked walking over to him. He didn't look at me until I was right beside him. "What is it, Romeo?"

There was nothing to see, but he was rooting around with his nose in the old grass clippings and mulch for all he was worth. I scoured the ground looking for telltale bunny poop. Nothing. I didn't remember seeing bunny poop anywhere on the field.

"Leave it," I said. Romeo looked at me and backed away from the fence. "Good boy."

I stepped in closer to see if I could find anything. I half expected a rabbit. He was still sniffing hard next to me. Didn't seem to be any obvious rabbit holes in the mulchy grass.

I scooted some off the top with my foot and a hand flopped out.

A hand.

Yuck.

Romeo sniffed harder, and closed in on the appendage. I clipped his lead onto his harness and moved him away.

A hand.

I could see the discoloured flesh and gross looking nails. I shuddered. Killing someone is one thing but finding a dead body is a whole new level of horrible.

I toed around the hand with my boot. Hand, led to arm, led to shoulder. I needed a head. There was a horrible feeling mounting that I knew whom the hand belonged to. My heart thumped hard in my chest. The crystal around my neck vibrated against my skin. The more I tried to convince myself it wasn't Justin the harder the crystal vibrated.

Crunching gravel caught my attention. A pale blue car rounded St John's Lane. That's all I needed. I knew the driver couldn't see the partially exposed body from where he was. I didn't want Daniel Shankle anywhere near Romeo's find.

I backed away from the body, taking Romeo to a tree a few metres to the right and pulled out my phone. I made a call to Steph.

"St John's Lane, he's just appeared and is idling at the end by the alley way to Ngata Grove."

"Where are you?" she asked.

"I've just uncovered a big problem in the mulch at the Fergusson Drive end of the church field."

"How big?"

"About six feet three inches and stone cold dead."

"Need a shovel?"

If I wasn't sure it was Justin, it'd be funny. Only a friend would ask that question. "I'll take care of the big problem. You deal with the stalker."

"Okay. We need to tag the Shankle prick's car, so we know where he is at all times," Steph said.

"Yes, we do. Can you run interference? I don't want him coming any closer."

"I'm pulling in behind him now."

I hung up and turned my attention to Romeo and the corpse. Steph would take care of Shankle. He wasn't my problem now.

Romeo sat and lifted his paw.

"You can't have the hand buddy," I said, patting his head. "Good boy for finding him."

Now what?

Do I call Reede and tell her one of her intelligence officers is dead? No, that would not be smart. Without getting a look at his face, I wasn't sure it was Justin. I tied Romeo to the tree and went back to the partially hidden corpse. I used my foot to scrap away the leaves and grass from where I thought the face would be.

Dead glazed eyes bulged from putrid skin. I swallowed hard and looked past the hideous death mask. It was Justin. He looked like he'd been dead for weeks. I was sure that wasn't right. I wanted to know how he died and how he came to be partially buried in mulch.

I covered his face back up. "Why didn't you come to me?" I said, pushing more leaves and mulch over his face. "I'm sorry, Justin."

Behind me, a loud male voice and the quieter more controlled reasonable voice of Steph resounded. I ignored them. Justin's death and involvement in the gnome situation baffled me.

Why would he hide the gnomes and not hand them in to Reede? Because he didn't trust her? Or because Justin wasn't playing for our team anymore? That didn't feel right. There was nothing to indicate Justin was rogue.

Ignoring the yelling male behind me was not easy. Romeo whined. I looked over at him. He turned his head to watch the commotion. I knew by his tail wag that he recognised Steph.

I made another call.

"Ben, we have a problem."

"We?"

"Yep, we. The person who planted the gnomes has

been planted himself."

"How do you know who ...?"

"I just do. You need to get your arse out here to me."

"Where are you?"

I gave him directions. "I'm running out of time." I hung up and stuffed my phone in my jacket pocket.

The noise behind me escalated and I heard another voice. Romeo whined louder and wagged harder. That could only mean Jenn had arrived. I looked over and confirmed that Steph and Jenn were talking to Shankle. They were facing me, which meant Shankle had his back to me. I took the opportunity to cover the hand and arm with the mulch and grass clippings. Then untied the dog.

"Come on Romeo, let's go."

He didn't want to move.

"Heel."

He fell into step beside me.

I sauntered over to the group. Romeo leaned on Steph then Jenn in turn before resuming his position next to me.

"Is there a problem?" I asked. The dog, stood straight, and puffed his muscly chest out.

"With your bitches," Shankle said, glaring at me.

I smiled. Jenn kicked him in the ankle. He squawked and hopped out of the way.

"What was that for?"

Jenn shrugged. "I slipped." She moved a bit closer to him and kicked his other ankle. Shankle fell. His large soft body wobbled for a few seconds.

"I'm going to press charges!" he blustered, trying to lift himself off the ground and failing.

"What for?" Jenn asked. "I slipped. Sorry about your ankle, it was an accident." She stepped back.

"Actually, Mr. Shankle. You go ahead and call police," I said enjoying the confusion in his eyes. "Some fat fuck in a pale blue car has been stalking me and left a threatening note in my letterbox today." With much drama, I flung my arm out and pointed to his car. "That car!" I said, "That's the one."

Shankle cowered on the ground.

"There's no need, I'm sure your friend slipped and the kicking me twice was an accident."

"No, I think she did it on purpose," I said. "Really we should report this."

Steph piped up, "I'll call police, shall I?"

Shankle clambered unsteadily to his feet shaking his head and muttering apologies.

"No need, no need."

He wedged himself into his car, started up, and drove in a wide arc across the grass and back down the lane.

Jenn laughed.

"Good job, ladies," she said as we all high-fived.

"Guess he doesn't want police pulling the plug on his PI license then?" I said with a grin.

"Guess not!" Steph replied with a chuckle. "I think we can have that license blocked without too much trouble."

Yes, we can.

"I don't think we'll need to, I doubt he'll get it approved," I said.

To be honest I didn't see him living long after today's ridiculousness.

Jenn was rubbing Romeo's shoulders. "What did he find over there?"

"A problem ...," I said. "A big, dead, smelly problem."

Steph frowned. "Who?"

"A guy I used to work with in the service." I couldn't think too much about who and how long I'd known him. To finish the job without falling apart I needed distance.

"Has this got something to do with your case?"

I nodded. "So does Shankle. He's become a thorn in my side."

"I bugged Shankle's car," Jenn said with a smile. "He was too busy looking at Steph to notice me stick a GPS unit in the back right wheel arch."

"Excellent, now we'll know where the fat bastard is at least. I'm going to need you two to monitor and follow him. Just like this morning."

"Okay," Steph and Jenn replied in unison.

"This case is close to being over and it's getting dangerous."

Another car approached. I recognised it as soon as it rounded the bend. "This is for me, you guys head off ... keep a close eye on Shankle."

I looked at Jenn. "If you see him using a cell phone ... it would be a shame if the signal was blocked ..."

Steph smiled again. "I like this game."

Ben sat in his car and waited for Jenn and Steph to

leave.

Once they'd gone, he climbed out of the car and joined me on the side of the lane.

Romeo leaned on him and received a pat.

"This way," I said and led the way to the burial site. "The body is under the mulch." I pointed to where I saw his head earlier.

Ben couched down and scrapped some of the garden material off the mound, revealing a face contorted by a painful death.

"Christ," he murmured, covering the face again and standing up. He looked at me, then back at the mounded mulch. "I need to make a call." Ben took his phone from his pants pocket and walked toward the building on our left. I stayed where I was. I could hear him talking, after hearing the words, 'clean up' I stopped trying to listen. Ben joined me again. We stood for a moment, just staring at ground.

"Can you find the last gnome?" Ben asked me.

"I know roughly where it is. So, yes, I can."

"Don't do it today. Do something unrelated, okay?"

"Wouldn't it be better to get it fast and get this over with?"

"Not with that man following you and not today. You know who is buried in the mulch here?"

I nodded. "Justin. He was a friend and a colleague for many years."

"And he hid the packages. Did he tell you what is in them?"

I shook my head. Dead men aren't very chatty.

"When I realised this situation had something to do with Justin I tried to find him," I said.

"What made you think he was involved?"

"A gut feeling." We had a gnome connection.

His eyes brightened as they looked at me. "That's it? A gut feeling?"

I nodded. "I was looking for him, meanwhile, something kept pulling me back to the church yard and the dog has been super interested in this place for days too." I paused, aware that I needed to be careful with my choice of words. "I wasn't getting any movement from Justin at all. Usually there's something, cash withdrawal or credit card use, or something."

I purposefully made it sound like I was tracking him using conventional methods.

It was easier than trying to explain how I can pick up energy via a quartz pendulum. People give off energy, vibrant energy that the pendulum can pick up. What I was getting while trying to locate Justin was akin to the non-committal energy the gnomes gave off. More of a, I'm here but I'm not, thing. I'm in the general vicinity but you can't narrow it down without legwork – type energy. Energy like that tended to mean something life ending.

"You never spoke to him?"

"No. I talked to his mother and she said he was in Australia with work." I walked away from the death and leaned on a big tree. Ben followed me. Romeo lay on the ground by my feet.

"He was an intelligence office for the NZSIS, but he reached out to us, not the NZSIS. Justin intercepted something world changing and didn't trust his boss," Ben said, explaining his involvement with Justin.

"How very dramatic. World changing or world destroying, Ben?"

"Both."

I was right about Reede. Justin didn't trust Reede. So she warned me the Americans wanted my help in an effort to stay in the loop because she knew she'd be shut out.

"Did you speak to him?" I said.

"No, we exchanged emails. He sent a picture of the gnomes but never had a chance to say where he'd hidden them. He said he was ill and needed to keep away from people."

"Ill?" That did not sound good.

Romeo whimpered as he stared at the fence line.

Ben followed the dog's gaze.

"Holy shit!"

We watched as something in the mulch moved.

"Could it be gas from the body causing that?" I asked, aware that my voice had lifted an octave.

"I hope so," Ben replied, not sounding convinced.

The movement became writhing. Grass clippings dislodged.

"What do you mean he was sick?" I asked, trying to control the urge to run as a hand emerged, followed by an arm. "What's in those fucking gnomes?"

"Two viruses and the third contains an antidote," he replied, drawing his gun from the holster in the small of his back.

"Which ones do you have?"

"One virus and the antidote."

The writhing and flexing continued from the mound at edge of the field.

"Now what?"

"He must've been exposed to both viruses."

"Then why didn't he take the antidote?"

"Maybe he did?"

Antidote that doesn't work? Great.

"You going to do something about this? Ring an ambulance or something?" Panic edged my words.

He carefully pulled back the slide and peered into the chamber then let the slide return to its proper position.

"We can't risk him spreading this." Ben pulled a black cylindrical object from his pocket and screwed it to the barrel of the gun in his hand. He walked toward Justin.

Over his shoulder, Ben said, "Take the dog and go home. I'll meet you there in an hour."

I wanted to both stay and go. Morbid curiosity soared through my veins. I wanted to understand what was happening.

"Go!" Ben yelled at me.

The dog and I walked to the beginning of the alleyway. I turned just in time to see Justin's reanimated body stagger from the ground and lurch toward Ben. A gentle pfft pfft followed.

Justin's head snapped back. He crumpled like a marionette with broken strings.

"Come on, Romeo. Let's go home." I held his lead firmly in my right hand and jogged toward home.

The disturbing events weighed heavily on my mind.

Two viruses.

Two.

Justin.

What sort of illness reanimates dead flesh?

None that I'd ever heard of. Not in life anyway.

This was horror movie stuff.

My thoughts switched to Romeo.

He'd found the body.

Touched the hand with his nose and vacuumed up the smells associated with Justin's death. Cold dread filled me. I had more questions.

So, how was the virus spread and was it a cross species type deal?

Or was it like the movies and you had to be bitten by someone who was infected. The last zombie book I'd read was apocalyptic and involved grey snow that turned out to be human skin. That wasn't something I wanted to think about ever. Bile rose. It was too late to put a lid on the whole grey snow thought.

I unlocked the front door, no messing around, no scanning the street for loser wannabe PI's. It felt safe inside with the door shut and locked. I unclipped Romeo's harness and hung it in the laundry. He headed straight for his water bowl while I put the jug on. A cup of tea was in order.

Hot sweet tea. That's what Nana would insist on for shock, along with a glass of whiskey.

While the jug boiled, I grabbed my laptop and fired it up. I stared at Google Chrome and wondered what I should Google to find out about the viruses. Google knows everything, you just have to ask the right question. I knew it wouldn't this time. I ditched the browser and opened one that allowed me access to the deep web.

I made a phone call to Steph while the internet searched for answers.

"Everything okay with you two?" I kept my tone light and perky, hoping I didn't come off borderline hysterical.

"Yes, Shankle is currently at KFC."

Where else would a fat bastard like him be at lunchtime?

"Good. This case has taken a wee bit of a turn toward not good." I paused. "Steph, we have a problem."

"Serious?"

"Could be."

"What do you want us to do?"

"Check out the first-aid kit, make sure there is hand sanitiser, masks, you know... make sure we have every-thing."

"Okay." Her turn to pause. "I think you should tell us what's going on."

"The things I'm looking for ... they're viruses."

"What are we talking here? Smallpox? Anthrax?"

I wish.

"I don't know what it is, but I saw Justin's dead body reanimate."

Steph laughed. "Good one."

"Really ..."

"That's not possible," she said. "Is it?"

"I did not think so, not outside television, movies, and books anyway. But I saw what I saw."

I had a horrible feeling that we were screwed.

Chapter 14
[A NIGHT OFF]

Ben came up with the idea to taking the rest of the day off. I found it strange but part of me understood his reasoning. If we had one virus and for the virus to be deadly you had to have both, then we were winning. Without our one, the bad guys, whoever they were, couldn't release a deadly virus. Considering what I'd witnessed and what was going on, my brain wasn't coping too well; maybe an afternoon off was a good idea.

He thought it would be fun if we went out for dinner and pushed the point.

Sure, yeah, why not?

My mate became a zombie. By all means let's go out for dinner and pretend like nothing happened here. So, being the good sport that I am, I searched my wardrobe for the perfect outfit and tried not to worry about Romeo becoming whatever the hell Justin became. Seemed smarter to avoid the zombie thought, because it really didn't help.

It wasn't strictly speaking a business dinner. Not that that helped my decision at all. It didn't help me move my thoughts away from Justin's death either.

I caught sight of my reflection in the mirror and growled at myself. "You've read way too many horror novels and seen way too many horror movies, and now you think it's all coming true."

No point arguing with myself. I'd win or worse, I'd lose.

It was so much easier when I was finding missing people. Funnily enough when we started our agency, we all thought we'd be taking photos of cheating spouses and doing background checks for the rest of our lives. The thought that I could involve us in something world destroying was never on the cards.

I pulled a black shirt from the wardrobe and paired it with indigo jeans and black boots with a two inch heel. Anything would've done. I just wanted to be away from the accusing looks I was giving myself from the mirror.

I knew I could not have saved Justin.

Maybe if he'd come to me early on. My brain hovered over that thought. If he'd come to me earlier on, we might all be dead.

I checked my laptop for any urgent emails.

Nothing.

Well, nothing of vital importance. Nana had sent a flurry of emails asking where I was and why I hadn't visited today.

There was nothing else for it. I emailed her back and said I had a dinner date.

That would shut her up until I saw her next.

Even if it didn't, I wouldn't be checking email until tomorrow anyway.

I tottered precariously on the unfamiliar heels to the living room and flicked the play button on the stereo remote.

Leonard Cohen blared from the speakers.

"Bloody hell!" I squawked and hit the off button. Nope. I removed the offending CD. Leonard Cohen was a dead giveaway that Donald had been lurking in the house again.

The case sat top of my CD rack. I carefully put it away, and set my iPod on the dock. I pressed play and scrolled until I found an Eric Clapton album. I pressed play and let 'Promises' fill the room.

As I listened, I poked through the contents of a camphor chest that sat under the window by Romeo's bed. In the chest, I found a handbag to go with my black and indigo outfit. I decanted the important things from my leather backpack. The knife required a thorough inspection.

It looked clean but just to make sure, I opted to clean it again. I went through to the kitchen and grabbed a bottle of bleach from under the sink. I filled the sink with near boiling water until about two inches of water lay in the bottom.

I pulled on a pair of heavy duty rubber gloves, tipped half the bottle of bleach into the sink and swirled it around. I wondered briefly why I chose to use bleach while wearing a black shirt and deciding to be very careful not to splash.

I opened all the blades and tools on the knife and sunk it in the sink, and then carefully scrubbed every surface with a dish brush, while keeping the whole thing submerged. I left the knife in the water as I pulled the plug and drained the sink. I rinsed the knife in hot water then in cold. I took off the gloves and put everything away. Using a clean tea towel, I dried all the components of the knife.

Something made me look up.

My heart leapt. Body jumped. Brown eyes looked at me from the outside the window.

"God! What do you want?"

Donald laughed.

"Just seeing if you were home yet," Donald called back. "Open the back door, I'm exhausted!"

The pounding in my chest slowed and resumed a more sedate pace.

"You nearly gave me heart failure."

I wrapped the knife in the towel and left it on the bench before going through to the laundry and opening the back door. Donald noticed my boots immediately.

"Oh yes, they're nice. Love that heel. You're looking good," he cooed, flapping past me and into the house. "Oh what a day I've had."

"No details!" I warned as I followed along behind, watching the floor for anything that could trip me and ruin the fabulous look I had going.

Donald put the jug on and busied himself making tea.

"It reeks of bleach in here," Donald said, swinging the kitchen window open. "What on earth were you doing, removing DNA from something?"

I ignored his question because yes, I was. I carried on drying my knife and folding away all its bits and pieces.

Donald spotted it in my hand.

"Oh now that's fab!"

"I know!" I replied, dropping it into my fancy black evening purse.

"Ah yes, what every girl needs on a date," Donald commented.

"Be prepared," I quipped.

"Dob, dob, dob, dib, dib, dib," Donald shot back giving the Boy Scout three fingered salute.

"Yeah, I can see you as a Boy Scout."

"Not me darling, I was in Boys Brigade," he said with a wide grin.

I should have guessed. "One of Dave's boys?"

"Yes, I was. Back before anyone knew what being one of Dave's boys, meant!"

My mind trawled over the Dave thing. For years, he was the leader of the local Boys Brigade and an upstanding member of the local church. Parents loved him; he put in extra effort with the boys that were deemed to be heading for trouble. He taught the young teens how to drive. He took them away for weekends. Then all the jokes about Dave's boys broke wide open when boys came forward years later and declared he was a pedophile.

"So it never left you with any emotional scars?" I sat at the table and waited for the tea to brew. "The whole pervert thing?"

"Well, sweetie, I was always a little different to the other boys."

"You don't say."

Donald slid a mug of tea to me and sat opposite. He held his mug in two hands, and blew across the surface of the tea. Then he looked up, beaming, and said, "He could be the one, you know!"

"Does he know?"

Donald winked. "Oh, I think so."

"Then congratulations, I'm glad it went so well for you today."

"It was pure magic. Of course, tomorrow I'm back to work and so is he. We're getting together after work, at my place."

"Where does he work?" I asked, making idle chatter but still interested in Donald's new love.

"He has a government job, something in the Department of Internal Affairs."

I perked up and was all ears. "Internal Affairs? Sounds exciting."

"Doesn't it? All very cloak and dagger." Donald came across all wistful and dreamy. "Do you think he's a spy? Like James Bond?"

"I doubt it. Internal Affairs isn't a spy agency. He's probably a clerk in the passport office or something."

What were the odds of Donald meeting someone who worked for a Government Department while I was embroiled in a gnome dilemma?

I considered the implications and promptly dismissed the idea as silly. But then a new thought emerged. If this new lover boy of Donald's was a spy, he could be going about telling anyone, lover or not, that he worked for Internal Affairs rather than GCSB or NZSIS. Back in my day as an intelligence officer, I'd said I worked for Internal Affairs a few times rather than tell the truth. But no one knew I was working this job.

But they did didn't they?

Reede knew. And Justin didn't trust her. I thought about the conversation with Reede. She did not know for sure that I took the job. She asked me, too, but I never confirmed with her that I had.

I looked up to discover Donald had been talking on and I had no idea what about. I nodded and smiled, and checked my watch.

"You need to go," I said.

"I want to meet the mystery man," he said with a pout that only Donald and maybe Elton John could pull off.

"Not today," I replied. "Next time. He's new."

He tried blackmail. "I'll tell Nana."

"You don't want to start playing that game," I warned with a grin. "Anyway I'd already headed that particular blackmail line off by telling her myself."

"Maybe you're right," he said with reserve. "People in glass houses and all."

"Glass? Oh no Donald, your house is made of spun sugar. You best hope it never rains."

Donald stood up, placed his cup in the sink, and swanned out of the room, cackling, "I'm melting, I'm melting."

I laughed and watched from the window as he galloped across the back lawn riding a pretend broom.

All that was missing were the flying monkeys. I grinned at the thought.

Nana had the flying monkeys safely with her in the retirement home.

I checked my watch again. Ben would be almost pulling up the driveway.

Once again, I checked my purse: wallet, keys, knife, lipstick, tissues. I was all set. I took my favourite tailored leather jacket, and pulled it on. Looping my handbag over my shoulder, I flicked my hair behind me and extracted strands from under the shoulder strap of my handbag. I glanced in the mirror. Everything was where it should be.

My attention moved to the house and I checked everything was in order. All the window locks were caught fast. I checked the back door and slid the bolt across, just in case. Back in the living room, I unlocked my desk drawer. My fingers followed the lines of the sleek black gun in the drawer. I picked it up.

It wouldn't fit in my evening bag. As tempted as I was to attach the holster to my belt, I didn't. I reminded myself that Ben was armed and put the gun away. A little voice in my head mentioned Roofies. Not helpful.

A car pulled up the driveway just as I shut the living room curtains. Butterflies danced in my stomach. I smiled at the feeling.

I convinced myself it wasn't a real date to ease the nerves. He's just like everyone else. Nerves jangled louder. I had a hard job getting past the fact that it was Benjamin Reynolds the actor who was walking up to my front door and taking me to dinner.

I smiled as I opened the door.

There he was standing on my doorstep, dressed entirely in black. Black shoes, black dress trousers, and a black belt. My eyes rose to a black shirt with thin, shiny black stripes among the regular ones, and a black tie.

Black on black.

"Hello," he said, smiling.

"Hello," I replied, trying to decide if I was underdressed or not. A man dressed in black on my doorstep, and it wasn't Gortex. It was a real a date. I wondered if he was still armed.

I stood for a moment looking out at the street.

Ben followed my eyes.

"I didn't see any pale blue cars," he whispered.

I nodded.

Like a true gentleman, he locked the door for me, then took my arm and escorted me to the car.

He opened the door and helped me in, then closed the door.

It was all very proper. I couldn't help but think how much Nana would enjoy it. I doubted Nana had ever opened or closed a door for herself when Grandad was around.

"We have reservations," Ben said, his voice filled with promise. "I thought you'd like to get out of Upper Hutt for a few hours."

"Sounds good to me. Where are we going?"

"It's a surprise."

I both liked and didn't like his last statement. Surprises in our line of work were rarely good, as evidenced by the morning's discovery. But this isn't work. This is a getting-to-know-each-other better dinner before some freak virus kills us.

He turned the radio on as he drove. I smiled.

"That's okay isn't it?" he asked.

"It's fine," I replied, watching the road ahead for some clue as to where we were headed.

My phone rang. It was Steph.

"Hey, we've been paged. Massive fire at St. John's. Four engines are on scene."

"Wait a sec," I said and touched the mute button. "Ben, is it safe for Steph and Jenn to attend the fire at St. John's?"

"Yes," he replied. There was zero emotion on his face or in his voice.

I unmuted the conversation and spoke to Steph, "Be careful."

"We're support, it's not dangerous making coffee," Steph replied.

I hung up and dropped the phone into my bag.

The coincidental fire that engulfed the church about the same time as Ben arrived on my doorstep wasn't something I wanted to think about.

The drive took over half an hour. We were definitely out of Upper Hutt and that was a good thing. The conversation in the car was polite, non offensive and contained no shoptalk. In short, I enjoyed it. I really did enjoy every second of Ben's company and his enchanting cologne.

He parked in a deserted area under the only streetlight for at least a hundred meters.

"This is not ominous at all," I said, smiling as I watched him get out of the car. "Where are we?" I asked as he opened my door.

I began to regret my choice of heels. I did however rejoice in having my Victorinox knife in my handbag. In hindsight, a torch would have been a better.

For the second time in as many days, I really wished I hadn't been reading a scary story to Nana.

The dark bush shrouded area in front of me felt ill omened. I shrugged the feeling away. At least there was no sign of the troll or anything reanimated and for that, I was grateful.

"So where are we?" I asked again.

"You'll see," he replied, in a voice laden in mystery.

"I'm sure I will," I replied, trying hard to keep suspicion from my voice and stay fun and date like.

He placed a hand in the small of my back and encouraged me along a rough path.

Ben used his iPhone as a torch.

In places, the path was completely broken.

It rose up, eventually becoming concrete steps that disappeared into the shadowy bush covered hill above us.

The climb seemed to take forever. I wished I'd known we were going hiking before dinner and had worn a pair of Doc Martens instead of trendy high heeled city boots.

What restaurant was up so many dark steep steps? In

my world, a reservation implied a restaurant.

Ben didn't talk much on the climb, he led me by the hand, and told me to watch my step as we rounded an obscured corner.

A magnificent old house loomed from the bush. Candle lit steps wound up to a balcony. So many candles. A square table sat in the middle of the deck area, draped with a pale pink tablecloth. Set for two.

Slightly off centre, a crystal vase held deep pink roses. White fairy lights twinkled from the balustrade and trees beyond. The entire scene enchanted me.

"Wow," I said. Lost for words wasn't a usual thing for me. I lost a few standing on the balcony with Ben. Best of all there wasn't a decomposing body in sight.

"Our table is ready," Ben said. With one fluid movement, he pulled out a chair for me.

I beamed a smile at him as I sat.

"This is amazing," I said.

He sat opposite me wearing a grin that made his blue eyes dance.

"You haven't even seen the menu yet."

"There's a menu? Where are we?"

"Welcome to my home away from home," he replied. He was obviously enjoying my reaction to the night he'd planned.

"You actors certainly know how to live."

"Champagne?"

"Thank you."

He picked up bottle of champagne from an ice bucket

in a stand at the end of the table. With a twist of his hand, the cork popped. Champagne fizzed.

He filled the glasses.

That was the moment that I realised this was a real date.

I was on a date with Benjamin Reynolds. Wow. That was not how I expected my week to go especially after the toilet block incident and then the church yard mess.

There are dreams and there are wild dreams and then there is the craziest dream of all, reality.

He picked up his glass and tilted it toward me, I followed suit.

"Salute," he said, as our glasses touched.

I took a sip of the cool bubbles and set my glass down carefully. Champagne could be lethal. I swear the bubbles go right to my brain.

"This is a great location," I said.

"It's Jared's home. He's back in the States and let me use his house while I'm here. He also left me the keys to his wine cellar," Ben said lifting his glass to his lips for another sip.

I followed suit despite being able to hear Nana's voice telling me of the dangers of liquor and men. It's champagne not bourbon, what could go wrong?

Another mouthful of bubbles washed Nana's words away. Relaxation was beginning to creep in.

"It's stunning," I replied.

I tried to imagine Jared as the owner a wine cellar. It implied he relaxed occasionally and perhaps even enjoyed life. Those were things that were one-hundred per-cent beyond my realm of comprehension when it came to Jared. To me he was a grumpy shit who snarled instead of talking, and whined about everything.

And most importantly, had absolutely no sense of hu-mour. I wouldn't have been sitting with Jared having a very expensive glass of champagne in a candle lit setting. I just bet they weren't his fairy lights.

"What are you thinking about?" Ben asked.

I raised an eyebrow. "Dangerous question to ask."

"Only if you can't handle the answer," he replied refill-ing our glasses. "I can handle any answer."

Such confidence.

"I was thinking ... about ... Jared drinking wine and living in this beautiful place."

"It struck me as out of character too." Ben placed the bottle in the ice bucket. "He's very good at what he does," he offered as if to ameliorate his comment.

"Yes, he is. Not so easy to work with though."

A shadow moved past French doors to the side of us. I watched with interest as a waiter appeared carrying menus and a carafe of water.

He introduced himself.

"I'm Gary, I'll be serving you this evening," he said, fill-ing the water glasses on the table, and placing the carafe on the table. He handed the menus to us.

I opened the menu and smiled. I discovered I had the choice between two entrees, two main meals, and four different deserts.

"You approve?" Ben asked, lowering his menu then shutting it.

"Yes," I replied, following suit. I already knew what I wanted.

Gary stepped forward, "Would madame like to order?"

"I'll have the seafood salad, and then the crayfish," I replied, placing the menu in his outstretched hand.

"Very good," he replied and turned to Ben, "Sir?"

"I think I'll have the same. Could you bring extra seafood sauce too, please?"

"Of course. Would either of you like dessert?"

"We'll decide later," Ben said and handed the menu up to the waiter.

Gary the server left.

I smiled and wished I could tell Nana about my date in glorious detail because it sure felt like a real date now. Ben was the sort of man that Nana would approve of. The evening stretched before us. I made a decision. I couldn't bring Justin back so enjoying the down time was the smartest thing to do.

Champagne and Ben removed all traces of any concerns I harboured earlier.

Being in the moment felt right. Everything else could wait until tomorrow.

Chapter 15
[DONALD]

It was late afternoon before I headed out to do the next phase of the assignment. Truthfully, it was more an extension of my assignment, but a quiet extension that Ben didn't know anything about. No one knew anything about it. We'd decided the final gnome could wait a day or two. We already had two and they were safe. Even if someone did find the second virus, it wasn't lethal without the other virus and that gave me a bit of breathing room. I drove evasively to my destination making good use of my knowledge of back roads and checked constantly for any sign of the troll.

Paranoid.

Unnecessarily paranoid. We'd GPS'd him. Steph and Jenn would alert me the minute he moved. I walked past the row of houses by the railway line, continued up the street, popped into the chemist for a bottle of vitamins, and then walked back passed the houses, this time on the other side of the road. I stopped on the corner outside the fire station and observed a mother pushing a pram heading toward the shops.

An elderly gent came out of the vet's, just before the shopping centre. A few teenagers headed toward the railway station. Several cars passed, some going into Silverstream, some heading back out the underpass and off on their business elsewhere.

There were no cars parked in the vicinity of the houses. No one moved about in the small gardens.

I half expected to see the gnome in question sitting in the garden on the pebbles by the Aloe Vera plant. As I watched, the door opened and Martha Johansen stepped out. She looked up and down the street but seemed to miss my presence completely. I was pleased to go undetected.

Martha's eyesight is failing, I thought.

I walked down the road and around the block. I opted to walk through the shopping centre car park. Once out on the road again I considered my options.

With a small smile, I ducked into the bar that bordered the shops and called Donald from my cell phone.

"I'm at Charlton's. Come on over. I'll buy you a drink."

"Sounds like a fab way to spend a Friday afternoon. I'm on my way home anyway."

"I'll grab us an outside table."

"See you in a jiffy."

I ordered two house white wines and took them outside to a table. I sat with my back to the windows of the bar, facing out into the street and with a twist of my chair directly at Martha's house.

There was nothing to see.

No visitors.

Martha had gone back indoors and drawn the curtains.

I watched the street, as I waited for Donald.

My promise to Martha that I would keep an eye on her house weighed heavily. By now, the other faction after the gnomes would know they had the wrong ones and I doubted they'd give up easily. The smartest option was to believe they'd keep looking in the hope of coming across the right gnome still in a garden somewhere.

Donald arrived about ten minutes after my phone call. He seemed pleased, very pleased.

"Spill it!" I said, passing him his drink.

"Bruce wants to meet you," he announced with glee.

That was pretty big news. None of his boyfriends to date had wanted to meet his family. Mostly, I thought, because they hadn't come out to their own families. I sailed back to the boyfriend's name, Bruce. Maybe his parents knew before he was born that he'd be gay, I surmised. Really with a name like Bruce, what else could he be?

I'd often thought that about Donald, never Don, or Donny, oh no. He was Donald, as dictated by his mother and father, my Aunt and Uncle. Did they know when they chose his name? Donald Henere-Tracey was born the same day as me. A family joke had us pegged as yin and yang. He was the brother I never had and I was the sister he deserved.

"So why are we here, and not at home planning a dinner for my lovely Bruce?" Donald asked sipping his wine.

"I thought it would be nice to get out."

Donald raised an eyebrow in disbelief. "You'll have to do better than that, love. Hello, we're in Silverstream!"

He had a point, it wasn't exactly a thriving metropolis, and Charlton's wasn't exactly roaring.

"I felt like a change," I offered, gazing down the street.

"Didn't Nana have a friend who lives along here?" Donald asked absently, following my line of vision.

"Still does. You remember, Martha," I replied.

"The gnome woman," Donald said, in a suddenly too interested way.

"Yes, I believe so," I said dismissively.

"Again with the gnomes."

"Pardon?"

"Just seems to be a lot of gnomes about lately."

"Maybe it's gnome season," I said. I saw someone walking up the street. The person paused across the road from Martha's and stood as if waiting for someone or something. I observed without being too obtrusive and quickly realised it was a man.

Donald saw the man too.

"He looks lost," he said, indicating toward the man down the street.

"He does, I guess," I replied.

A few minutes later, a car pulled up and the man climbed in. I memorised the license plates, then pulled a notebook from my backpack and wrote the number in it, with a description of the car. A silver Mitsubishi.

"How was that even remotely interesting?" Donald asked, observing my writing.

"I'm not sure," I replied.

"What are we doing here?" Suspicion laced his words and indicated he wasn't buying my earlier story.

"I could tell you but then I'd have to kill you," I replied, letting mystery resound, because I knew that's what he wanted. He got that from Nana.

Nana shared more with Donald than with me, personality wise.

Nana and Donald shared a love of the dramatic, hypochondria, and an inability to leave well enough alone. Those three things also drove me to distraction.

"What is it you do, exactly?" Donald asked. He leaned across the table looking for juicy titbits.

The gleam in his eyes reminded me of a hungry wolf.

"You know what I do. I'm a private investigator. I find people. You know missing aunties, and people from the past."

"That's all?" he seemed slightly disappointed.

"Pretty much," I replied fiddling with the edge of the coaster under my glass. "I also gather evidence of cheating spouses and do a bit of loss prevention in stores. But mostly, I look for people."

"You wouldn't know anything about gnomes, because they're not people?"

"That's right, Donald. They just fish in ponds and look freaky. They don't get lost and they're not people."

"And your midnight cowboy, he's your new boyfriend?"

"Yep." Maybe. Perhaps. Hell, I don't know.

"Maybe we should have the boys over for dinner, you meet mine, and I'll meet yours."

"Sure," I replied using a noncommittal almost dismissive tone.

That'll happen when pigs fly. Watch closely, children, the pigs are growing wings. Imagine the mess those bastards will make of cars. Pigs roosting in trees, and everyone thought pigeons were bad.

I peered into the gathering darkness. The car from earlier did a drive by.

Interesting.

But it made sense.

They had the wrong gnomes and didn't know if we had the right ones.

So they had to keep an eye on the places they thought the gnomes were.

For the third time I watched the same silver car slowly drive by. This time, the occupants took more notice of the bar and afforded me an opportunity to commit descriptions of the occupants to memory. None of them were Shankle so that was a plus. Three men. Dark haired, tanned, no facial hair. Not much of a description but better than nothing.

I had a thought about the package I was expecting. I was down a gnome and needed a fresh replacement to swap for gnome number three.

"Donald, did a courier come by this morning?"

"Yes and there was a bit of a mix up," he said, squirming uncomfortably in his seat.

"A mix up?" I smelled a rat big time.

The car circled back around, for the fourth time.

"I thought it was a package I'd ordered from TradeMe, and I opened it before I saw your name on it," he confessed.

"Hold that thought," I told him and pulled my cell phone from my bag. I chose Ben's number; he answered the phone quickly. "Check this out. Tango, Echo, Oscar five four five. Silver Mitsubishi. It's hanging around. I've seen it drive by four times."

"Where are you?"

"A bar in the vicinity of package one."

"I'll get back to you."

"Thanks," I said and hung up.

"Now that wasn't suspicious at all!" Donald crowed. "Any more so than that parcel that arrived today, at any rate. Do you want me to tell you what was in it?"

"No need." I looked up at him. "As I said, I could tell you what I do but I'd have to kill you." I smiled displaying my usual understated charm.

Donald didn't look too sure. It was almost as if he believed I would kill him, or even that I could kill him. That brought my mind back to gnome number two. No one had reported a murder, to my knowledge. There was nothing in the newspapers about the body in the Pinehaven Park toilet block.

So, missing gnomes make the newspaper, but not people. That was puzzling. He was a designer, and yet no one cared that he hadn't shown up to work or come home for three days. I sipped my wine, and watched in case the car returned. There was no point pondering on the fate of the dead designer. It's not as if he was a nice person who hadn't deserved to come to a sticky end. Eventually it would have happened with or without my help. He was just another cog in the murder machine. I hoped he'd stay dead. I became aware of Donald's attention in an unusual way. It happened when he leaned over the table, into my space, and mouthed words at me.

"Say the words Donald," I said. "I'm too tired to play lip reading games tonight."

"You're a PI," he stated with the normal earnest conviction he displayed when stating the bleeding obvious. His voice dropped to a harsh whisper. "You can find out things about people, can't you?"

"Uh huh," I replied as a young man put fresh glasses of wine on the table. Donald must've ordered us more drinks while I was thinking. I hadn't even noticed I'd finished my glass but there it was being carried away by the young man, empty.

"Could you find someone for me?" I knew he hadn't lost anyone. I nodded my affirmation and waited for the real question.

"Or more importantly, find out about someone for me?" Donald asked in a slightly louder whisper.

"Who'd you have in mind," I answered toying with the now worn edge of the coaster under my glass.

He peered intently at me.

"Donald? I need to know or I can't do it."

"Bruce," he said, his eyes darting around the tables near us.

"You want me to run a background check on your new beau?"

"He wouldn't have to know, would he?" he asked, I detected nervous tension in his voice.

"Nope."

"Well, then, yes, I'd like you to do that."

"Care to tell me why?"

Now I knew why Donald had arrived so quickly; he wanted something. It wasn't just about the box containing a gnome he'd found on the doorstep. He was intent on creating a drama where possibly none existed, typical Donald.

"I never seem to have much luck with men," he said.

Rats! I couldn't dispute that. He had a dreadful record of zero accomplishment in the relationship segment of his life.

"Fair enough," I said with a small sigh. I couldn't explain it but part of me was disappointed Donald hadn't created some dramatic scenario regarding Bruce. He was almost acting out of character.

"Really?"

"Yes. I will need more than his first name though," I told him, smiling at his relieved expression.

"What do you need, exactly?"

"Full name and date of birth, are the absolute minimum." I studied Donald for a few minutes. "How much do you want to know?"

"There are depths?"

"Oh yeah, and breadths, you can barely imagine."

The silver car reappeared on the street catching my eye. Pulling my phone out again I redialled the same number.

Ben answered so fast I never heard the phone ring.

"What's up?"

I heard road noise over the phone.

"They're back."

"I'm right here," Ben said.

Right then, I saw his black Camry cruise up behind the Mitsubishi, in a casual and non threatening manner. It wasn't easy to look non threatening when there was no other traffic to blend with.

Although I suspected if I saw Ben cruise up behind me like that, I'd feel threatened, especially if I had something to hide.

I ended the call and placed my phone on the table by my drink.

Donald was watching me with open unrepentant curiosity.

"No, Donald, I can't tell you. Surely you know the rest by now?" I told him as he moved in conspiratorially. It was easy to sense his impending questions. Nosiness beamed from his face and glinted in his brown eyes.

"What if I guess?" he suggested with a wicked smile.

"Well I can't stop you from guessing," I said and settled back to see if Ben was still in view. " Just be warned I can neither confirm nor deny."

No sign of Ben. The red light on my phone wasn't flashing. No missed messages. Donald fired words at me at the rate of knots and I couldn't keep up. Ben's absence occupied my mind.

"Ronnie?"

I shook my head slightly and looked back at Donald. "Sorry, what were you saying?"

"I was wondering why you weren't writing down the information I have been busily divulging to you?"

Colour me confused. I thought he'd been rambling on trying to guess what my conversation with Ben was about. Maybe I should pay attention.

"Oh, I'm sorry Donald. Here ..." I passed him my notebook and pen. "You write down everything you think I might need."

I stood up. Ben was too quiet. My stomach twisted into a tight knot.

"Where are you going?"

I looked over the deserted road. "It's getting chilly, how about we go inside?"

"Good idea," he agreed. "Won't be as much to distract you in there."

"I'm not distracted," I replied.

"Oh darling, you are super distracted. If I didn't know better I'd think this was about the mystery man. Not just work."

"Good thing you know better."

I glimpsed suspicion in his eyes.

We gathered our things and went into the bar. Declaring it was warmer and more comfortable away from the draft of the door, I chose a table as far into the bar as possible. Donald wrote in my notebook while I checked my phone. Nothing.

Five minutes later Donald was still writing. I slung my backpack on my shoulder and said, "Toilet break, be back in a few."

He didn't even look up.

I headed for the toilet, once out of Donald's line of sight; I ducked out the side door.

Noting the time on my watch before I hoofed it up the street to Martha's house to make sure I wasn't gone longer than three or four minutes.

Donald would grow suspicious if I was too long in the bathroom.

He had a terrible habit of barging into ladies rooms at bars, flapping wildly, and demanding to know why I was taking so long. His theory was no one was going to follow me in and attempt anything nasty, with the threat of him flying in after me. He was probably right.

I approached the gate. The still silence of the night weighed heavy upon me. Almost as if something was about to happen. There were no cars, or people on the footpath. I could see right down the road and it appeared deserted.

I remembered the gate didn't squeak, but opened it slowly anyway. Deciding safe was better than sorry, I held my breath involuntarily as the gate opened. I stepped through, and carefully closed it again. I stood away from the gateway, obscured from the street by the high fence, and watched.

The kitchen light blinked out.

The hallway light flickered on. I knew it was the hallway as the subdued rays didn't quite reach out the kitchen window.

Old people tended to retire to their beds early. I never could understand why. All the oldies I knew seemed to do was complain that they couldn't sleep, which to me indicated they weren't tired and hadn't done enough during the day to warrant toddling off to bed so early.

It wasn't exactly late, and Martha was off to bed.

I poked about in the dark, checking that her house was secure and that no one had broken in during Coronation Street. I didn't know for sure that Martha watched the show, but it seemed likely. I also imagined the volume would be high enough to hide the sounds of anyone breaking into the house.

All was well.

Just to make sure, I shone my tiny torch around the garden, checking on the whereabouts of the rest of the creatures that inhabited the small space. I kept the beam low and semi concealed in my hand, filtering the light to avoid drawing attention to my presence. Several of the other gnomes were lying down, revealing their hollow bottoms. A few were disturbed from their resting places. I set about putting the garden to rights. It wouldn't do to have Martha find her gnomes were in peril during the night.

I wondered how anyone got in the garden without me noticing. Why would someone check the gnomes if they already knew we had two of them.

Maybe they didn't know, I thought, maybe they only

suspected. Maybe the car had dropped someone off on the other side of the railway track, in the McDonald's car park for example. A person could cross the tracks and enter the yard from the back. How would they know exactly which house? I growled internally, Shankle the troll and his freaking pale blue car! I was sure his job was to follow me and report back to someone.

I let myself out the gate, just as the hall light went out. The house plunged into darkness behind me. I peered up and down the street.

I could see no sign of the silver Mitsubishi or Ben's black Camry. I couldn't even hear car engines in the distance. I checked my watch and ran across the road. Almost out of time, I had to sneak back into the bar before Donald discovered I wasn't in the bathroom. I walked quickly, ready to slow down and stroll at the first sign of another person or car on the street. Luckily, there was no sign of either, as I ducked back into the side entrance, and emerged by the toilet door.

Donald seemed not to have noticed my absence. He was still writing in my notebook.

I sipped my wine and wondered where Ben and the silver car went. It puzzled me. Did he have back up with him, another car standing by to block the silver Mitsubishi? Maybe now that the terror cell was out in the open, so to speak, they'd made an arrest. I didn't see any other cars, but someone could've bypassed the bar by going down a different road.

Watching Donald fill several pages didn't help calm my

mind at all. I considered the possibility that he was writing a novel and hoped it wasn't grubby. On the plus side, with screeds of information it would make running the background check easier.

I shifted in my seat. Toyed with the stem of the glass in front of me. My right foot tapped against a table leg.

"You're shaking the table," Donald said. "Do you mind?"

"You're taking forever," I replied, crossing my legs. Waiting for the phone to ring was not on my list of favourite things. I needed to disguise my impatience before Donald caught wind of it.

"Do you want coffee?" I asked Donald as I stood up.

"Cappuccino please, with chocolate, not cinnamon," he replied, putting down the pen and closing the notebook.

"Large?"

"Of course."

I went over to the bar to order and didn't wait long as the bar wasn't overly busy.

There were approximately twenty patrons, spread out over the whole interior and no one was sitting at the bar itself. A small group of youngish men had gathered in one of the window filled corners. They were the noisiest of all the groups but even then were not disturbingly so. As far as bars went, it was a very pleasant one.

The friendly atmosphere, comfortable and well designed interior combined to create something quite special.

I toyed with the idea of moving to Silverstream just so

Charlton's could be my local watering hole.

Back at the table, waiting for the coffees to arrive. I found myself contemplating buying a house in Silverstream. I voiced this to Donald, "What do you think about me moving down this way? Buying a house here?"

He looked up at me and smiled. "It's a nice area, I'd go further in though, maybe the Silverstream side of Pinehaven but further up than this part."

"I was thinking that."

I thought back to the drive the other night, the streets Ben and I travelled to the second gnome pickup. I'd seen For Sale signs all over the place, but one in particular stood out. A house down a long driveway. I couldn't even see the house, and that appealed, especially after visiting Ben's bush sanctuary. The idea of being well off the road and backing onto hills covered in bush not houses felt secure. I liked the idea of being away from prying eyes and trolls.

Donald leaned in, and then sat back as the coffee arrived. Once he'd finished adding a mountain of sugar to his cup, he leaned toward me again.

"You have a house in mind, don't you?"

"Sort of," I replied.

"Sort of?"

"I haven't seen it yet. But I know where it is."

"It's pricey down this way," Donald said idly.

"I know. But it's getting pricey everywhere in the upper Valley now."

I stopped short of saying it didn't matter. I could afford it. The work I did for agencies paid well. I'd been doing it a long time, even before I left the Service, and had a healthy bank account. When it came time to buy I'd consider whether or not I'd pay cash, or put half down and get a mortgage like a real person. The idea of being a cash buyer and owning the property outright appealed more than the thought of ongoing debt.

I finished my coffee. My phone lay on the table next to the notebook and pen. I gathered the notebook and pen and dropped them into my bag, while willing the phone to ring. If I willed it hard enough, he'd call, I knew he would.

The phone lit up. Before it could buzz and ring I snatched it up, pressed answer and said, "Hello?"

"Can you meet me?"

"Where?"

I listened intently, trying to determine from the background noise and his tone if everything was all right. I didn't hear any stressors in his voice.

"Go out to the car park behind the shopping centre. You'll see me, I'm over by the supermarket," he said.

And there was a stressor, the way he said see me, told me there was something off. Probably not enough for anyone else to recognise and not something I could testify to in court. My stomach twisted. There was something wrong.

"I'm coming. Two minutes. Anything you need to tell me?"

"No. I'll wait."

Ending the call, I dropped my phone in my jacket pocket. From my bag, I took my knife. Donald's eyes widened as I slid the red knife into my other jacket pocket.

Flipping through my notebook to the page with the license plate number of the silver car. I wrote a description of the car, and two occupants, underneath the number. Then I wrote Ben's license plate number from memory, and car description. I also wrote a phone number and a first name. I ripped the page off and passed it to Donald.

"If I don't ring you in five minutes, call this number and ask for him." I pointed to the name at the bottom of the page.

Donald nodded. "Should I come with you?"

I looked at him in utter amazement. Yes, that's what Donald should do, come with me, and flap wildly in the general direction of any imagined danger while squealing like a girl.

That was his go-to move when threatened. It wasn't pretty.

"No, you need to stay here. If I don't call you ring this number ... give the man that answers all this information," I told him. "And one other thing, tell whoever answers that the last traffic cone is in jeopardy."

"Traffic cone?"

"Yeah. Trust me. He'll know what that means."

"All right. Take care."

"When I call, and you are sure everything's okay, burn the paper."

Donald looked relieved. "I thought you were going to say eat it!"

"If you want," I said with a smile. "Whatever floats your boat, Donald."

I kissed his cheek and hurried out the back door and through the paved pathways to the car park.

I cursed quietly as I walked. Why hadn't I thought to check the car park earlier? I saw Ben's car parked by the supermarket. I watched the car for a minute. It was well away from any other cars. The other cars were much closer to the doctor's office, which was the outer wall of the shopping complex. I squinted into the night. There were no streetlights by Ben's car. He didn't have the interior lights on. I tried to determine if he was alone in the car.

I thought I could see only one head.

I made my way around the edges of the car park. It was the long way, but preferable to walking straight across in the open. Better to be safe than sorry.

It didn't pay to take undue risks. I'd taken enough already with this assignment.

The list was growing, Nana's friend being one of the houses they hit, then Kirsty and the dead guy, and Justin buried in the garden. I avoided anything in my mind that linked me directly to his death. There would be time enough for processing that special hell later.

Chapter 16
[TROUBLE]

I approached Ben's car from the right hand side. That way I could clearly see him, and determine if anyone was in the car that shouldn't be. It looked okay. Ben was looking around, probably trying to locate me. When he spotted me, he waved and smiled.

A flood of relief flowed over me.

He opened his door, got out, and leaned on the roof facing me.

"Okay?" I asked.

"Yes."

"Someone searched through the gnomes in the first garden tonight," I told him.

"Maybe they weren't so sure then."

"That's what I was thinking. Seen any troublemakers?"

"I saw one, but he's a little tied up right now."

As if on cue, I heard a thump from the boot. Now I knew why he liked to drive a Camry, they had a spacious boot. Plenty of room for a man. Or a couple of men, if they weren't big.

"The silver car?"

"This guy sort of fell out of the car," Ben replied with a cheesy grin. "And I scooped him up."

"Do we know where the car went?"

"It headed further into Silverstream. How many roads out are there?"

"Four."

"You don't have your car?"

"I do it's parked over by the school under a street light."

"We can cover two exits."

"The third leads over to Whitemans Valley. Unless they know where they're going, they won't risk that. And the fourth leads back toward Upper Hutt."

I looked back toward the bar. "I need to make a call, before Donald calls in the cavalry."

"Donald?"

I dialled his number. While I waited for him to answer I said, "My cousin."

Donald answered.

"Burn it now, or eat it if you wish. I'm going to be busy. Can you get home okay?"

"Yes," he said then added, "What religion was Nana born into?"

"Roman Catholic," I replied without hesitation. He was checking I really was okay. Bless him and his attempts at covertness.

"Okay, see you later, be careful," Donald replied. He sounded satisfied that I was all right and all was well.

The call ended and I shoved my phone in my pocket.

Ben smiled as I looked up at him and said, "I take it Donald was your backup?"

"More like flap up," I replied, grinning. "You'll meet him if you're very lucky."

Ben smiled.

"Jump in. I'll drive you to your car." Ben strode around the car and opened the door for me.

"Do you think they're still here?" I asked, slipping into the passenger seat.

"I think they want the packages and their pal here," he replied shutting my door. His door opened and he angled behind the wheel. Ben pulled out of the car park, looking for traffic, and more importantly looking for the silver car.

"And we're going to do what?" I asked as he pulled up alongside my car.

"If we're lucky we can get the driver," Ben said as I opened the door and climbed out.

"I'm not armed like you are," I reminded him.

He smiled, reached into the glove compartment, and pulled out a holstered weapon. He handed it to me. "Glock 17, now you're armed."

"Jesus Christ!" I took the gun, and clipped the holster to my belt, moving it around until it was semi hidden under my jacket.

"I know you're proficient in small arms. I know you prefer a Glock," he said. "Now let's do it."

"You want to set up a road block?"

"That would be ideal but I don't think we can," he replied, watching me with interest. "Unless of course you know something I don't know."

"I know Silverstream. If they headed into Pinehaven, the only way back to here is a forked intersection. If we set it up there, they can't get down this far, it limits their choices."

"More manageable," he said with a nod. "I'll follow you."

"Okay."

I unlocked the door and slid behind the wheel of my car.

There was a major flaw to my plan, which neither of us had discussed but we were both aware of. If the car we were after wasn't in Pinehaven but lurking in Sunbrae, we wouldn't find them. They could make their escape with ease.

Likewise, if the car had gone up over Chatsworth hill they could get out by travelling the back roads to the nearest railway crossing in Trentham. Then they could take one of the two main roads south.

It wasn't a perfect plan.

Ben's insistence that the car would stick around gave me hope as I drove up Whitemans Road, being sure to keep to the speed limit. There was really nowhere to park near to the forked Blue Mountains Road - Pinehaven Road intersection. Either we could go down Pinehaven Road and park near the intersection, or separate and one take Blue Mountains and the other take Pinehaven. I had an idea.

I called Ben on his cell phone.

"You take Blue Mountains road, I'll go Pinehaven. They've seen your car, not mine, so we'll leave my car visible."

"Good idea," he replied.

"Let's keep this line open," I said, and turned the speaker on before I laid my phone on the passenger seat. I turned up a driveway and reversed out to park facing the intersection.

From where I parked, I could see Ben do something similar. Although he pulled back a little from the corner, rendering his car difficult to see until it was too late.

"Is it always this quiet up here?" he asked.

"Pretty much," I replied. "It's a nice area. Always has been."

"I need to check on my cargo. It hasn't moved much in the last ten minutes."

"Leave it," I said.

"I knew you would say that."

"Figure you should wait until we find this freaking car," I said.

"Yeah, good plan. No sense risking an injury now. And if the scum bag dies in the meantime, well that's just too bad."

"My thoughts exactly."

Ben laughed. "Heads up, I hear a car."

I watched my rear vision mirror. There was no one behind me. Then I heard it too. However, I couldn't determine from where. Was it behind me or behind Ben? Maybe even coming toward me. The hills that surrounded the small Pinehaven valley caused sound confusion.

I flicked my eyes from the rear vision mirror to the view out the front, where I could see both Ben's chosen road and Whitemans Road stretching away to the left of us. Nothing.

I zapped my window down a few centimetres. The engine sounds grew.

"See anything?" I said.

"Not a thing," Ben replied.

The noise suddenly amplified, and I realised I could hear it from the outside and inside. I looked at the phone. The noise seemed to make it jiggle and vibrate on the seat.

"He's coming up behind you," I said.

"Crap." he replied.

The noise intensified to a screeching of tires and a sickening crunching of metal.

"Ben?" I said, loudly.

I shoved the car into gear and put my foot down.

Rounding the corner my headlights illuminated twisted metal. I slowed. Light beams shone at weird angles from crumpled wreck.

What seemed to be one car wasn't.

Not unless Ben's car was two tone, silver and dark blue. I knew it wasn't. I turned my car until the headlights shone right into what was left of Ben's, and clicked my hazard lights on.

The silence from my phone filled me with dread. My breathing almost stopped as I threw my car door open and jumped out. Leaning into my car, I grabbed my phone and disconnected the call to Ben. I pressed 1-1-1 into the keypad but didn't press dial.

Ben's car. I could see him, slumped in his seatbelt. I

pulled on the door handle. Metal groaned. The door stuck. Closer inspection showed it was buckled.

Shit.

Think.

I ran back to my car and fumbled keys as I opened the boot. My fingers felt along for a crowbar I knew I had in there. Finding it, I slammed the boot shut and hurried back to Ben. The metal graunched as I used the crowbar to prise the buckled steel apart. It moved in small increments until I could pull the door open and get to Ben.

Blood ran down his head onto his shirt collar.

I felt for his pulse and felt it strong and steady. I lifted his head up and tried to wake him up. "Hey!"

His eyes flickered, they didn't open, but they flickered inside his eyelids.

I heard moaning from behind me.

"Wake up!" I tapped his sternum. "Come on Ben. Wake up."

He groaned.

"Say words and open your eyes," I said as the moaning from behind me grew louder. "I need to know you're okay before I check the other car."

"Go," he said, lifting his head.

"I'll be right back."

I left Ben, removed the gun from the holster I wore and carefully approached the other car. The moaning became louder. It wasn't coming from the boot of Ben's car, I checked, there was no boot anymore. Whoever was in there, was pulp or as near to it as mattered.

The noise came from the back of the silver car that was firmly wedged into Ben's car.

As my eyes began to make sense of what they saw, I realised it wasn't the back of a car, it was the remains of the front, forced into the back. I holstered the gun.

My gut told me no one that survived the crash in that car was going to be in any position to fight.

I tried pulling the doors, but they were so badly buckled they wouldn't budge.

Smashed glass sparkled in the light emanating from streetlights above the crash.

I peered into the back passenger window. There was a man still wearing a seat belt but lying in an odd position. He was in the front seat, or what used to be the front seat, trapped by one leg. All I could smell was blood. Looking closer the origin became obvious.

His other leg was severed above the knee. I turned away for a moment and took a few breathes. The man groaned.

"Who are you?" I asked, holding my phone ready to call emergency services.

"Help me," he said, his voice weak.

"Who are you?" I repeated.

I scanned the interior of the car, looking for anything suspicious. There seemed to be only wreckage, glass, and blood. So much blood that I could taste it in the air. I hated the metallic smell of blood and wasn't thrilled about smelling it for the second time in a matter of days. It was like walking into a slaughterhouse, or in this case, leaning through the window of one. There were other smells too, ones I didn't care to think about. Accidents are not clean things to happen upon, especially ones that caused grievous bodily harm. I saw the edge of something sticking out of a pocket in his jacket.

"Michael," he said.

I leaned in the broken window. There was another smell, and something I recognised but couldn't place right away. I pulled the object I saw in his pocket out. It was a wallet. Straightening up, I jammed it into my jacket pocket.

The other smell as almonds.

That was bad. I ran back to Ben and unplugged his seat belt.

"Wake up!" I ordered. Pulling on his arm. "Come on, Ben, this is bad!"

His eyes were closed. All of a sudden, his eyes flickered open.

"Get out!" I yelled at him, tugging his arm with more force and grabbing him by the lapel at the same time.

"What?" he said, I could tell he was trying to understand what I wanted. Thoughts weren't forming very fast for him.

"Bomb!"

This time he understood, as I pulled his arm he moved toward me. Ben stumbled from the car. I semi dragged him to my car and shoved him in the backseat. I jumped into the driver's seat and peeled out of the danger zone. I was half way back to Silverstream when an explosion rocked the area. I pulled over and hit dial on my phone.

"Which emergency service do you require?"

"All of them," I replied.

The woman at the other end stuttered.

I rethought and said, "Fire."

I gave the approximate address and hung up without leaving my name. Then I saw the troll's pale blue car moving toward me. He stared in the window as he passed. I flipped him off.

"Bastard!" I growled. "Hairy fat bastard!"

He must've found the GPS unit and removed it, or one of the girls would've let me know he was out and about.

Ben moved in the back seat, and then climbed into the front passenger seat. He slid down and put his seat belt on.

"Does your cell phone trace back to you?" he said with amazing clarity of thought.

"No, it does not."

"Good. Let's get the fuck out of Dodge."

"You need your head looked at," I told him, as I drove sedately down Whitemans Road and turned right at the end. An enormous explosion resounded from Pinehaven. "Think that was the wreckage."

"Good call," Ben replied. He looked out the window. "Where are we?"

"Taking the back roads out of the area to avoid emergency services seeing you covered in blood and my car leaving the area."

Sirens filled the still night air. We followed the deserted back roads.

"Covered in blood," Ben said, confusion clouded his words.

"Your head hit something. You're bleeding," I replied. "Open the glove compartment and get the first aid kit. Might pay to clean that up a bit."

He took a zippered container from the glove compartment.

Ben flipped the front visor down and lifted the flap to reveal a vanity mirror. While I drove, he inspected the cut on his forehead.

"It's not bad, just bloody."

"Head wounds bleed like a stuck pig," I replied, glancing over at him. "Use the antiseptic wipes and clean it up, before, someone notices a car with a blood covered man in it."

"Good point," he muttered, wiping as much blood up as he could with the aid of wipes and the vanity mirror.

He should think himself lucky he's never had to use a mirror like that to apply makeup.

Chapter 17
[LATE NIGHT WITH NANA]

"Where do you want to go?" I said, as we came up to the Trentham railway crossing. Lights flashed, bells dinged and the arm came down.

"Can you take me home?" he asked, wiping his face, trying to get the bloody streaks off his cheek and chin.

I was all for getting out of Upper Hutt, especially after seeing the troll. If he told anyone I was in the vicinity of the crash and had a bloody passenger things could get very messy indeed. I hoped he was close to the cars when they exploded. Really close.

"Home, to that fabulous house on the hill in the bush, or home the embassy, where you can get medical attention without raising too much suspicion?" I enquired. "Sure. We'll take River Road via Upper Hutt. Don't fancy taking Fergusson Drive south at the moment." I figured police would be heading that way any minute.

The barrier arms raised and bells stopped. I carried on over the railway lines and up the street. Seconds after I got through the traffic lights and headed north, my cell rang.

I tried ignoring it but the song grew louder and louder, or maybe it just seemed to get louder.

"You going to get that?" Ben asked lifting his voice over the noise.

"I don't want to," I replied, hoping voice mail would

kick in before we were deafened.

"Just answer it," he said, pressing a wound dressing to his head.

I wrestled the phone from my pocket while driving. It slipped from my fingers and landed on Ben's knee. He picked it up and answered it, "Hello?"

Cold spikes stuck into my stomach lining.

"Oh God," I said. "That was a bad move. Give it here."

Ben grinned as a voice crackled back at him so loudly that I could clearly hear it. Nana.

"Who are you, and where is my granddaughter?"

I snatched the phone from him as he chuckled.

"Nana, I'm right here," I said pulling over to the side of the road. "Isn't it a bit late for you?"

"Usually dear, but Martha called and woke me up."

My heart sank. Martha called. When I checked earlier, I was fairly certain Martha was tucked up in bed for the night. I guessed the explosion and subsequent sirens woke her.

"Really? What was Martha doing up so late?" I replied, trying to maintain a sense of moderate curiosity in my voice.

Ben listened as he stuck the wound dressing to his head using paper tape. It was much easier for him to fix himself up with the car stationary.

"Some dreadful noise woke her, an explosion, she said. And then I couldn't get back to sleep with all the sirens," Nana explained.

"Do you know what it was that exploded?"

"No. she couldn't see anything outside, apart from fire engines roaring past."

"And you are ringing me because?"

"I thought you might be able to check it out and let us know?"

I picked up on the us.

"Not really Nana, I'm on my way home." As soon as the words left my mouth, I realised Ben answered the phone, and trouble would follow if Nana thought I was going home with a man. "As soon as I drop my friend off," I added, hoping that would satisfy Nana.

There was an intake of breath on the other end of the phone.

Damn, it didn't work.

"Are you in the habit of taking strange men to your home?" I could hear tutting in the background. More than one tut. The cronies were definitely awake and I suspected I was on speaker.

"No I am not," I replied. "And you know that Nana."

"Well, you let strange men answer your telephone, how I am to know what else you do?"

"Nana!" I said with force. "What exactly did you want from me tonight?"

"Martha was worried that the gnome thief was back," Nana said.

"I doubt it, Nana. Tell Martha I'll drop by tomorrow and check on her."

"I'll get no sleep."

Nana would get no sleep and that was about to become

my problem, even though just want to get Ben home before something else went wrong.

"I'm sorry, Nana. There is nothing I can do tonight."

"You won't check on her?" Nana pulled her trump card out. "She's old and frail. But if you are too busy to help one of my oldest and closest friends ... well then."

I let out an audible sigh. Closest friends? I'd hate to hear what she said about people she didn't like, if Martha was one of her closest friends.

"Donald might still be in Silverstream," I said. "We were having a drink there earlier. I'll ask him to check on Martha."

Right away Nana spun my words around to suit herself.

"I see, Donald gets to meet your friend but I don't."

I chose to ignore my comment. "Do you want me to send Donald?"

"I suppose that would be all right," Nana conceded.

There was more, I knew there was more. Nana had caved too quickly. I waited. I could hear the three old crones chattering amongst themselves.

"We're not going to be able to get back to sleep until we know Martha is safe. You'll have to come and sit with us." And there it was, hell in a retirement home.

"I can't Nana, not tonight."

I looked at Ben, who was grinning like a Cheshire cat. The grin alone was enough to make me change my mind and subject him to The Cronies of Doom.

"I need to go Nana. Unless you don't want me to call

Donald before he leaves."

"We'll be expecting you."

"I said not tonight," I replied firmly.

"About half an hour, I'll have some tea made. I told the girls about that story you're reading me. They'd, love to hear it."

"I don't have the magazine with me, Nana."

"You could pick it up."

I sighed. Nana's life flashed before my eyes. Was it really so hard to indulge an ancient woman? No. It wasn't. I hung up. I scrolled through recent contacts and chose Donald's number. Seemed to take forever for him to answer.

"Ronnie?"

By the background noise, I knew he was still in the bar.

"You still in Silverstream?"

"Yes, big excitement here, darling! Apparently there was a serious traffic accident and the cars exploded."

"Wow," I replied hoping to convey shock and horror in a single word.

It didn't work.

"You know something?"

"Hush, Donald. I need you to go over the road and check on Nana's old friend."

"Oh please, you're sending me to visit a crone?"

"Please, Donald?"

"If I go … you have to tell me the gossip later."

He drove a hard bargain but I had no intention of telling him anything important.

"Sure."

"What house?"

"The one with the really the low gate and high fence. Front yard is full of unsavoury ornaments."

"You owe me!"

"Love you, Donald."

I pressed the end button and dropped the phone back onto Ben's lap. "Take care of that for me, will you?"

"Sure, Ronnie. You want I should answer it if it rings again?" The Cheshire grin was still plastered across his face.

"No, once was enough, thanks," I replied, pulling back out onto the road. Subject change coming right up. "How's your head?"

"Not too bad. The bleeding has stopped." He looked over at me. "We could swing by your Nana's if you like."

"When pigs fly," I replied.

"How bad could it be?"

I peered up at the sky and pointed. "Did you see that?"

"What?"

"Nothing ... no flying pigs, no nothing."

He laughed.

We stared at one another when the phone rang again.

"That's the same song," Ben said reaching between his legs and picking up the phone.

"Don't answer it," I squealed, trying to grab the phone from his hand before he hit answer.

He held it in his left hand out of my reach. Either I had to pull over and practically climb him or admit defeat.

I chose defeat. I'd get my own back when he wasn't injured.

"Hello, is that you Nana?"

My stomach flipped as Ben called my Nana, Nana. I could imagine my Nana's horror struck face and terrifying reaction.

There was nothing else for it, but to abandon all hope and head to Nana's, as Ben introduced himself over the phone.

Ben's delightfully witty banter tightened the knot in my stomach. The temptation to open the door and puke was great. I impressed myself with my ability to control my vomit. Then I remembered the magazine. If I turned up without the story, she'd use the visit to interrogate us both.

Detour.

I pulled up my driveway and jumped from the car.

"Stay here," I said to Ben and ran inside. I returned two minutes later carrying the magazine. I dropped it onto Ben's lap and drove off again.

He was still talking to Nana.

Ten minutes of listening to more of his conversation with Nana later I said, "Hang up. We are here."

He said into the phone, "We're here, June."

I parked, grabbed the phone, and disconnected the call. I sat in the car in the dark and dared Ben to speak.

He didn't. He tapped the magazine on his leg as if waiting for me.

I flipped the stereo on, a familiar song cranked out of

my speakers.

My Chemical Romance was singing 'Teenagers'. I sang along, hoping to find they were caught in some weird black hole and weren't at my Nana's retirement village at all.

I found I'd adjusted the words slightly to make myself feel better.

"Old people scare the living shit out of me!" I sang at full volume, aware I couldn't hold a note to save my life and not caring a jot.

Ben laughed until tears welled up in his eyes.

"She can't be that bad, Ronnie? She sounds so sweet on the phone," he said while turning the volume down to a reasonable level.

I wailed at him and let forth with more of the song.

"If we don't get out of the car, those three old women over there are going to come over here and demand to know what is taking so long."

He was right.

I saw the three of them gathered by the front door of the reception area.

The harbingers of doom peered in our direction. I wondered how good their eye sight was, and if I would be in trouble for sitting too long in the car with a man.

It seemed reasonable.

I seemed to always be in trouble.

Enough trouble that I occasionally had to stamp my feet and declare I'd been an adult for quite some years. That really upset the apple cart. Tossing my toys out of the crib simply served to remind my Nana how I was at three, four, five, fifteen, and twenty-five. It always ended badly for me, badly being how it ended when Nana was involved in any area of my life. But she means well. That's the thing with Nana, she means well. If I keep telling myself that, one day I'll believe it.

"Let's do it," I said. I removed the keys from the ignition and with them the temptation to start the car and drive away. "Bring the magazine."

Ben got out of the car before I could open my door. He walked around to me and made a show of opening my door for me.

I glared at him. He smiled.

"Careful I don't whack you on the other side of your head," I whispered. "You have no idea what you just did, do you?"

He shook his head, linked his arm in mine. "I'm doing what any gentleman would do," he replied, and escorted me to the door.

I tried to shake his arm off. "I can walk without being escorted, thanks," I growled.

"You won't run?"

I shook my head and leaned in to whisper, "Nana will now think we are an item." I sighed. "And that you have probably bonked me senseless already."

Ben looked confused. "From me opening the door?"

"Oh yeah, and this." I indicated with a nod at our linked arms. "That lovely sweet old woman is quite adept at filling in the blanks with crap." I sighed. "There'll be talk about why you would want to buy the cow if you can get the milk for free."

"What does that even mean?" Ben whispered.

"It means she'll start muttering how you won't marry me now, because I'm used goods."

Ben bit his lip hard. By the smirk on his face I guessed it was to stop himself laughing aloud. His shoulders shook with amusement.

I pinched his arm. "Oh, it isn't funny."

We stopped at the blocked doorway, unable to proceed until the crones parted.

The gathering parted, letting us through. They filed down the hall behind us.

Nana spoke, "Go to my apartment, dear. I've made tea."

"It's down this corridor and then a right at the end," I told Ben. "You asked for this, just remember that."

"Yes I did," he agreed. The chattering of women behind us seemed endless as we walked through the corridor. "If we use longer strides they won't be able to keep up."

We lengthened our stride just enough to put some distance between us and the gaggle of oldies.

"Was this the smartest thing to do?" I whispered.

"We're off the street," he replied.

I nodded in agreement. "Although personally I'd prefer to take my chances with any possible police road blocks."

"I doubt they'll know much yet."

"Body in the boot," I whispered. "Even charred that

will be recognisable as a body."

"I didn't think I had a trunk left," Ben said. "By the way, boot is a stupid word."

"Yeah, because trunk makes sense?"

"It does. The model A Ford had an actual trunk on the back of the car behind the rumble seat. You know like a steamer trunk. Feet go in boots."

"Thanks for the explanation. Anyway, it was the back-seat you lost. The contents of your boot ended up where the back seat used to be," I said, and came to a stop outside a door. "This is it." I tried the handle and the door opened. We went inside and made ourselves comfortable in the small living room. It was a few minutes before the gaggle arrived.

Nana fussed around then made a show of going to pour the tea. My phone rang.

I looked at Ben and said, "Donald."

"I'm now wondering what my ring tone is," he said. "I do have one, right?"

"Yep," I replied and answered the call hoping he never ever found out what his ring tone was.

The more time I spent with him the truer I found the song.

"Martha is stark raving mad and I am not impressed with having to baby sit the old trout," Donald spouted into my ear.

"We have a dinner with friends soon, remember?" I lowered my voice to a whisper at the mention of friends and hoped like mad none of the gaggle had turned their hearing aids on.

It amazed me how quickly old folk could pick up on anything you didn't want them to hear, and yet in the supermarket they blocked aisles and apparently were all completely deaf when anyone politely asked to get by.

Donald ranted on about how I owed him and it was going to be more than a dinner.

He also parted with some information regarding the crash.

When Donald started talking about the crash, I perked up a little. "Police were everywhere and someone in the pub said police discovered a body in the back of one of the cars."

"Really? That's awful." I used every acting skill I possessed to let surprise resound in my voice. I was nowhere near as good at it as Ben.

"I know!" Donald replied.

"If all is well at Martha's you should probably wait for the police to ease off, then get along home."

"Why wait?" he asked, obviously keen to leave as quickly as possible.

"No real reason, I guess," I replied trying very hard to maintain control and not laugh.

"Then I'll go now."

"Sure, you do that. Don't come crying to me when you get hauled into the station."

"Why, would that happen?"

"Because they'll stop you in the road block and take one look at your Tuhoe arse and assume this was an act of terrorism," I delivered my line with cool precision, and was delighted in my ability to do so.

Donald chuckled on the other end of the phone. "How long have you been waiting to use that one?"

"You have no idea," I said with a small laugh. "It's been years."

"I might wait, just in case," Donald replied and hung up.

I had a sudden cold chill and called Donald right back.

"The piece of paper I gave you, did you destroy it?"

I hoped he didn't just ball it up and leave it on the table at the bar.

There was a weird silence then he said, "I ate it."

"Seriously?"

"Yes, just like in the movies."

"Good job," I replied. "I'll buy you something sparkly."

I ended the call.

Nana shuffled over with cups of tea. She handed Ben a cup and commented, "That must be a nasty cut you have."

"It's not too bad," he replied. "Thank you for the tea."

"I wondered if Americans drink tea, but Ester assured me you would say if you didn't."

"We're not so different to regular folk," he said with a disarming smile.

"Veronica is reading me an American story. It's quite fun, I am enjoying it."

"That's nice," Ben said pushing the magazine down the side of the chair.

I watched the exchange and could finally get a good look at Ben in full light. He was a mess. Never mind his head and face, which he'd cleaned up. Bloody streaks covered his shirt. He had bloodstains on his hands. His pants were ripped and shirt torn.

I waited for the trio of doom to question him regarding his appearance. Who would be first, I wondered.

I didn't have to wonder long.

Frankie piped up, "You are in a state, young man. What happened?"

Ben grinned sheepishly, "Bit of an altercation, I'm afraid."

I cringed, knowing what he was going to say next.

"Someone insulted the lovely Veronica, what could I do?" He gave a resigned look and slight shrug. "I had to defend her honour."

All three women nodded in agreement and murmured about honour. I grimaced. Internally, I readied myself for a barrage of questions from my Nana.

"Oh dear," Nana said. "Perhaps you'd like to clean up."

"Yes, I would. If you don't mind?"

"Not at all. Veronica will show you to the bathroom."

"You're a real mess," Ester commented at Ben stood up.

"Yeah, but you should see the other guy," Ben quipped with a cocky smile.

I did my best to fight back the desire to laugh aloud. The other guy was a crispy critter. We left the room to a chorus of mutterings about real men and how there needed to be more men like him and less of the wishy-washy type that were good for nothing. I couldn't dispute that, at all. I'd often wondered what happened to all the real men. Ones that weren't Neanderthal, and weren't Donald. Not that there was anything wrong with Donald if you're so inclined.

I gave that some thought. Who was I kidding? He was a raving fruit loop and a pillow biter. He went for the rugged, all-man type, too. It wasn't easy sharing my type with him. Not that there was ever any real overlap. The thought alone scared the hell out of me. I'm a fairly caring and sharing person but there is a limit.

Then along came Ben.

I realised the entire time I was agreeing mentally with the crones I was staring at Ben like he was the other white meat. He met my gaze and broke the spell.

"Did you want to hold it or shake it?"

"What?" I asked unaware where we were. I glanced down and saw the porcelain throne. "Oh my. I'm sorry," I said, feeling heat rising in my face. "I was thinking. I'm sorry," I turned and hurried from the room, shutting the door behind me.

Ben called after me, "Wait for me."

I had no choice, I could hardly go back to the living room with my face flamed to the colour of beetroot. That would be too much.

"Bollocks," I mumbled to myself. I was sure I'd come across like a complete idiot and made a fool of myself in a bathroom. I drifted into the recesses of my mind to try to find less embarrassing moments to ponder while I waited for Ben to finish up. This would not have happened if Jared was still handling incidents on New Zealand soil. He would be in the freaking office for one thing, and not traipsing around the countryside after gnome thieving terrorists. For another, he'd never ask to meet my Nana, not ever. I stared at the photograph of my grandfather on the wall opposite me. "How did I find a good looking American with a sense of humour?"

My granddad didn't answer.

He stared down from the wall with a no nonsense look plastered across his black and white face. Even in death, he seemed to show his disapproval. I smiled at him, he was right of course. There was no such creature, well not in my field anyway. You got one or the other; it was either good looking or a sense of humour. Ben was an anomaly. I felt heat rise in my face again. Ben was an actor. I willed calmness and breathed slowly, trying to dissipate the colour before he stepped into the hallway. I heard the handle turn, a slight squeak, and the door opened.

Ben stepped out, looking slightly better than he had when he stepped in. I almost didn't want to make eye contact, but found I couldn't help it.

To my horror unchecked words tumbled from my mouth.

"I was waiting in case you needed me to hold some-thing."

He grinned. "If I'd known you were waiting here to help, I would have called you back in."

He draped an arm casually about my shoulders, and kissed the side of my head. "Now back to Nana and her entourage," he said smoothly. "Do you mind if my arm stays where it is?"

"Not at all. You are playing my boyfriend for the evening. I'm fairly sure Nana allows draped arms but you best keep your lips to yourself."

Together we entered the living room and met with the scrutinising stare of the three old women. When they didn't immediately begin tutting and managed to keep the pursing of lips to a minimum, I understood that to mean they were okay with Ben draping his arm about my shoulders.

I sat on the sofa wishing I were somewhere else, but with a certain amount of conflict involved in the wishes.

We were relatively safe with Nana, certainly compared to being out on the road.

"While you are here ..." Nana started, turning her faded blue eyes to me. "Did you talk to Donald about any lady friends he may have?"

Ben looked from Nana to me. Confusion clouded his face. He saw the warning glance I slipped him and said nothing.

"I haven't really had a chance, Nana. We had a few words. You know Donald, he's very particular about things," I lied through my teeth and hoped lightning wouldn't strike me down. At least this time as I considered being struck down it wasn't for stealing an old woman's gnome. It was for lying to an old woman, but for a good cause. As long as the end justified the means, I could live with it.

"It's just that Frankie's granddaughter is coming by tomorrow afternoon and I know Donald will be here."

To anyone else that would sound innocent. From anyone else that simple statement of fact probably would be innocent.

"You're going to spring the poor girl on him aren't you?" I looked from Nana to Frankie and back. At least Frankie had the decency to show embarrassment at the surfacing plan.

Ben nudged me and said, "But I thought we were going out with Donald and his friend tomorrow night. Doesn't he have a beau already?"

I raced over the words that tumbled from his mouth. He never said boyfriend. It was going to be okay.

Thinking on my feet I said, "Oh, how did I forget that? Thank you, for reminding me."

He squeezed my shoulder. "No problem, that's what I'm here for."

A chorus of approving clucks circled the room. Ben was their new favourite. Lucky he was pretending to be my boyfriend or he would find himself set up with Frankie's granddaughter.

I leaned closer to his ear and whispered, "They'd eat out of the palm of your hand. For some reason I find that sickening. Could be because they're ancient and have more wrinkles than eyelashes."

Ben stifled a chuckle. Suddenly all eyes were on him,

expectantly. He knew they wanted to know why he made strangled noises of merriment. It was like being back in school. I was certain one of the crones was going to ask that he share his amusing anecdote with the class. Panic gripped me. The man, who tackled a very interesting and often dangerous job without faltering, wilted under the stare of old ladies.

I watched Nana as the old woman readied herself to speak.

"How did you meet each other?"

It would have to be an honest answer. I smiled sweetly. As tempting as it was to inform my Nana that Ben was a random stranger I'd picked up in a bar I didn't think that a smart move.

"We worked together," Ben interjected, before I could find the right words.

"Yes," I agreed readily but not too fast as to cause suspicion. "We worked together."

All three women leaned in, their frail bodies poised with the joy of gossip.

Ester asked, "Where was that?"

I wondered if the woman remembered I was a private investigator. A flash of brilliance crossed my mind. The truth, sort of, began to emerge.

"We can't tell you exactly," I said, leaning closer to the oldies and glancing around furtively for good effect. "I can't talk about clients."

The women backed off, disappointedly.

"Yes, yes, I understand," Ester muttered.

You're lucky you don't.

"I have the magazine, Nana. Shall I read?" I offered knowing that reading would stop any further conversation for a little while at least.

"Yes, yes, yes," Nana said. "You'll love this ,girls! Remember how I told you about the story so far."

The two old crones nodded. I pulled the magazine from the side of the chair and found the correct page. The reading began. I stopped a little while later and gauged my audience's reaction. Enthralled seemed to fit.

"What a marvellous mystery," Ester said. "No wonder you like this story, June. You're good with mysteries."

I nodded. "Yes, Nana is quite the sleuth."

Ben checked his watch.

It felt like we'd been holed up in the retirement home for hours.

He saw my questioning glance and showed me his watch. My stomach sank to find it was only an hour. Not long enough. We needed to stay longer to avoid road-blocks. Although if stopped we at least had a legitimate, easily verifiable place of origin.

"Nana, do you mind if I make coffee?" I said, rising to my feet.

Ben moved his arm and commented on my decision, "Coffee would be great."

"Of course, dear, go ahead," Nana said, but her manner suggested she might have offered resistance but for Ben's expressed pleasure at coffee.

"Does anyone else want more tea, while I'm in the

kitchen?"

I looked at the coordinated women, and for the first time noticed, they were all wearing slippers. They'd dressed after Martha's phone call, but were wearing slippers.

Slippers that matched their outfits. I had a feeling they had matching handbags too.

I was beginning to feel like a prisoner in an ancient version of a Nancy Drew novel.

The mystery of the garden gnome.

The crones all made approving clucks at the mention of more tea. Ben stood up to help. He and I gathered the cups and took them through to the kitchen.

I put the jug on. "You okay?" I asked.

"Yes, don't seem to be suffering any adverse effects."

"Good." I opened a cupboard and took out a container of coffee. "It's instant, I'm afraid."

"That'll do fine, Veronica."

I looked at him as I opened the container. There was something about the way he said my name that warranted me looking at him. He looked okay. He looked better than okay. I turned my attention to the tea and refused to let my mind draw me into the realms of fantasy.

"It's a good story," he said.

"I've been reading to Nana for years. She proudly tells people she's never read a book in her life. Which is true; I read them to her."

Ben grinned. "She is lucky to have you."

He washed cups and put them on the bench. I tipped

out the teapot and made fresh tea. I smiled to myself at the domestic scene we'd created in my head. A wave of exhaustion washed over me. I yawned.

"All right?" Ben asked.

"Bit tired," I said.

"To be expected after an adrenaline rush."

"Of course," I replied, knowing that was something I should've known. "That makes sense."

"Let's get some coffee down you and spend some more fun time with Nana," he replied.

"Or you could drive," I said. "And we could leave."

"I could, but I have this head injury," he said, feigning a staggered collapse, but grabbing the bench at the last second and stopping the momentum of the fall.

"Don't tell me, you're enjoying being centre of attention?"

He chuckled. "When I'm as old as that lot, I'd be happy to have half as much spunk."

"I guess being that old and still functioning is a rather cool achievement." I moved closer to him to share an observation. "Did you ever read Nancy Drew mysteries?"

He stepped back. "I'm a guy, or had that escaped your attention?" Ben sidestepped the question.

"Oh, I know you are, but have you?"

He nodded. Due to the subtlety of his head movement, it was almost lost in the coffee-making exercise.

"You have?"

"Yes," he replied with a sheepish smile that indicated I'd stumbled upon a guilty pleasure or dirty little secret.

"My kid sister had Nancy Drew books. I may have read a couple during my childhood."

Sure. A couple. Not buying it.

"When we go back out there," I said, waving a hand toward the other room, "Tell me if the Trio of Doom aren't exactly what those girls from Nancy Drew would look like in their dotage. Matching outfits, the whole deal."

He gave me a long penetrating look, which pierced my soul. "Your mind is a very strange place."

"I'm serious, you'll see."

He cupped my face in his hands. I froze. In one fluid movement, he bent his head and kissed me briefly. Without any conscious thought, I returned the kiss. Then it was over.

He smiled and carried on with the preparation.

I carried the cups of tea back to the living room. I insisted that Ben sit down, and I went back for our coffee.

"See?" I whispered in his ear as I sat.

He smiled as he took in the scene in front of him and nodded ever so slightly. I could tell he knew I hadn't imagined it. They really were geriatric Nancy Drews.

"Veronica, dear. There are cakes in the tins. Pop something onto a plate and bring it in, will you?" Nana called.

"Sure. Any preferences?" I replied copying her tone.

"Just a little something for supper, dear. You choose."

I took two tins from the cupboard and chose a few slices. I smiled to myself and thought about poor Martha's terror at serving up bought packet biscuits to my Nana.

Here I was dishing out what everyone thought were homemade slices, but I knew were from one of the bakeries in town.

I took the plate through. Like the dutiful granddaughter I was, I did the rounds with the plate of cakes. Ben first, as he was the newest guest, then clockwise around the room. I finally took a slice myself and sat down. Amusement bubbled as I listened to the crones complimenting Nana on the delicious cakes and lovely manners of her granddaughter.

Ben thwarted my temptation to yell, "I'm right here, and I'm not ten!"

"We should probably head off once we've finished our coffee," he said.

"Yes, we should. It's quite a drive to drop you back at your place."

"It is."

The crones looked on, eating their cakes and sipping their tea.

Frankie eventually spoke, "Will Martha be all right?"

"I'm sure she will," I assured her. "Donald checked the house. And it was probably just a car crash anyway."

They all nodded.

"Nasty businesses, car crashes," Ester said. I sighed. "Not that I ever got to attend one. It wasn't what policewomen did in my day. I did hear the stories from the boys when they came into the canteen for their breaks, though."

Ben listened with interest, as did I. I suspected I would not have coped well back in Ester's day. I would have been run off the force for refusing to follow orders and stay in the station.

"How long were you on the force?" I said.

"I did a good twenty years," Ester replied, proudly. "I was often in hot water for asking for more responsibility and wanting to get involved in policing rather than filing."

She paused; I could see her thinking before she spoke again. "I see the policewomen these days out on the beat or driving police cars and wearing those new stab proof vests and I think it must be a lot more interesting for them now."

"You were a pioneer," Ben told her. "If it wasn't for women like you, female officers would still be behind desks."

He was right.

If women like Ester hadn't stood up and been counted, then women today would still be in the kitchen. I considered that; it also related to me. If Ester hadn't been a police woman, I wouldn't be a private eye. Women spies were nothing new, but being a private investigator and working in what was a traditional male role for so many years, now that was only possible because of the Esters of the world.

Ben stood up. He placed his cup carefully on the table and leaned down to Ester with an outstretched hand. They shook hands.

"It was my pleasure to meet you," Ben said smoothly as the handshake came to an end.

"You're a lovely young man," Ester replied.

So as not to irritate the other two women, he made the rounds, choosing Frankie next.

"It was a real joy to meet you, Frankie," he said shaking her hand.

"I did enjoy the evening," Frankie replied with a smile. Old thin lips pulled taut over yellowed teeth.

Nana was last. "June, it's been a delight to meet you. Your granddaughter is quite special," he said, taking Nana's hand in his. "And now I should get her home."

"You are most welcome to visit us again," Nana crooned, her eyes bright with plans. "Most welcome."

"Don't walk us out," he said as the cronies began struggling to their feet. "Veronica can show me the way."

I stood beside him, and leaned over to kiss Nana on the cheek. "I'll call you tomorrow."

"More story tomorrow, don't forget the magazine." Nana said pressing the folded magazine into my hand.

"I should leave it with you Nana," I replied.

"No, dear, you take it."

Chapter 18
[HOME WITH BEN]

I handed Ben the keys; he took them. They jangled in his hand as he walked me toward the car. He pressed the button on the fob unlocking the doors, then without fuss he escorted me to the passenger side, opened the door, and waited until I'd clicked my seat belt on.

"You didn't have to do that, you know," I said, looking up at him. "No one is watching."

He smiled and shut my door firmly.

I watched with interest as he skirted the bonnet and opened the driver's door. I suspected a smile lay on my lips, but no longer cared if he saw it or not. So, I enjoyed the view, no harm in that. I ignored the warning bells in my head.

If the virus has escaped we'll all die?

He was humming as he started the car. I recognised the tune. 'We've Gotta Get Out of This Place.'

There was no traffic in sight as Ben headed south.

He sang. I joined in.

When we finally reached the end of the song, laughter erupted.

"I think we'd be better lip syncing with the radio," I said. "You sure you're okay to drive?"

"I'm fine."

I turned the radio on, and he settled into the task of driving.

Two minutes passed and he said, "I hate to ask this. But can I crash at your place?"

I looked at him, carefully studying his face. "Yes, I have a spare room."

"Thank you," he replied.

There was relief in his few words, which struck me as odd for a second. How odd could it really be? Would I feel like driving into the city after being in a car crash and nearly exploding? The answer was no, I would not.

"You said you were okay."

"I am, I think - just tired. Better to be safe than sorry."

Fair enough.

I offered directions from Nana's to my home. He happily followed my directions and even managed to decipher my left, right, no the other left confusion.

It was a relief to be parked up my driveway.

"Can I have the keys?" I asked, climbing out of the car. I stretched my hand out.

"Sure," Ben said dropping them into my palm. I closed my hand around the keys and swung my door shut. The area was silent until my door closed with a sharp click. I hurried down the driveway toward the road and the big double iron gates. As I shut the gates behind us and locked the padlock, I felt a sense of relief. Ben waited on the front porch. I noted he too looked relieved. It was quite a night. I stepped past him to unlock the door, but in true gentlemanly form, he took my keys and opened it himself. I heard Romeo stretch and shake. He appeared around the corner of the kitchen door. His tail smacking into the door frame as he wagged it.

"Hey Romeo. You been a good boy?" I asked, rubbing his head and ears.

He yawned, sniffed at Ben and then went back to his warm bed. I followed him and tucked his blanket around him.

Ben locked the door and gave the handle a gentle shake, then followed me into the house. Ben stood in the middle of my spacious kitchen.

"Drop the keys in the bowl on the table," I said, I tossed the magazine onto the table then switched lights on and closed the kitchen curtains. "I'll just close the rest of the curtains."

"Okay," he replied. "I'll just sit here?"

"Yeah, good idea," I said. I heard him pull out a chair and sit down as I moved through the kitchen to the main living areas. It didn't take long to check everything was in order. I opened the door to the guest bedroom and found the bed freshly made. I added folded towels to the end of the bed, and put an extra blanket on the chair under the window. Satisfied my hostess with the mostest job was done, I joined Ben in the kitchen.He did look tired. There was still blood on his clothing, and stuck in his hair.

I thought for a minute, and remembered I had a few of Donald's more normal shirts in the laundry. I recalled at least one regular man type tee shirt and a button down shirt.

"I'll be right back," I said and disappeared into the laundry. I emerged seconds later carrying a grey tee shirt.

"I think this will fit. Hand over that shirt you are wearing, I'll soak it and see if I can get the blood out."

He looked at me with a slight amusement in his eyes. "

You're a lot more domesticated than I would have thought," he said.

"I have my moments. Take your shirt off." I smiled. "Why don't you have a shower, and wash the blood out of your hair as well?"

"I think that would be a good idea," he said, standing. "Point me to your bathroom."

He undid a couple of buttons, then hauled his shirt off over his head, revealing a taut flat stomach and impressive six pack. I averted my eyes and held out my hand for the shirt. Having him half naked in my kitchen was tempting fate big time and I knew it. There was a massive temptation to reach for my phone and Instagram the sight in front of me. The little voice in my head that said we could all be dead in a few days. It wasn't helping.

"Down the hall, on your left. There are clean towels on your bed ... down the hall first door on the right."

"Thank you," he replied gratefully.

I hung the shirt over the back of a chair. I intended to give it a good soak but first there was something I needed to do.

While Ben showered, I fired up my laptop.

I took it to the kitchen and sat down at the table.

Visions of death filled my head. I shook the thoughts away. We had to get that last gnome before whoever else was after it found it.

Something cold and dark edged into my consciousness. I needed to check my email. Nothing I'd seen made much sense. A virus that reanimated dead people was not a comforting thing. Justin didn't look good as a zombie. According the internet the virus was fictional. Well, that didn't explain what I'd seen or help me at all. I don't think I'm in a movie. Of course, I could be wrong. I thought once death got its icy claws on a person that was the end. Dead people are supposed to lie down quietly and not cause a fuss. Nothing came up online that even remotely suggested reanimation was a real thing. I gave up the search.

In the laundry, I become a domestic goddess. I dropped the shirt in the laundry tub and ran cold water on it. From the shelf above the tub, I took a bright pink container of nappy soaker. I added a heaped lid of the white powder to a clean bucket, filled it half full of cold water then swirled the shirt into it. There was something oddly satisfying about being domestic.

Back in the kitchen, my email chimed, time and time again. I found twelve emails waiting. One and only one bore a flag and a subject that required immediate attention. I looked at the time stamp. Within the last hour. I opened it, and read it, and then stood up. I walked slowly down the hallway and stopped outside the bathroom door. At first, I hesitated upon hearing the water running and not wanting to disturb him. I listened to the water for a few seconds. My mind began to wander into the bathroom. With a sigh, I reined my thoughts in and knocked once on the door.

"Ben?"

I heard the water shut off, and a voice say, "Do you make a habit of standing outside bathroom doors?"

"Apparently, I do," I replied. "Meet me in the kitchen ..." As an afterthought, I added, "When you are dressed."

"Sure," he replied.

For a second I thought he'd asked a question. I replayed his reply in my head. "Sure?" was wishful thinking on my part. I went back to the kitchen and read the email again. From the wording and experience, I had a fair idea what the actual message would say once it was decoded. I opened another computer program, then copied the email into it and clicked the start button on the screen.

A few seconds later, the program revealed the real message.

"Damn," I murmured.

I looked down the hall, Ben had yet to appear.

I waited, tapping my foot on the linoleum floor, thrumming my fingers on the table, willing him to hurry up. I read the email for the fourth time, paying special attention to every single word. Ben appeared. I glanced up at his clean face. For the first time I could see the cut on his forehead. It was longer than I thought, covering a good three centimetres.

"Sit down, I'll get some wound closures and see if I can close that gash for you," I said.

He looked a lot better without the dried blood all over his face and clothes. I pulled a first aid kit out of a cupboard under the sink bench. I placed it on the bench top and opened it up. I took out a packet of wound closures and some antibacterial hand wash, and a pair of latex gloves. I cleaned my hands, pulled the gloves on, and then carefully held the edges of his wound together. I stuck two of the sticky closures evenly across it. It held, better than I thought it would.

"Glue would probably be a good idea too, but I don't have any," I said.

I tossed the backing from the strips and my gloves in the kitchen rubbish bin. "Feel okay?"

He frowned a little then smiled, as if checking how much they pulled. "Feels fine."

I turned the laptop to face him. "Read this, I'm going to make coffee."

He read in silence. I opted for real coffee. I found my plunger pot and made the coffee, filling the kitchen with a delicious nutty aroma.

"Smells good," Ben said. He read the email twice then leaned back in his chair and waited for the coffee.

"White chocolate and macadamia from Gloria Jeans," I replied, sitting the plunger on the table in front of him. "The email?"

I sat down.

"How big was the explosion?" he asked.

"I don't know. Are you asking if your DNA is recoverable?"

"Yes."

I shook my head. "I don't know."

"They traced the license plates and are not amused to find the car registered to Lord Voldemort," he said peering over the laptop at me.

"Imagine that."

"How the hell did Jared get back involved in this," Ben whispered.

I smiled. It was almost as if he didn't want to say his name louder, in case he suddenly materialised. Never say it three times in a row.

"Is that rhetorical?" I sat up straighter and looked at him over the screen. He didn't react. "Your car exploded. I'm guessing here, but I suspect that event would send a bit of a ripple through the pond."

"I thought he'd retired."

"Does anyone fully and irrevocably retire from the agency?"

He shrugged. "Guess not. I need to contact him and tell him I'm alive, and can finish the mission."

I blinked. That was the first time I'd heard him say the word mission. Up until then I was happily avoiding what this really was. I was playing a game and now I was at war. Even when the car exploded, I'd avoided thinking about suicide bombers and terrorism. This was a mission. A cold chill spread through me. How many people did Justin infect before he knew he was sick?

"Ben, how many people were infected before Justin knew about the illness?"

He rubbed his forehead with his fingers.

"I don't know. I need to get hold of Jared."

"Use my laptop. It's running agency software and some fandangled NSA encryption doodad," I said.

"They'd be technical words then, fandangle, and doodad?" he asked, closing my email program and navigating his way to a bulletin board they were using for the mission.

"Absolutely."

I poured the coffee and watched him in silence as he gathered information and sent messages to Jared.

When Ben looked over at me, I smiled but I doubted it was convincing.

"This is not beyond our realm of expertise, you know that?" he said, typing.

"Really?" I replied. "You've come across mutant fucking killer viruses before then?"

"Yeah, I have, just not this particular combination though," he said. "Time I filled you in on some of the details here.

"That would be nice."

"The Intel this time came from chatter picked up from Islamabad," Ben said.

"Islamabad chatter refers to packages in New Zealand? Jesus!"

"All hell is breaking loose in Pakistan right now," Ben said. "And Syria and, well you name a country over that way and there's trouble there."

I nodded and interrupted him, "I know. I watch the news." At the mention of Syria a horrible feeling wound its way up my spine and into my brain and chilled me from the inside out. "Does this have anything to do with ISIS?"

"We can't confirm that at this point."

"Do you think they're involved?" I asked.

"It's possible. Let me tell you what I do know."

"I'm listening."

"It was Justin who came across the Intel and then discovered the packages."

"I gathered that. He hid them. What I don't get is why he didn't go to Reede. She's his boss."

Ben gave me a questioning look. "Reede called you, yes?"

I nodded. "She told me you'd be calling."

"We all already knew about you. Through MacKinnon. It was his idea to let Reede know we wanted you and for her to make first contact. She was directed to make sure you were on board."

"Why?"

"Because Reede trusts you. She doesn't like you much but she trusts you. You have a relationship with her and she needs to know where the packages are."

It's not a great relationship. I never liked her and I've never trusted her. Wasn't something I could talk about while she was my boss, but she was instrumental in my decision to leave and go private.

"She's a traitor," I said as it all fell into place with a thump. "That was the chatter that Justin overheard."

"Yes."

My phone rang. I had a horrible feeling. I answered the

phone.

"Wherefore Art Thou, Ronnie speaking."

"Veronica, it's Reede."

Guess she felt a disruption in the force.

"How can I help you Reede?"

Ben's eye brows rose then dropped into a frown.

"I was wondering how you were getting on with the American issue."

"The case really didn't appeal to me. I sent them packing."

Ben grinned.

"That wasn't wise, Veronica. They asked specifically for your help."

"Turns out I didn't need the aggravation."

I hung up.

"She's not going to like that," Ben said.

"Tough, I don't like her, and I don't like her thinking she can weasel information out of me."

Ben wisely changed the subject. "How close are you to finding the exact location of the third package?"

"I know the suburb, but it's hard to pinpoint it exactly. There isn't a big energy field for me to tap into."

He gave me a quizzical look. "Do I want to know what that means?"

I shook my head. "No."

"Okay." He was concentrating on the screen in front of him. "I may have found something. It's possible that the location message is on the board." He turned the laptop to face me. There was an encrypted message left by

Justin. "Do you know what that says?"

I held up one finger. "Give me a minute."

I closed my eyes then opened them. The message on the screen began to pop out of the words he'd used. Within a few seconds, I could read the message. We'd used this encryption many times.

Supposed location. "Okay, awesome, I got it. Not as helpful as I'd hoped. I was hoping for an actual address but I suppose that was too dangerous. We have a series of street names. One of them will contain our package."

He hadn't narrowed it down much more than I had using the energy fields but I knew Justin and there were probably clues once I got to the area.

"Is it helpful at all?" Ben asked. "Can you use the information?"

"Yes and yes. It narrows the search area from an entire suburb to a group of streets roughly in the middle." I read the message again to make sure I had it right. I did but I also had a question. "Who's to say they don't have the same Intel we do?"

"We don't know if they do or not. As far as I could tell, they didn't know exactly where the first two packages came from and everything we've intercepted so far indicates they don't know we have the second package."

"That's good."

"Them not knowing could indicate their Intel is either lacking or slow. I do know that this package won't give them much of an advantage if they get it. It's the second virus and they need both."

"Explain the two virus thing to me," I said. I was having a hard job getting my head around what I'd seen happen to Justin.

"Separately the viruses would be no worse than a bad flu. Some people would die, and some people wouldn't get sick at all," he said. "It's an influenza type illness."

"Okay, so one won't kill normal healthy people?"

"That's right but together they combine and mutate within hours to form something deadly. And judging by Justin, the supposed antidote isn't that good."

"Do we know what the plan was?"

"Yes, that's how Justin managed to steal the viruses. He found a plan or a plot if you like. New Zealand was going to be the testing ground."

"What?"

"It's an island nation. Borders are easier to shut on an island. They were going to release the viruses at two different primary schools, then sit back and watch as it spread. That way, they could track the movement of the virus."

I had a flash of a game I'd played on my phone that was similar. Frightening to think someone was playing with real lives and watching the progress.

"We were to be guinea pigs for a terrorist organisation?"

"Yes."

I looked at him from under my dark lashes. "And my price has gone up."

He smiled. "It's already authorised. A substantially

larger amount will be credited to your account tonight."

"I was kind of joking." What good is money if we all die anyway?

"Jared did it, without me saying anything."

"Do you suppose I'll get to spend it?"

"You will," Ben replied. He never faltered.

"And you know this?"

He ignored my question.

"We should get onto this third gnome ASAP," Ben said.

"Neither of us are going fossicking about anywhere in the wee small hours, after the whole explosion thing," I said. "We'll start again tomorrow."

Ben's phone rang. He answered it quickly and walked into the hallway listening. He came back with his mouth set in a grim line.

"What?" I asked, knowing by his expression that it was bad.

"They found two more infections."

"That's what we're calling them ... infections?"

"Well they're not people anymore," he replied sitting at the table.

"Where?"

"The vicar and his wife."

I breathed a sigh of relief. It wasn't a supermarket worker or someone from a fast food restaurant, or a kid, it was the vicar and his wife. Surely that was confined. If it were in a supermarket then clean up on aisle four would take on a whole new meaning. I imagined someone with a flame thrower walking through the supermarket torching everyone and everything in sight. What scared me was that that scenario wasn't out of all reason.

"How many more could there potentially be?"

"Four million."

I blinked. That was the population of New Zealand.

"There is a team going through the rectory now, trying to determine the movement of the deceased couple and who they came in contact with in the last week."

"You might want to find a parish list, regular church goers and a list of services." I had an idea. I typed St. John's Anglican Church into Google. The services page held more horror than I'd imagined.

"Two Sunday services, two midweek services, two morning prayers and they take services and four different rest homes once a month but in the last fortnight they only held services at one rest home."

Nana's home was not on the list, I checked three times to make sure. I remembered her rest home came under St. Hilda's parish. I fired off a silent prayer of thanks and apologised for the laptop smiting request.

"That's a lot of potential infections," Ben said.

There are going to be a lot of major fires in Upper Hutt.

"How can we stop it?" I rocked in my chair and thought about Romeo, and how he touched Justin's hand with his nose. "What about animals?"

"As far as we know these particular viruses are not transferable to other species."

"Not like swine flu or bird flu, you're sure?"

He shrugged. "Justin got sick and we don't know how. He shouldn't have come into contact with either virus let alone both, and he had access to an antidote, yet he's dead."

"Hold on. It takes both viruses to start the initial infection, yes?"

"Yes."

"But once someone is infected with both and it mutates, that person is then contagious?"

"Yes."

"I liked it better when I thought you could only catch it contracting both viruses at once." I powered down my laptop and closed the lid. "Welcome to the end of the world."

"We can contain this," he said. I almost believed him, then I remembered he was an actor.

"They better move fast and start shutting down that rest home," I said. "Norovirus would make a great cover."

Ben nodded. "They will."

He made a call from his cell phone but this time didn't leave the room. There really was no point trying to hide anything. I listened as he passed on the information we'd found online about the parish.

I knew by the replies he made that someone already knew everything we did, but it didn't hurt to make sure.

Ben hung up. "You heard?"

"Yes."

I was right. There would be many big fires in Upper

Hutt tonight which meant Steph and Jenn would have a super busy night. My turn to make some calls.

I rang Steph first.

"Sorry, I know it's late, but this is important. Do not answer your pager tonight."

"Why?"

"I can't tell you, but don't answer it. Be unavailable, be sick, be anything, but do not go out."

"Has this got something to do with the body in Trentham?"

"Yes."

"The virus thing?"

"Yes."

"All right. Will you ring Jenn or will I?"

"I will."

I hung up and called Jenn straight away. I told her the same thing. She agreed to stay home.

It was time to stop thinking about the worst case scenario. I remembered Nana telling me that wisdom was knowing what you can change and accepting what you can't.

I couldn't change what was happening but people were out there working on containing it. I had to trust them.

Ben and I had to do our part.

"Meanwhile?" Ben asked. "You okay?"

"Yeah, I just need sleep." I tried to smile but it didn't feel convincing. I tried again, same result. So I tried logic. "There is nothing we can do about any of this. As far as we know, police didn't get anywhere with the rego from your car, so let's let that sleeping dog lie, and that was the biggest worry tonight. We have enough potential problems without going looking for more."

"Rego?"

"License plates – registration – rego."

"Makes sense," he replied.

I gave him a sly look. "Unless of course you are Lord Voldemort?"

"Nope, last I time I checked I was real." He touched his cut forehead gingerly.

"I think you're real too. Bed?"

He grinned, raised an eyebrow, and then grimaced as it pulled his cut.

I smiled.

"Serves you right for thinking improper thoughts," I said. "Let's go get some sleep."

"Yes, ma'am."

I pointed him to the door. "Get moving, mate."

He sloped off. I could tell he was grinning as he headed for the guest room. I went into the laundry and emptied the contents of the bucket into the washing machine. I added a scoop of Surf laundry detergent and switched the washer onto a short cycle.

I waited until it was finished, and hung Ben's shirt in the laundry. He needed a shirt for the morning.

I hurried out of the laundry before the overwhelming compulsion to reach for a bucket and mop grasped me.

There was a danger of me becoming Martha Stewart or worse, my Nana. I inspected the kitchen floor before I sat back at the table.

It didn't look filthy dirty but the soles of my socks told a different story. It could wait for a few days. It may not matter at all soon.

Before long, the shirt was hanging on a coat hanger in the laundry and I was crawling into my bed alone.

Chapter 19
[HATCHING A PLAN]

The world woke slowly. My corner of it fought the waking process with a vigour I hadn't experienced often before. My alarm switched from annoying beeping to the radio. I lay dozing half listening, wishing sleep would overtake me again. The radio beeped. I rolled over as the hourly news started.

The announcer's smooth voice said, "Leading the news this hour. What first appeared to be a fatal car crash in Pinehaven last night ..."

I sat up, and turned the radio up. It crackled loudly then settled as the announcer said, "... is now a murder investigation after traces of an explosive were discovered in one of the cars. Two bodies were found in the wreck-age, and one driver is missing."

I listened intently, hoping for more information but he moved on to a stabbing in the central city. Moments later the announcer swung back to something interesting, "There were two fires in Upper Hutt last night. A horrific fire at a local rest home has been attributed to arson. We have an eyewitness report that the doors were all locked and barred from the outside."

I lay back down and stared at the ceiling until I felt more like facing the day. Another full day of hunting gnomes ahead and the horrible thought of seeing burned out buildings that were once buzzing with life. Sure, it was old life, but it was life. It was life that shouldn't have ended like it did. I hauled myself from my warm bed and hit the shower. By the time I emerged I could smell coffee, not instant coffee either, the real deal. I opened my bedroom curtains and let the daylight swamp the room. I towel dried my hair then ran a brush through it. I swiped mascara over my lashes. The reflection staring back at me in the mirror appeared tired. I sighed. What a way to start the day, already looking like I'd worked a full one. I glanced in the mirror again. A reflection of two women walking across the street toward my house gave me pause. They stopped in at my neighbours'. Door knockers. Probably religious nutters. I walked into the kitchen. Ben was pouring coffee. I sat at the table.

"Good morning," Ben said, placing a cup of coffee on the table for me.

"The old people didn't burn to death did they?"

"No, the only way to stop the viral effects on the body is to take out the brain. So no, not burned to death. They were all shot before the fires were set."

"Good to know."

To be honest I had no clue if he was lying to me or not, but it seemed smarter to believe him. The alternative was too horrific for me to comprehend.

I sighed and plugged the laptop into the power cord that hung next to the table. I followed the cord back to the switch on the wall and flicked it on.

"You all right?" he asked.

"What about visitors to the rest home?" I turned

around stood facing him.

"Taken care of. They're tracking everyone who signed in and everyone who worked there. They'll get them all."

"God!"

It was a given that I'd know some of those people.

"Don't turn the radio on again today," he said.

I tried to quash all the thoughts that crammed into my skull at once about the end of the world as we knew it. They fought back but I was stronger. With them banished to the dark corners where they belonged, I concentrated on the day ahead.

"Did you sleep well?" I said, sitting back down at the table. I took a sip of the hot coffee. "This is good."

"I did sleep well, and thank you," Ben replied.

"We'll get going in about half an hour, I've had an idea how we can poke about Totara Park."

"How?" he asked, sitting at the table.

"Two ideas actually. The first involves reflective vests, clip boards and a measuring wheel," I said. "The second involves tidy clothes and a couple of Watch Tower magazines."

"I'd sooner pretend to be street surveyors than Jehovah's Witness."

"We should be prepared. We'll cover both possibilities. For all we know, the council could be surveying the streets already or the Jehovah's could be out in force."

"True."

"So we'll hopefully get to be surveyors. As long as we write a few numbers on the clipboard and count a few paces every now and then, no one should care or take a blind bit of notice."

"Equipment?"

I smiled. "I have vests and a wheel. I can get a few copies of the latest Watch Tower magazine from the JW's when they knock on the door, about now."

There was a knock on the front door.

Ben grinned. "Spooky."

"Spooky I am, but scary is what I want you to be. About a minute after I get the magazines, rush to the door and do something to get me out of the hole I would have had to put myself in to get the bloody things."

"You got it."

"Just don't scare the dog. Probably best if you shut him in the living room before you come out guns blazing."

"I will."

I chuckled as I made my way toward the knocking. On the porch, I found two women, and as I had rightly guessed, they were two Jehovah Witnesses.

"Could I trouble you for a few copies of your Watch-tower magazine," I enquired with what I hoped was a genuine interest and sincerity.

"Of course," the older of the women replied, she fished several copies from the large shoulder bag I carried. "Can we help you understand your path? Perhaps some study sessions?"

I cringed. I knew my simple straightforward request was going to end in harassment of giant proportions. The women pushed for my name.

I resisted.

From down the hall I heard a bellow. "What are you doing at the door? Your place is in the kitchen making my breakfast!" Ben yelled his voice getting louder the closer he got. "Not opening the front door and chatting to your ill favoured friends."

The two women appeared somewhat nervous.

One woman stepped back. The other, although nervous, held her ground.

"Get that door shut!" he roared.

"I'm sorry. I have to go," I said, with mock terror and a brilliant but shrinking display of subservience.

Ben strode to the door. He grabbed the magazines from my hand. "Not in my house!" He yelled at me then wrapped a hand around my arm and addressed the women, "I'm sorry, you have wasted your time. My wife doesn't make the religious decisions. Say goodbye."

"Goodbye," I said quietly.

Ben shut the door. We tiptoed to my bedroom and watched the women scuttle down the path, through the gate and across the road. They didn't even glance back.

"Guess they thought I had that coming," I said, watching them hurry to the next house.

Ben shook his head. "I didn't hurt your arm did I?"

"No, I'm fine. I can see why you get so many award nominations though. If I didn't know you were acting I would've been scared."

"All in a day's work," he said and winked at me. Ben handed me back the magazines. His rough treatment didn't crumple them too much.

"We have our second cover," I said with a smile, holding the magazines up.

"Ever read one?" Ben asked.

"Once I skimmed through one, but found the ideas it contained drove me to violence and copious vomiting."

He laughed.

We went back to the kitchen and the coffee.

"We're set?" Ben asked.

"We're set," I replied.

"Gnome?"

"Laundry in the box on the floor under the tub," I replied. He was still wearing Donald's shirt. "Your shirt is hanging in the laundry. Should be dry."

"Thank you." He smiled, revealing straight white teeth against a tanned background. His eyes lit by the smile, sparkled. Pale blue like aquamarines.

I liked his smile and enjoyed how readily that smile appeared. It was infectious, and more fun than catching a cold or an evil killer virus from hell.

The morning newspaper sat on the bench. I hadn't even noticed it.

"Did you get the paper in?"

"Yes," he replied. "I haven't had a chance to read it yet."

It was so easy having him in my house. So easy, it felt normal. We moved around each other like a well oiled machine or long time married couple. The level of ease suddenly made me uncomfortable. I found the situation ironic. I flicked through the newspaper as Ben went to fetch his clean shirt.

"While you're in there, can you grab that gnome? Should be a backpack hanging on the back of the door. You could put it in that." I carried on looking for anything that might hand Intel to the other side or news that would make their day harder.

"Anything interesting?" Ben asked as he came in, buttoning his shirt. "I did as you asked and left the backpack by the front door."

"Thanks. Something has stirred up some recapping of past transgressions by China. There is a huge article on all the awful things they've done to consumers. With a lot of time spent on how they've, in the past, made used condoms into hair ties," I said.

"That was the worst," he replied.

"Yep they win the grossest product on the market award," I said.

"I don't get why people are so scared of terrorists when they have this kind of thing becoming more common place," Ben said.

"Me neither."

Lead paint on kids' toys, used condom hair ties, antifreeze in toothpaste, stuffing kids' toys with old bandages. Extreme levels of formaldehyde in our clothing, melamine in baby formula, all that makes the occasional car bomb look clean.

He pointed to an article on another market place disaster. "I'd forgotten about that one ..."

Someone was dragging up old stories as examples of how screwed our world really was. I read the passage about how Bindi beads became GHB once ingested. I laughed.

"I'm sorry. It's not funny, really, but I can't help but wonder how many adults wanted Bindi beads that Christmas. A new party favour."

He chuckled. "I could do with some. Might be easier than locating Rohypnol for spiking water bottles when I'm out and about with you."

"I think we can safely say that today is a slow news day. Between the recapping of old stories in the wake of massive amounts of baby formula being shipped to China, dropping milk prices, and more carrying on over the Auckland housing crisis, there isn't much happening." It was weird. The radio was reporting the retirement home fire in Upper Hutt overnight but not the newspaper.

"Good. Let them go on about old stories and leave us alone."

"Wonder how many gangs rushed out to buy up Bindis before they were pulled from shop shelves?" I imagined them dishing out the brightly coloured beads in small zip lock plastic bags and selling them to druggies. Visions of people busted for having a bag of beads on their person amused me.

"Enough crazy shit, is there anything at all in the paper that hinders our movement today?" Ben asked.

"Can't see anything so far. It seems strange. The fires alone should have been all over the paper this morning.

The radio was talking about it earlier."

"It was only a matter of time before they figured out that people were dead prior to the fires. Unless the government stepped in," Ben said.

"My government or yours?"

"Both. I imagine they would have taken control of the fire scenes last night. You don't have a spare toothbrush, do you?" Ben asked running his tongue over his teeth.

"I actually do," I replied. I opened the cupboard under the sink and pulled out a box. After a good deal of rummaging about, I found a toothbrush still in its packaging and handed it to him.

"You go do what you need to do. I'm going to pack the car," I said.

He thanked me and with the toothbrush clutched in his hand, he disappeared down the hallway.

I gathered everything we would need for both cover stories. I took note of the day as I walked to the car. It wasn't overly warm. There was a definite chill to the wind. I stowed all the equipment in the boot of my car. There was a measuring wheel, the reflective vests, a clipboard, and two plain dark blue baseball caps, and the magazines I'd scored from the women at the door. Back inside I went and checked my email.

There was nothing from Jared. At this point, I deemed that good news. I took a warmish jacket from my wardrobe and put the laptop away. The jacket was perfect for a surveyor, not so good for a religious nut job. I dug deep in my wardrobe, reaching way back into the dark recesses, and came up with a sensible long black button up coat. It was demure and religious looking, possibly why it was so far back in my wardrobe.

The last thing I put in the car was the backpack with the gnome in it.

I removed my cell phone from its charger and dropped it into my small leather backpack. Then reconsidered and opted for a large black handbag. There was something religious sect looking about that particular handbag. I emptied my backpack contents into the enormous handbag, knowing I could easily take a few important things from that and shove them in my jacket pockets if we decided we were surveyors. I slung the bag over my shoulder, gathered up the coat and jacket and headed back out to the car, only to be foiled by a greyhound.

Romeo had stopped pacing up and down and was blocking the front door with his long body.

"Come on, Romeo, out of the way."

He lay down.

"Not funny. Go to bed!" I said firmly.

He stood up and skulked off. I felt mean. I dumped everything on the porch and went back inside. I knew if I gave him a treat, it'd keep him happy until I got back and could walk him.

Romeo watched me approach. He could see the treat in my hand. His tongue flicked over his doggy lips. I held the piece of dried duck out. He took it gracefully.

"You'll have to wait until we come back for that walk, Romeo."

The dog didn't care. With my conscience eased, I went back to putting everything in the car. I was hoping Nana would be sleeping in due to the late night activities, but as I'd learned over the years, one could never tell with Nana.

Nana.

Familiar ringing resounded from my handbag. Instantly knowing I'd jinxed myself by thinking about Nana, I fished my cell from the bag.

"Veronica dear, did you hear the terrible news?" Nana said as soon as I answered.

Time to play dumb.

"What news Nana?"

"Oh, dear, one of the newer rest homes in Upper Hutt went up in flames last night. We don't know what happened. Ester had friends at that home and can't find out any information."

"I haven't heard anything, but I'll look into it."

"They said arson on the radio this morning," Nana said. "Arson, who would do such a thing to old people?"

"I don't know, Nana."

"You wouldn't have time for a little bit of that story, would you? It's just that the girls and I are here and thought you might read to us, to take our minds off it all." As if she sensed my reticence, she added, "It could have been us dear, in that fire."

Yes, it could've been and that scared me. We weren't done yet. It could still be my family on the line.

"I'm on my way out, Nana."

"Not even five minutes?"

"No, Nana, I can't. I'll come in later and read then. I promise."

Ben appeared without my needing to go back and get him.

He whisked the phone from my hand.

"Veronica is driving me today. I can read on the way," he said with a silky smooth voice.

He disappeared back inside then reappeared with the magazine continually talking to Nana.

I watched with interest as he took the car keys from me and unlocked the gates. He gave them back and waited for me to back out before shutting the gates.

I thought I could get very used to having someone so handy about the place.

"A few pages are all I have time for, June. Are you ready?" Ben said.

"Yes, we're waiting."

"Right, here we go ..."

Ben's voice filled the car as he picked the story up where I'd left it last night. I liked what he was doing. It must have been scary for Nana and the cronies finding out about the rest home fires. She's right. It could've easily been them. And I'm not ready to be without my Nana.

"Oh it's getting more and more exciting. When can we hear more?" Nana chirped so loudly I could hear her.

I reached for the phone and spoke to Nana, "How about a thank you Ben for reading to you?"

"Oh dear, my manners are remiss. It's the shock, you know."

I handed the phone back in time for Ben to receive a gushing thank you chorus from the cronies of doom.

"I'm sure Veronica will read you more later. Bye bye for now."

He hung up and grinned at me.

"They're a lot of work, aren't they?"

"If by work you mean constantly demanding, then yes, yes they are. Only today I don't blame them at all."

Chapter 20
[JUST MY LUCK]

"So this is Totara Park," Ben muttered as we crossed the bridge.

"And this is the only way in or out by road," I replied. "There is a foot bridge that goes over the river at the other end to Harcourt Park. I'll head toward the interior."

"Good idea."

"We'll do a drive around and look for houses with obvious gnomes or ornaments," I said. "Probably best to start in the middle and work our way outward."

"Pull over, I'll grab the clipboard. We'll need to keep track of the houses and streets," Ben said.

I did as requested. He found my clipboard and a list of possible streets that I'd written down. Justin didn't believe in making things too easy for us but he hadn't made it harder either. I knew if I kept my eyes peeled, I'd see something that gave me a clue.

We carried on our merry way, making sure to go slowly but not too slow as to raise suspicion. I noted many For Sale signs and smiled. There was yet another cover if needed. A couple of newlyweds looking for a house to buy. Newlyweds, yes, newlyweds were a nice touch.

Ben wrote down all the addresses of interest. There were quite a few more than expected but nothing that screamed 'Justin was here'. Not only was Totara Park the supposed wife swapping capital of Upper Hutt but it seemed to be where old gnomes went to die. It was possible that the gnomes were breeding. Eventually they would find their way to some derelict old building and lurk about with the scary life size plastic horses that used to inhabit The Mall.

"Ronnie?"

"Yes," I replied, trying to give the impression I hadn't tuned out.

"There's another gnome filled yard."

I glanced over. It was a doozy.

"Hope you wrote that one down," I said.

"This place is like a maze or maybe a rabbit warren," Ben commented, his pen scratched on the paper.

"How many houses so far?" I asked.

"Thirteen."

"How many gnomes in each yard, do you think?" A rough guesstimate was all I was after.

"More than we'd like. It's not going to be easy spotting the one we're after."

The next three streets netted another four gnome filled delights of gardens.

"Okay, we have seventeen possibilities, yes?" Ben said.

"You were the one counting," I replied. "Were any for sale?"

"One, I think."

I pulled into the New World car park and chose a suitable parking space, not too close to anyone else but not so far away as to promote interest. We opted for the surveyor's cover story. I tugged on my jacket, then one of the reflective vests.

Grabbing both blue caps, I handed one to Ben, then jammed one on my own head.

I slung the backpack containing a gnome on my back. Ben pulled on the other vest and zipped it up. He had the clipboard under his arm and took the distance-measuring wheel. We checked each other out, and declared we would do. I locked up the car and pocketed the keys.

Ben rolled the measuring wheel across the car park to the street. He asked, "You just happened to have this lying around?" He picked the wheel up.

With a straight face and deadpan delivery I said, "You never know when you'll need to accurately measure out a rugby field."

He nodded. "You Kiwis do take your rugby rather seriously."

"It's a serious game."

"You were joking, weren't you? About you measuring rugby fields?"

"Oh yeah."

We walked down two streets. There weren't many people around.

He touched my arm. "We're approaching the first gnome garden."

"Okay, get set to look official."

He passed me the clipboard and muttered, "Another four meters this way and we'll take new measurements."

I pointed a few times in different directions. We walked past the garden. I casually glanced in and took stock of the gnome inhabitants.

"I'm sorry, I missed that last measurement," I said in a normal speaking voice.

Ben turned and walked past the house again and said some random number. I followed him, and on the way back I got a better look at the gnomes.

I caught up to Ben and said, "None looked like ours."

"I think the next garden isn't for another three hundred meters."

"I have to get a good look on the first pass this time. We can't risk anyone noticing we back track only at houses with gnomes."

"Tie your shoes. You do have sneakers on, right?"

"I do," I said, looking down to check.

A dog barked as we crossed a road and moved steadily forward toward the second gnome home. A car pulled out of a driveway, almost knocking Ben down. The woman behind the wheel glared at him. Ben knocked on the hood of her car but didn't speak, conscious that his accent was unusual and therefore memorable.

I was under no such restraints. I glared back and said, "Maybe you should get glasses."

The woman drove off without a second look. I suspected she felt guilty and knew she was in the wrong.

"Stupid bitch must have got her license from a Weetbix box," I said under my breath, making Ben throw me a questioning look.

"Weetbix box?"

"You don't know what Weetbix is?"

"I've seen the boxes but never eaten it."

"Remind me, I'll make you Weetbix next time you stay over," I told him with a wicked grin.

I continued, "Donald can eat seven in one sitting. Myself, I can only manage two."

"I don't know if I want you to. That grin of yours was the evilest thing I've ever seen."

"Don't be a girl. The All Blacks eat Weetbix."

His right eyebrow rose. "If they're good enough for Richie McCaw..."

I was quietly impressed that he knew who Richie was.

"How far away are we from the next place?"

"Next house, I think," he replied.

We slowed down so I could get a good look. Ben was watching the wheel and the footpath like a surveyor should.

A dog flew at the fence as we approached, barking, snarling, teeth bared. I jumped.

A male voice from by the house yelled out, "Shut up, you idiot animal!"

Perfect, I thought. I watched the dog and still got a clear look at the yard. Fishing gnomes sat on a little bridge over a small creek. Several other gnomes lurked under large ferns and around a pond. Thankfully, none was similar to our viral gnomes.

Relieved, we moved on.

I tugged the brim of my cap down slightly, concealing more of my face in the shadow it cast. I was shaken by the barking, snarling dog, and getting thirsty - not a great combination. I looked around in hope but there was no diary or shop anywhere. We'd parked by the only shops in the area. I looked back and could no longer see the car park or the shops.

"We should've dropped a trail," I said. "We may never find our way back."

"Come on, Gretel. I'm sure we won't be lost in Totara Park forever."

"As long as you are sure."

A car rounded the corner in front of us.

"Not much traffic during the day over here," Ben commented as the car drove toward us then passed our position. "Not even foot traffic."

"Maybe everyone's either left the area to work or bonking at home."

He shot me a sidelong glance, and obviously wanted an explanation of my comment.

"It's just that, once, before the advent of multiple telephone companies and different phone numbers, it was easy to tell what area a phone number came from. You looked at the first three digits. For example, Silverstream was 289, and eventually became 5289 as more and more numbers were added to the network and so forth. Trentham was 284 or 5284. You get the idea."

"Yes, carry on."

"I noticed that Totara Park was overly represented in the personal columns of the local and regional newspapers on a regular basis."

"Are you saying this quiet, seemingly sleepy place, is a

den of immorality?" He cast his eyes around the empty suburban street with carefully manicured lawns and tidy weed free gardens. "This place?" Disbelief resounded in his voice.

"Oh yes, this charming little gnome filled rabbit warren was a seething cesspit of low standards and perverts."

A car passed us. We watched as discretely as possible, while apparently discussing measurements or whatever people expected us to discuss.

"Cesspit has a nice ring to it," Ben said, peering over my shoulder as if he needed to see the clipboard.

Another car passed. It was a different car than before.

"I hear tell there is more than one brothel out here," I replied, pointing at the pieces of paper clipped down to the board.

I noticed the passenger.

"Trouble," I said. We walked without looking at the car as it passed it.

"What?"

"The male passenger was driving the previous car," I said.

Ben laughed, throwing his head back, as if I'd told him a hilarious joke.

"The female driver looked scared," I continued.

The car was gone.

"I would be, too, with that evil looking asshole in my car," Ben said.

"We need to get her out."

Ben looked at me.

"We need to find the package."

I listened to the tone he used. It spoke so much louder than his words. It was fate of the world stuff.

"Then let's get moving. We'll grab it, and get her," I said.

We stepped up the pace, knowing the car would be back and the chance of us being seen removing the gnome, or even being stopped, was increasing by the second.

"Justin was right to be careful. They couldn't have found us this quickly without surveillance or maybe cracking the code on the message board," Ben said, increasing his stride length to cover more ground.

I followed suit.

We had a lot more gardens to check.

The direction we were moving in gave too many helpful clues to whomever it was who wanted the next package.

"Where's the next place?" I said.

"Around the road a bit more, why?"

"I think there are alley ways connecting the streets. We can use them to make ourselves disappear."

I scanned the area. We could both hear an approaching car. Across the road, I saw a gap between houses, flanked by hedge and fence. "There," I said pointing.

The car engine noise grew louder.

Ben picked up the wheel. We hurried across the road and into the alleyway, moving quickly and staying out of sight. I ripped off the reflective vest. Ben followed suit. I crept toward the entrance of the alleyway and watched for the car, remaining low and in a concealed position. I was on the wrong side to see the passenger but got a good look at the driver.

The same scared looking woman.

I watched as the car turned at the end of the street and came back, slowly. Obviously, the passenger hadn't expected us to disappear. I saw him peering at the houses as they drove by. I ducked back and stayed out of sight until they passed.

"Ben?" I whispered as the car disappeared around another corner.

He crept up behind me. The car was moving further away.

"He lost us. Do you think he'll give up and assume we found the package?" I knew that I sounded a little too hopeful.

"No."

I stood up and looked out at the street. On a diagonal from our position, I could see the very edge of a garden and spotted the telltale point of a gnome hat. I stood on tiptoes to get a better look at the pointy hat.

I gesticulated wildly with my hand and said, "That's the next one, right?"

"Right."

"Can you see the points? There seem to be a few the same colour as our previous gnomes."

He nodded.

"I'm going. You stay here. They're looking for two people wearing reflective vests now, not one woman."

"Okay."

I took the cap off my head, letting my hair fly free. I removed my jacket, in case they recognised the colour from the sleeves, and turned it inside out.

"Reversible," Ben said with approval as I stood in front of him wearing a pale blue jacket made of fleece and not the dark green waterproof one I'd worn minutes ago.

I took the gnome out of the black backpack.

"If you liked that, you'll love this," I said. I turned the backpack inside out. When I was finished, it was a pale pink messenger type bag. I shoved the gnome back in and clipped the folded top over it. I took a pink shoulder strap from one of the pockets on the bag and clipped it to the D rings on the top corners.

"Damn, that's cool," Ben muttered.

I took a hair tie from my pocket and pulled the top half of my hair back into a ponytail, letting the back remain long.

"You look completely different," he said with approval.

"That was the plan," I replied.

We watched and listened for the car. It was no longer audible.

"I'm going. Watch for me."

"Be quick."

"Will do," I replied. Ducking out from the alleyway, I headed quickly across the road.

I didn't look back. If I had, I might have seen Ben trying to attract my attention.

As I approached the curb right in front of the garden, an empty cigarette packet in the gutter caught my eye. Normally I'd think rude thoughts about disgusting smokers, but this time I wondered why it was there. The blue and white packet of Winston lights seemed to point me in the right direction. There was no other rubbish in the gutters. We'd come across other cigarette packets on occasion, mostly screwed up and tossed without thought. This one wasn't damaged. The top was open, and it pointed to the garden. This one wasn't what I expected to see. It was an American brand, from North Carolina. Not the usual Rothmans, Pall Mall, or even Holiday brand. A notably American brand that Justin preferred.

I looked over the low fence. There were a lot of gnomes.

Buggery bollocks.

I quickly surveyed the house. It wasn't possible to tell if anyone was home. I'd just have to rock up to the front door and knock. If someone were home I didn't want to be caught tipping over gnomes and risk creating a fuss. Tipping gnomes. Ha! With a backward glance at the cigarette packet I moved on with my plan.

I squashing the notion that I should call Ben. I didn't know exactly I'd say to him. Seemed best to just get on with it and not worry about the pack of Winstons pointing the way. I didn't recall seeing any cigarette packets anywhere near the other gnomes. Could be coincidence.

I opened the small gate even though it'd be just as easy to step over it. Why would anyone bother with decorative gates? I decided it was an elderly person thing, for whatever reason. A smooth concrete path led straight to a large solid wooden door. No peephole. My mind wandered as I approached the door. I considered pulling out my phone and having Ben on the line, just in case it all went pear shaped. I got as far as fishing my phone from my pocket and holding it in my hand.

The door opened before my hand knocked.

An elderly lady startled at the sight of me on her doorstep.

"Sorry. I didn't mean to give you a fright," I said with my best mannered smile at the ready. "I live down the road and was wondering if you needed any weeding done?" It was the best I could come up with on the spot. The sight of another elderly woman almost made me turn and run.

The lady took a moment to look me up and down. Then she said, "I'm Mrs. Cosgrove, what's your name dear?"

"Veronica Tracey."

Then a horrible clawing sensation started in my stomach. Cosgrove? What were the odds? Could my Nana really know every old woman in Upper Hutt? I took a breath and asked, "Are you Lillian Cosgrove?"

The woman smiled, a taut fleshless smile stretched across her off white false teeth. An involuntary shudder raced through me and I hoped it wasn't obvious.

It had to be this garden and this was Justin's idea of a joke. First Martha, now Mrs. Cosgrove.

"Yes, dear. Have we met?"

"Probably a long time ago, I'm June Tracey's granddaughter."

Mrs. Cosgrove appeared slightly confused.

The taut smile slipped away, then reappeared with more conviction. "June Tracey! Why, I haven't seen her in several years. How is she?"

Still alive.

"She's well, thank you."

"Now, dear, what did you want?" she asked, walking to the edge of the porch and grasping the sturdy handrail.

"I just wondered if you'd like a hand with your garden." I said lightly, trying to sound as casual as I could.

"I don't have much to offer you, and a bit of weeding would be such a help."

"I'd settle for a cup of tea," I replied. "Show me what you want weeded and I'll get on and get it done."

I could feel Ben's eyes watching intently.

I glanced at my phone, imagining I'd missed a message or call from him. There was nothing there.

Mrs. Cosgrove clutched at the railing as she hobbled down the two steps and onto the smooth path. Now I knew why the path was so smooth, so the old lady didn't trip.

As the woman showed me around the front flowerbeds, I called Ben's phone but didn't speak, leaving the line open so he could hear what was happening.

Taking special note of any gnomes that were similar to

our gnome, I listened to Mrs. Cosgrove talk about the flower beds. The noise of a car coming closer made me look up. Before I could see it, I crouched down to ask about a flower, taking myself out of view until the car passed. I stood up once the engine noise began to fade past Ben's position.

"Have you always collected gnomes?" I said.

"Yes, I have. It started as a joke. My late husband bought me a gnome one Christmas as a joke."

"Oh I see."

"It snowballed; he began buying me gnomes for Mother's day and Christmas from then on."

I smiled. "You're probably lucky you didn't get them for your birthdays too."

"Yes, I think I am."

Mrs. Cosgrove moved toward a gnome that looked very familiar. "Goodness, where did you come from?" she asked.

"Is that not one of yours?"

"I don't think so," I replied. "I don't seem to remember this one at all."

"Maybe it came for a holiday. This does look like a gnome-friendly place to be," I commented, with a smile. "Looks like this flower bed needs more attention than the others. I shall start here, with the interloper."

"Very well, dear. I'll pop inside and make us a nice cup of tea," Mrs. Cosgrove said, hobbling back up the path.

I didn't expect there would actually be any popping going on. Mrs. Cosgrove seemed a great deal frailer than my own Nana.

The phone in my hand made a noise. I lifted it to my ear.

"Everything all right?" Ben asked

"Another one of Nana's cronies. I can't believe my luck," I said. "Give me a second."

"The gnome?"

"I have it," I said quietly, replacing the garden interloper with the gnome from my bag.

"Excellent, let's get out of here, before our pal in that car comes back around."

I hesitated then sighed and said, "I kind of promised I'd do the garden." I cringed and waited for an explosion from Ben, ready to cut him off if it got too bad.

His voice was calm as he said, "Does that mean you've forgotten about the woman in the car?"

I was impressed with his ability to press my buttons. I hadn't so much forgotten as blocked it temporarily as my mind assimilated another one of my Nana's cronies.

"The problem is," I started to say as I heard a car and Mrs. Cosgrove simultaneously. I looked toward the house. The old lady was hobbling along the porch. I glanced to the road. A car was approaching too slowly. "Ben, the car."

I made a split second decision to go for the old woman. If the car's occupant saw me and realised what I was doing in the garden, I sure as hell didn't want to explain to Nana why I was visiting Mrs. Cosgrove at the same time the old woman was killed in a drive by shooting. Bad enough the whole gnome connection would be of great interest to Nana and her cronies. I picked up my messenger bag and closed the gap between the lady and myself in matter of seconds.

I called out, "Mrs. Cosgrove, may I use your bathroom?" not wanting to alarm her at the rate at which I approached and to get her back inside without a fuss.

"Oh yes, dear," she said and turned back to the front door.

I stepped up behind her, hoping we'd get into the hallway beyond the door before the car levelled with the front gate.

Ben spoke from the phone in my hand. "Get as far away as you can from the front."

I kept moving until I was inside the front door and the old lady was well in front of me, heading down the hallway.

"I'll shut this. We don't want any uninvited visitors," I said and shoved the door shut. It was surprisingly dark inside the hallway.

"Along the passage, dear, second door past the last bedroom," Mrs. Cosgrove told me. She hobbled along toward the back of the house. "I'll be out the back, in the kitchen, pouring the tea."

I let out a slight sigh of relief. Mrs. Cosgrove kept moving. I dropped back and headed for one of the rooms that faced the road. A living room.

The car cruised by. Ben spoke again. I lifted the phone to my ear. "It's coming back. She's doing a U-turn now.

The windows are rolling down."

"Can you get a shot?"

"Maybe," he replied. "But from this side of the road, I'll hit the driver, not the passenger."

I closed my eyes for a second. That wasn't the outcome I wanted. "I can do it."

I remembered the Glock he'd given me the night before. I'd hidden it in the jacket I wore. I'd been meaning, of course, to give it back, but thankful I hadn't. I struggled out of the jacket, undid the secret internal pocket, and removed the gun.

I racked the slide, let myself out the front door, and ran down the side fence, hidden from the road by a hedge and camellia trees. I made it to the road as the car pulled slowly along the curb. The passenger window was down. The passenger had something in his hand. My phone fell to the ground.

I aimed and fired, hoping I got the angle right, and the 9mm round wouldn't hit the woman driver. All I heard as the gun fired were the words in my head that I'd heard many times before, "Shoot the hostage."

The car braked sharply, the passenger slumped forward, and the driver screamed.

I squeezed my eyes shut, then flicked them open. Ben yelled from the ground where I'd dropped the phone. "Ronnie!"

Footfalls pounded on the footpath coming toward me. With the Glock in my hand, I approached the car. I couldn't tell if the passenger was dead, wounded, or playing possum.

The woman driver screamed again. Tears rolled down her face. I made eye contact with her.

"Are you hurt?" I said.

The woman shook her head.

"Get out of the car," I said calmly. "Keep your hands where I can see them."

I felt Ben move up beside me. His gun was trained on the passenger.

"Have you checked him?" he asked.

"Not yet," I replied. "We need to move. Someone will have called police."

Ben opened the car door. A gun fell into the gutter. He reached in and felt for the man's pulse.

"Dead," he announced. Ben rifled through the dead man's pockets, looking for his wallet and any forms of identity he might have on him.

He looked at me. "Where's the package?"

"Inside," I replied, watching the shaken woman alight from the vehicle. I addressed the woman, "Walk around the back and come over to the footpath."

"Get it now, we need to get out of here," Ben said without looking up. "Go!"

"You take her," I said and took off into the house.

I snatched up my phone on the way in. I found my messenger bag in the living room, shoved my gun into it and slung the bag over my head and slid it to my side.

I called out to Mrs. Cosgrove, "I'll be back later. I didn't realise how late it was. Sorry. I've got a lecture."

"What's that dear? You have a picture?" she called back.

I shook my head and smiled as I let myself back out the door. I'd had more than my fair share of old folk of late, and each one was more of an adventure than the previous.

At the curb, I found Ben talking to the woman. I considered she was approximately sixty years old and the morning had come as one hell of a shock to her.

I made eye contact with Ben. He nodded, and then he offered the woman a drink of water from a pump water bottle he carried in his pocket.

That old trick again.

I suggested the woman should sit down on the curb.

Ben inspected the documents he'd found on the male's body. He took his cell phone out, walked away a few feet, and made a call.

A few minutes later, he walked back to me and the now semi-conscious woman.

"We can't leave her like this. Anything might happen to her," I said.

"Our car is too far away. We are going to have to," he replied looking around. The area was silent, and deserted. "How many alley ways like the one we hid in are there?"

"Lots, I think."

"Enough that we can get back to the car without being in the open for too long?"

"I think so," I replied watching the woman sway.

I lay her down on her side, and put her in a recovery position.

"Good thinking," Ben replied. "Let's get out of here."

He took my hand and hurried back to the alleyway.

"We have to get to the car before the police and paramedics arrive," Ben said in a hushed whisper.

At the entrance to the alleyway, we scooped up the reflective vests we'd been wearing. There was no time to shove them into the bag. Ben grabbed the measuring wheel and tucked it under his arm. We ran, quietly, through the alleyway. At the other end, I surveyed the street. No traffic, no noise. I looked for another alleyway entrance and saw one about a hundred meters away.

"Down there," I said.

We walked fast, across the road and down to the alleyway.

Once inside the long, cool, tree-lined alley, we stopped. I removed my bag and jacket. I turned everything back the way it was.

If anyone had seen the car and the shooting, they'd be looking for a girl in a pale blue jacket with a pink messenger bag.

Aware that we'd left the car looking like surveyors, we needed to return looking the same.

Reflective vests back on in preparation.

We negotiated two more long alleyways before hearing the traffic on the main road into Totara Park. There was a lone siren winding in the distance.

"They haven't made it over the bridge yet," I said as we

crossed the road to the car park.

We stowed our equipment, reflective vests, and the backpack in the boot.

I looked at Ben and said, "You drive."

He nodded, and took the keys.

We made our way out of the car park, and around the roundabout. As we started across the bridge a police car rushed toward us, siren wailing, and lights flashing.

Neither of us looked back.

I knew that when the police arrived at the scene, road-blocks would go up. To shut Totara Park it was as simple as closing the bridge. One police car parked across the entrance of the bridge would do it.

"Let's get into the city. Before some smart-ass recalls your license plates," Ben said, negotiating the traffic as we emerged from the light controlled intersection onto River Road.

He eased his cell phone from his pants pocket and pressed a number.

Then he hit speaker and set the phone down on the console between the seats. The phone rang twice and was answered on the third ring.

"It's me. Assume the car is compromised and get the registration details changed, ASAP," Ben said.

"Give me the license plate," the female voice on the other end replied.

Ben told her.

"I'm doing it now. Any traces entered into the system will result in a fictitious name and address. A new SUV will be waiting at Percy's Reserve car park."

"Thank you."

Ben hung up.

"New car?" I said. "Awesome."

"We can't hang you out to dry, can we?" Ben said with a smile.

I wondered if maybe he would, in different circumstances. All things considered, it wasn't outside the realms of possibility. I don't know whether that concerned me or not.

We approached the end of River Road and merged onto the Western Hutt Road. There was a usual amount of midweek traffic, and no one took any notice of us.

Within twenty minutes, we were pulling into the Percy Reserve car park. A phone call told us the medium blue Ford Expedition parked there was for me. The keys were in a magnetised case up under the right front wheel arch. We were to leave the other car. Someone would take care of it.

We transferred everything to the new car. Ben took a polishing cloth and a spray cleaner from the new car. He quickly and carefully wiped down all the obvious places our fingerprints might be, inside and out of the car we were leaving. A truck pulled up behind my old car. Two men in overalls jumped out. They took the keys from Ben and told us to leave.

As we pulled out and headed toward Wellington city I saw the men load my former SUV into the covered truck. I knew I would never see it again.

I sat back in the very comfortable leather seats. "This is nice," I said.

"It's not bad at all," Ben replied as he, too, relaxed a little.

My phone rang. It blasted forth a familiar tune. I fished it out of my pocket and answered, "Hello Donald."

"Oh stop that!" Donald replied.

I chuckled, imagining him swatting the air in annoyance. "Did you need something?"

"You won't believe this," Donald said in mock horror. "I just had the weirdest phone call."

My heart sank. Now what?

Donald continued, unaware of the terror he was causing.

"Some chick called Christine rang from Countdown. She's your personal shopper or something?"

My heart bounced back up.

"There is a supply problem with the Clinkers you ordered with your groceries."

"Countdown rang about lollies?" I said in disbelief. I wondered immediately if there was some secret code for the day that I'd forgotten and the call was really from Steph or Jenn.

"Apparently the Clinkers are unavailable, and they'd like to know what you would like instead?"

I frowned. "There is no substitute for Clinkers," I replied. "Tell them not to worry. I'll live without my Clinkers."

Lollies seemed so frivolous in light of current events,

but then again we could all be dead by morning and I would've died wanting Clinkers.

"I shall relay that message for you," Donald said sounding every bit the personal assistant. "I'll leave you to it and hear from you later?"

"I'll call you when I get home." I had a thought. "When were those groceries going to arrive?"

"Between two and four. Shall I be here?"

"If you could, that would be great."

"Bye bye now."

I hung up. I sensed Ben's internal fight throughout my conversation with Donald to remain composed but could take no more.

"What in hell's name are Clinkers?"

"Have you ever had biscuits called Squiggle Tops?" I said by way of an answer.

He shook his head. "I don't believe so."

"Then I can't explain what Clinkers are. We need to locate a diary or supermarket, obviously not a Countdown."

"Where would one be?"

"Take the Thorndon exit off the motorway. We're going to New World."

"We shouldn't be going anywhere except straight into the office."

"And you don't want to die without trying these, trust me."

It seemed that curiosity got the better of him and he pulled off the motorway at Thorndon and found his way into the supermarket's underground car park.

"Stay here, I'll be right back," I said.

I patted my jacket, and located the pocket my wallet was in, and then hurried to the stairs up to the supermarket. Taking the stairs two at a time, it wasn't long before I was moving quickly through the well lit building.

Smells from the bakery and delicatessen made my stomach growl as I searched for the confectionary aisle.

It didn't take me long. I found the sweets, and then found the Clinkers.

Clutching two packets of deliciousness, I moved to the biscuit aisle where I picked up a packet of Squiggle Tops. I was through the checkout and back in the car within five minutes. If we're all going to die then I'm eating lollies and chocolate, frivolous or not.

As I buckled my seat belt I said, "Biscuit or lolly?"

"Biscuit, I think," Ben replied. "I still can't get used to eating biscuits like you call them."

I opened the packet and gave him one. He gave it a cursory inspection. "It's not right. Biscuits mop up the gravy," he muttered. Once satisfied that there was no gravy to be found and chocolate wasn't ideal for mopping up anything anyway, he took a bite.

"This is a good cookie," he replied and took another bite.

"The lollies on the top are the same as Clinkers," I said. "It's a biscuit."

"You and your lollies and biscuits. We have cookies and candy, so much simpler."

Our drive continued.

Before long, we were safe in a secure car park under a protected building in the middle of the city. And again, my phone rang. This time it was Nana and she wanted more of the story. I reached around and grabbed my backpack from the back seat. In it I found the magazine.

"Okay Nana, but no interruptions, because I'm on my way to a meeting and have only got five minutes."

I looked over at Ben and mouthed the words, 'Hope you don't mind, won't take long.'

He smiled and with a husky whisper replied, "Looking forward to the story myself."

"Have you got your hearing aid on, Nana?"

"Don't be cheeky. We're ready when you are."

I sighed and opened the magazine at the marked paragraph and began to read. Five minutes later I was done.

"Oh my," said Nana.

"Yes indeed," I replied.

"Thank you, dear. Later?"

"You're welcome Nana, and yes later. I'll ring you."

I am the good granddaughter. I expected a sainthood to be offered at some point, should we all live long enough.

Chapter 21
[SAVE THE WORLD]

Flanked on either side by black Gortex and Kevlar-wearing, automatic-rifle-carrying guards, we travelled up an elevator from the basement car park to the thirteenth floor.

The elevator dinged and the doors opened slowly. Ben stepped out. He took me by the elbow. The armed guards disappeared with the closing of the elevator doors.

"They're intense," I commented. Way more intense than when I used to work for the Security Intelligence Service.

A long wide hallway stretched in front of us. The deep blue carpet bore a large fancy insignia that took up the entire space between the elevator and the reception desk. It was the gold, deep blue and white Agency seal.

The receptionist nodded. She handed us a visitor pass each. We clipped the passes to our jackets, then signed the visitor book.

"Down the hall to the meeting room," the receptionist said. "It's room thirteen-thirteen."

Of course it is.

We didn't speak. Ben took my elbow again.

Outside the room with the ominous number thirteen-thirteen, we paused. I took a second to gather my thoughts and take a breath.

Ben whispered, "Take the backpack off."

I nodded. I was wearing it slung over one shoulder. I dropped it down, catching the handle at the top in the palm of my hand. The bag hung a mere six or eight inches above the floor.

He knocked once.

The door opened. We were ushered into a spacious room with a central highly polished oval dark wood table. Round the table were enough chairs to seat twelve people. Only one person sat at the large table. Jared.

Jared rose to his feet from the end of the table.

"Congratulations on achieving your goal," he said with a slow southern drawl. He moved forward to shake both our hands. He reached for Ben's hand first.

I placed the backpack on the shiny table and waited my turn.

Jared shook my hand firmly. "Well done," he said with a half smile.

"Thank you, Sir," I replied.

"Now, sit. We have the debriefing to take care of," Jared said with a firm instructional tone.

We sat, together across the table from Jared.

Jared glanced at the backpack. "Is that the package?"

"Yes," we replied.

"Pass it over," Jared ordered.

I took the gnome from the bag and placed it on the table. Its reflection on the surface reminded me of a pond. For a moment, I thought it was funny that none of the houses with so many gnomes had ponds for them to fish. I considered the insanity of that thought while listening to Jared expound my virtues and delight in our team-work.

The man by the door stepped forward and took the gnome to Jared. He inspected it carefully then put it back on the table.

I had a sense I was waiting for the other shoe to drop, and rightly so considering the number of incidents that had potential to raise their profile during the mission.

"Veronica?"

The name was familiar but I was slow to recognise it.

"Veronica?" the voice said a second time.

This time I reacted. "Yes, Sir?" I looked up.

Jared stared at me. His cold grey eyes burrowed into my head, as if trying to reach inside my brain and read my thoughts.

"Did you have any questions?"

"The girl, Kirsty, is she all right?"

The corner of Jared's mouth curled up. He wasn't surprised I'd asked. "Yes, she is, she's making a good recovery and remains in Wakefield Hospital. Her family is with her. The strangest thing happened. She can't remember anything of the night she was brought in, or who helped her."

"And the assailant?"

Jared's lip curled again. "As much as I hate to say it, it appears that you may have rid the world of a sexual predator."

"Really? That wasn't a one time thing then?" I smiled, I'd done something good whether he liked it or not.

"Yes. I had some agents look into his background."

"Good," I murmured, knowing there was more information still to come.

"There was also the peculiar instance of no one reporting him missing. From what they've uncovered from his recent past, I'd say women in the Wellington region can breathe easier and sleep safer."

"Good to know."

Jared's eyes clouded with a new coldness. "That doesn't justify what you did. Your behaviour jeopardised the mission."

I cast my eyes downward. "Understood."

Ben spoke, "I would like the outcome of this incident to reflect in any future work we do with Veronica. Her instincts are good, and she acted out of humanity. The only person she risked was herself."

"Duly noted," Jared replied. "And for the car bomb? How would you like that to be explained?"

I cringed. "I had nothing to do with the car exploding."

"Her only part in that incident was to save my life. A commendation would be appropriate," Ben said.

Jared almost smiled, his lips curled then returned to the thin line they'd grown accustomed to.

"And today's development? The dead body in the car, and the unconscious civilian, and the old lady still waiting for Veronica to return to finish the garden?"

"The old lady waiting?" I felt sick. I hadn't thought about anything except getting the gnome out of harm's way. I'd quite forgotten Mrs. Cosgrove and the mess in the street outside her house.

"She mentioned to police she was waiting for her friend Ruby's granddaughter to weed her front garden."

"Did she say I had already been there?"

"No, she did not."

Confusion crowded in. "Why not? And my Nana isn't Ruby."

"As luck would have it, your sweet old Mrs. Cosgrove is days off being railroaded into a retirement home by her loving son and daughter-in-law. They've been trying to tell her and everyone else that would listen that the poor old dear is not fit to live alone."

I frowned. "That's hardly fair. She's a little lame and slow to move, but not senile, not the woman I saw anyway."

"I sent an agent to chat with Mrs. Cosgrove. She is by no means senile, Veronica."

"Did they get there before the police interviewed her?" I smelled a rat.

"Yes, I believe so. The police were busy with the terrible scene on the street and didn't notice one of our young men go in through the backdoor. What a wonderful place that is, with all those alley ways."

"So you told her to say Ruby?"

"I think the names may have been confused. The description might have caused a few problems, too. Now that I see you, I can plainly see you're not a blonde Scandinavian type at all," Jared said with mock surprise and wide eyes.

I could barely believe how deceitful he was, and hadn't ever figured on him actually misleading police or officials or twisting things to their end like that.

"So will she be forced from her home?" I said.

I hoped that she didn't end up in the same retirement home as my Nana and the crime-busting Cronies of Doom. That really would spell trouble. But in light of the destruction of one of the new retirement villages, I imagined there would now be a shortage of places for the elderly, so maybe she'd escape that particular hell for now.

"It seems not. We managed to convince the son he should back off." This time Jared did smile.

I had a feeling it was because he was getting long in the tooth as well, and could see the day coming when one of his kids might try shunting him off to a retirement home in Florida. Out of harm's way? Probably not, I concluded. Not after what had happened here in the last week.

"Am I allowed to know how this all happened and what's the connection to Reede?"

"The viruses were manufactured right there in Upper Hutt at the National Centre for Biosecurity and Infectious Disease (NCBID) in Wallaceville. Justin intercepted chatter, but he also managed to trace one of the interested bidders on the viruses to Reede. She was not bidding on behalf of New Zealand to try to prevent the viruses leaving the country." He paused for a moment to give me time for the information to sink in. "Justin sent me a file, automatically, when he failed to sign into a special account for three consecutive days. It contained all the information he'd uncovered about his superior officer. I knew when I got the file that he was dead or dying."

Ben looked at me. "This was very close."

"Yes. I know. Do we know if anyone else was compromised?"

"To be safe, there were a lot of fires in Upper Hutt, and teams from this office spread out locating anyone and everyone who had any contact with the church."

"But are we safe?"

"As far as we can tell, Veronica. There's no way to be totally sure."

"Does the antidote work?"

"Yes, it does."

That didn't seem right.

"But ..."

Jared held up his hand to stop me.

"We have the antidote and the original virus. Scientists are working on a vaccine. We are manufacturing an antidote now at the very place that created these viruses. It will be distributed throughout the Wellington region in the next few days via various means. We can't offer a vaccination because there are people who will refuse for whatever reason, so we're working on a more subtle distribution method."

Interesting.

"So if the antidote works, then why did Justin die?"

"He was infected by someone ..."

"So there is someone else out there?" Ben asked.

"Not anymore," Jared said. "We traced the person.

They were cleansed and so was their trail of contact."

Ben and I looked at each other for a few minutes, in an awkward world saving silence. "And Reede?" I asked.

"Already arrested for trying to procure the viruses for future sale."

"Good."

"Get out of here, you two," Jared said with good humour. "You've earned a drink or two, and Ben; I heard you got a part in a new series being filmed here."

Ben grinned.

"Guess I'll be sticking around for a while then."

Until next time ...

About the author

Cat Connor is a prolific crime thriller author hailing from New Zealand. Her expertise in the genre is reflected in her engaging and suspenseful narratives, which have garnered a loyal following. Her work is known for its intricate plots, dynamic characters, and relentless pace, keeping readers on the edge of their seats until the very end. She has authored multiple books, including the popular "Byte" series, which follows the exploits of an FBI unit that investigates serial crime.

Cat's passion for crime and espionage is evident in her writing, as she strives to create a world that is both authentic and thrilling. Her meticulous attention to detail and extensive research have won her critical acclaim and accolades from readers and peers alike. In addition to writing, Cat enjoys speaking on topics related to writing and publishing. Her talks are known for their candidness, humour, and practical advice. With her unique blend of talent, expertise, and passion, Cat Connor has established herself as one of the most exciting and accomplished authors in the crime thriller genre.

Her other passions include music, reading, tequila, red wine, coffee, and chocolate. When she's not writing she can be found binge watching TV shows and spending time with her much adored animals; Diesel the mastador,

Patrick the tuxedo cat, Dallas the tortie Birman, and Jimmy the thug.

You can follow and contact Cat at the following places:

Website: www.catconnor.com
Twitter: @catconnor
Facebook: @cat.connor
Instagram: @catconnorauthor

Acknowledgments

With much gratitude, I would like to thank Margot Kinberg (crime author) for reading this book for me. For loving the characters, and for sending through the most wonderfully useful edit suggestions. You, one-hundred percent, rock!

Thank you!

If you haven't read Margot's work (you really should!) ... here's a link to her website:

https://margot-kin-berg.com/